PENGUIN BOOKS

The Gingerbread House

Carin Gerhardsen was born in 1962 in Katrineholm, Sweden. Originally a mathematician, she enjoyed a successful career as an IT consultant before turning her hand to writing crime fiction. *The Gingerbread House* is the first title in the Hammarby series, novels following Detective Inspector Conny Sjöberg and his murder investigation team. Carin now lives in Stockholm with her husband and their two children. She is currently working on the seventh title in the series.

The Gingerbread House

CARIN GERHARDSEN

PENGUIN BOOKS

PENGUIN BOOKS

Published by the Penguin Group
Penguin Books Ltd, 80 Strand, London WC2R ORL, England
Penguin Group (USA) Inc., 375 Hudson Street, New York, New York 10014, USA
Penguin Group (Canada), 90 Eglinton Avenue East, Suite 700, Toronto, Ontario, Canada M4P 2Y3
(a division of Pearson Penguin Canada Inc.)
Penguin Ireland, 25 St Stephen's Green, Dublin 2, Ireland (a division of Penguin Books Ltd)
Penguin Group (Australia), 707 Collins Street, Melbourne, Victoria 3008, Australia
(a division of Pearson Australia Group Pty Ltd)
Penguin Books India Pvt Ltd, 11 Community Centre, Panchsheel Park, New Delhi – 110 017, India
Penguin Group (NZ), 67 Apollo Drive, Rosedale, Auckland 0632, New Zealand
(a division of Pearson New Zealand Ltd)
Penguin Books (South Africa) (Pty) Ltd, Block D, Rosebank Office Park,
181 Jan Smuts Avenue, Parktown North, Gauteng 2193, South Africa

Penguin Books Ltd, Registered Offices: 80 Strand, London WC2R ORL, England

www.penguin.com

First published in Sweden by Ordfront 2008
This translation first published by Stockholm Text Publishing 2012
First published in Great Britain in Penguin Books 2013

001

Copyright © Carin Gerhardsen, 2008
This translation copyright © Paul Norlén, 2012
All rights reserved

The moral rights of the author and translator have been asserted

Set in 12.5/14.75pt Garamond MT Std
Typeset by Jouve (UK), Milton Keynes
Printed in Great Britain by Clays Ltd, St Ives plc

ISBN: 978–1–405–92582–2

www.greenpenguin.co.uk

The Gingerbread House

Katrineholm, October 1968

The brown Queen Anne-style villa is a stately building, perched at the top of a grass-covered hill and surrounded by tall pine trees. The white corner posts and window casings, with their rounded corners, give it an inviting, fairy-tale shimmer. In summer the pines offer shade to the children playing around the house. But now, in autumn, they look almost threatening, like stern guards tasked with protecting the preschool against the winter cold and other unwanted guests. The first snow sits on the ground like a wet rag and has not yet melted away. All is silent, except for a dog barking somewhere in the distance.

Suddenly the door flies open and out swarm the children: boisterous children in clothes new and old, neat and tattered; tall and short children, skinny and round; blond children, dark children, with braids, freckles, glasses or caps; children walking and jumping, chattering and listening; children running ahead and children following behind.

The door slams shut, then opens again, and out walks a little girl with a white fur cap and red quilted jacket. Behind her is a boy in a dark-blue quilted jacket, with a scarf and a red, white and black Katrineholm SC cap – KSC has to be your team, at least in this part of town. The two children do not speak to each other; instead the girl, whose name is Katarina, walks quickly down the hill until she reaches the big, black iron gate. With some effort, she opens the gate just enough to slip through before it closes. Right behind her comes the boy, whose name is Thomas, and before he opens the gate to squeeze out he stops for a moment and takes a deep breath.

Once out on the pavement, his fears are confirmed: all the children have clustered on the opposite street corner. He sees how Katarina, apparently without hesitation, crosses the street, right into the jaws of the wild beast. Thomas makes a quick decision and, instead of crossing the street, turns left to take a detour home. He has taken only a few steps before they are on her. One of the girls, the resourceful Ann-Kristin, always with a sarcastic smile and a malicious gleam in her eye, tears off Katarina's cap and throws it to Hans – 'King Hans' – as the other children shout and laugh with delight.

Thomas stops, wondering whether he should help Katarina, but before he can complete the thought the children catch sight of him. At a clear signal from Hans, they rush eagerly back across the street and throw themselves on Thomas. The rest of the children follow like bloodthirsty dogs, and Katarina remains behind, astonished and relieved: for whatever reason, it was not her turn this time. She leans over and picks up her no longer particularly white fur cap, puts it on anyway, then crosses the street to view the spectacle at close range.

Where does this resourcefulness come from? And this unfailing bond that unites twenty-one, sometimes twenty-two children out of twenty-three? And the obvious but unspoken authority of the leaders when half the group, acting suddenly and enthusiastically as one, ties a terrified little boy to a lamp-post with skipping ropes and scarves, while the other half gathers stones to hurt him?

Thomas, incapable of offering resistance, incapable of screaming, sits on the wet, cold asphalt. Unmoving, silent. He looks at his schoolmates. A few throw rocks at him, at his head, his face, his body. Someone bangs his head against the lamp-post over and over again while another whips him with a skipping rope. A few of the children are laughing, others whisper with condescending, knowing expressions on their little faces, and a few simply stand there impassively and watch. One of those is Katarina; she gets to be one of them now – her schoolmates.

At some point during the assault the teacher herself passes by on the pavement. She casts a quick glance at the tied-up boy and his playmates, and raises her hand to wave goodbye to a few of the girls standing closest.

*

Just as suddenly as it started, they are done. In half a minute the children have scattered and are once again just ordinary, delightful kids on their way home from school. They go their separate ways, one by one, or two by two, perhaps three or four together. Left on the pavement is a six-year-old boy with an aching body and an insurmountable sorrow.

Stockholm, November 2006, Monday Evening

It was only four o'clock in the afternoon, but it was already dark. Snow was falling in large white sheets that melted as soon as they touched the ground. Passing cars blinded him with their headlights, and he had to take care not to get splashed as he walked along the pavement. Why were the cars going so fast that they sprayed him with dirty water? Drivers weren't supposed to splash pedestrians; that was in the Highway Code. But maybe they didn't see him; maybe he wasn't visible walking in the darkness, with his rather unassuming, short body, in his dark clothing. His posture was perhaps not the best either; he probably did look a little silly because his feet pointed outwards, like a clown's. But he was not a clown.

He was a quiet person who never got into arguments, probably because he never contradicted anyone. This was not really all that remarkable, since he seldom saw anybody. Except at his job, of course, out in Järfälla, where he worked in the post room of a big electronics company. He delivered internal and external mail to all the engineers, secretaries, managers and everyone else who worked there. That was all he did; he was not entrusted, for example, with sorting the mail. There were other, more qualified persons who could handle such things, who could make important decisions, like deciding whether the mail was properly addressed.

He was very bad at making decisions. When he thought about it, he seldom had an opinion of his own about anything. If, on some random occasion, he was asked what he thought about something, he could not come up with a satisfactory answer. His only real desire was to be accepted by those around him. He was forty-four years old and, as yet, this had never happened.

The question was: If this one small desire were to be fulfilled at some point, would he then move up a rung on the ladder of his needs and suddenly start asserting opinions about other things too? Do you automatically get to do that when you are a valued person?

He looked up at the windows of the building on the other side of Fleminggatan. They were illuminated and pleasantly inviting in the autumn darkness, with potted plants and curtains, lamps with beautiful shades, colourful fans and other decorative objects. Some windows already displayed Advent candleholders, as if to further underscore the picturesqueness of the scene, and behind every illuminated window a happy family, a happy couple or at least a happy individual could be found. This was clear from the warm light and cosy setting.

His own window, on the other hand, gaped dark and empty, except for a sparsely foliated Ficus and the cord trailing from a blind. The kitchen window was, likewise, completely bare, except for an old transistor radio sitting there in lonely majesty. He did actually read the occasional home decorating magazine with interest. Not because he was looking for inspiration for his own home. Why waste effort on an apartment that no one else was ever in? Just him, one small, insignificant person – or maybe no one at all. He was not visible to the cars that splashed water from the gutter in the autumn darkness, and he was not heard – in fact, he hardly heard himself. No, he read home decor magazines for the same reason he looked up at other people's windows. In his imagination he moved to another world, a world of friendly people with warm smiles and big, soft, colourful cushions on their couches.

Today he had almost been offered a piece of cake at work. It didn't happen often, for in the post room there was never any reason to celebrate. Besides, he was almost never there for more than a few minutes at a time, when he picked up freshly sorted mail to be delivered to other departments.

However, when he dropped off the mail at section eleven, the workers were all sitting around eating cake, for some reason unknown to him. He always felt a little uncomfortable delivering mail to section eleven in particular. They always seemed to be having a coffee break right then, so they could see him as he arrived, in his ridiculous post-room uniform. Maybe 'uniform' was too grand a word – it was just a pair of blue trousers and a blue jacket, but in any event, he was the only one dressed that way and it was never good to stick out.

And so they saw him there, or to be more precise *one* person saw him. A real joker, who made fun of everything and everyone, and had lots of opinions. The others laughed at his jokes and seemed to share his opinions for the most part, for he was never contradicted. 'Hey there, Mr Postman!' he said today, sitting with his arms crossed and his legs stretched out under the break table. 'Would you like some cake?' Without expecting an answer he continued, 'If you do, then you'd better get going on your little scooter and fetch that circuit board from the hardware division first, like I told you yesterday and the day before yesterday. Is everyone in the post room a little slow or is it just you?' Laughter from the others at the table, maybe at the mail deliverer, or maybe out of habit. There would be no cake for him, for he had no authority to act as a courier and run errands for people. His task was simply to dole out the mail that was assigned to him.

Mentally, he was not slow. True, he had had no education to speak of, but he did read a lot. He was probably not of above-average intelligence, but he was not slow. He had done quite well in school for the first few years, but that had to come to an end. In Katrineholm, you did not do well in school; it was absolutely forbidden. Actually, you weren't supposed to be good at anything, except bandy and football and that sort of thing. There were definite, unspoken rules for everything: what you could be good at (sports), what you should not be good at (music, languages, crafts, conduct), what you should be mediocre in (any other school subject), what you should wear (store-bought clothes of the right brands), what you shouldn't wear (caps, glasses, anything hand-made), where you should live (apartment building), what political values you should have (Social Democrat, but definitely not communist), and what bandy team you should cheer for (KSC, not Värmbols). Above all, you were not allowed to excel or be different in any way.

But for a grown man in Stockholm, other rules applied. Here, individual ideas were appreciated; a deviant appearance was often positively accepted. Above all, education and self-confidence were necessities.

Life was hard. His mother had died when he was very young, and his father was a shift worker at a printing company and did not have much time left over for his son. He was a loving father, but lacked the skills to run a household or bring up a child. After decades of chain smoking, he too died at an early age, leaving behind a great void.

From the very start he had been different, but he had never been able to figure out exactly how. Well, he had the wrong dialect to start with – he had spent the first few years of his life in Huskvarna. He was also forced to wear a cap, but still – that was probably not the main reason. No doubt there was something wrong with his personality, even then. As a little boy he had been happy

11

and outgoing. He liked people, but he had realized early on that people did not like him in return. And this soon took the individuality and good humour out of him. It was probably there – in preschool, the year that Swedish children start formal schooling before entering primary school – that he began to turn into the person he was today. The constant physical abuse, interspersed with ostracism and name-calling, had not only transformed him into a silent shadow, it had deprived him of all self-confidence as well.

Even so, the next year he started primary school as an enthusiastic, curious and interested seven-year-old. But raising his hand to answer questions caused problems from the very start. You had to be careful not to think you were somebody. If he was asked a question that he could answer, the other children giggled and exchanged looks. If his answer was wrong, there was laughter. Several of his old tormentors from preschool were in the same class, and the other children were quickly initiated in how he should be treated. At playtime they beat him up, made up mean rhymes about him, or else he stood alone, watching the other children play games. Sometimes he did not even go to school, but stayed at home in bed, either sick – headache and stomachache – or pretending to be sick. His marks suffered, and at sixteen he dropped out. He was given a so-called extended trainee position, which he did not choose himself, in a haberdasher's shop where he did what he was told.

As far as he was concerned, his schooling was a wasted decade, but maybe things were better for children growing up now. On the TV news the other day there had been something about the successful 'Katrineholm Project', as the news anchor called it. In the interview, the pompous county councilman Göran Meijer called it 'Project Forest Hill', after the primary school (and former preschool) where the successful anti-bullying programme had first been introduced. He wondered whether the new methods, described with big phrases like 'respect for the individual', 'physical contact', 'adult supervision' and 'mentoring', might even allow a Husk-varna dialect and Värmbols caps.

After his stint in the haberdasher's shop he moved to Stockholm, where he lived with his great-uncle in a studio apartment on Kungsholmen. Here he completed his education at night school. Against all odds, and without further qualifications, he managed to get the job he still had. His great-uncle was long since dead and the apartment was now his.

Suddenly his thoughts were interrupted and he stopped short on the zebra crossing, standing in the middle of the street outside his own apartment building. There was something very familiar about the man who had just passed, and without knowing why he turned and followed him. The clear blue eyes and blond, curly hair, the somewhat eager but purposeful expression, a scar by his left eyebrow, the way he walked – everything added up. But was it really possible that after all these years he would recognize a person he had not seen since he was six or seven years old? It was probably just that he had been thinking right then about the attention given to the Katrineholm Project, making him see ghosts.

This uncertainty was based on common sense, but emotionally he had no doubts. In his mind's eye he saw that man almost every day. There was no doubt that it was him.

The man took the stairs down to the metro and rapidly approached the turnstile, where, with a practised hand, he slid his railcard through the reader and pushed through. He walked all the way down the long escalator that led into the underworld. On the platform he pulled a newspaper out of his jacket pocket and thumbed through it, waiting for the train.

He kept ten or twelve metres from the man the whole time, and then sat down on the bench behind him. Thoughts were flying through his head and he could not give any reasonable explanation for his actions. During the last twenty years he had not done anything out of the ordinary: going to work, going home, shopping, eating, sleeping, going to the movies or taking an occasional walk, reading and watching TV. And then suddenly he found himself down in the metro, on his way to an unknown destination, following a man he had not seen in almost forty years. He was filled with an unexpected sense of well-being.

Something was happening in his life; he was on an adventure, and he was enjoying it.

* * *

It was always pleasant to settle down in the carriage with a newspaper on the way home from work. He began his day at the estate agency at seven in the morning, so that he could be home before the day was over and spend some time with his kids before they went to bed. He had to be up by five-thirty and seldom got to bed before eleven-thirty, so he suffered from a constant shortage of sleep. But he had learned to live with it, and in a few years the kids would more or less take care of themselves. Then he and Pia would be able to sleep in on weekends.

They had three children, three wonderful children who, despite their stubbornness and their whining and their unlimited energy levels, still made him feel very good. It was the same with Pia, whom he had met at college, although they did not get together until eight years later when they met again at a party. She worked part-time as a dental hygienist in the suburb where they lived, and their relationship was still exceptionally good after fifteen years. They were best friends and could talk to each other about almost anything.

He was basically happy with his work too, even if he did not always like having to show properties on weekends. The company was doing well, and that was the main thing. Work as an estate agent meant freedom and variety, and he and his partner took home a good salary every month, so he wasn't complaining.

With the odds he had started with, it had been by no means certain that he would grow up into a happy adult. He was the only child of a single, semi-alcoholic woman who supported herself by hairdressing – when she did work – and whose only interest seemed to be men of all types. They moved a lot and never really settled down anywhere. Various stepfathers came and went over the years, some more serious than others. When he was little, he was considered noisy and unruly, and his childhood was marked by countless fights and detentions. He must have been a real handful. Of course, it affected his schoolwork; but in high school he began taking his studies seriously.

There everything changed. His mother moved again soon after he started high school but he decided not to go with her. He lived alone in a studio apartment and had to take care of himself. On weekends he worked at a petrol station and the evenings he devoted to studying, football and household chores. He really matured during this time and graduated from high school with excellent results. In fact, he did well enough to be able to study economics at the university.

And here he was now. En route *from* his well-paid job at the firm he and his partner had built up themselves, en route *to* his dear wife and beloved children at home in a cosy townhouse. He indulged himself with this thought, and his contentment was reinforced when he looked at his drab and dreary fellow passengers, noses deep in some vapid free newspaper or vacantly staring out of the snow-blurred window. In the window he saw the reflection of one poor soul who was actually staring at him. Was his happiness that obvious? Was that a problem? Whatever. He could live with that.

* * *

Thomas sat down a little in front of the man – none other than 'King Hans' – in the carriage, with his back to the direction of travel so that he could watch him. Not directly – he sat strategically placed at an angle, with people between him and the object of his interest – but he could see the man's reflection very well in the window.

Hans looked relaxed and self-confident. Submerged in his own thoughts, with the newspaper folded on his lap, he looked distractedly out of the window. It almost appeared as if a little smile crossed his face from time to time. Thomas stared in fascination and wondered what it was that made him so happy. Was there someone waiting for him? Someone who was pleased to see him when he came home? Maybe he had curtains in the window and cushions on the couch?

The man's gaze swept across the people in the carriage and for a moment their eyes met in the window reflection. Was that contempt he saw in Hans's blue eyes? If so, it was not surprising, considering Thomas's hunched posture, unkempt hair and frightened eyes. He was a wretch, who glanced furtively at the people he met, if he dared to look at them at all.

The light in the carriage suddenly blinked and it was completely dark for a few seconds. When the light came on again the man had gone back to investigating the water drops flowing together on the window. Thomas could continue studying the ghost from his childhood undisturbed.

He thought about all the caps that had disappeared on the way home from preschool, tossed on to roofs and passing truck beds. He thought about the drawings he would take home to show his father at the end of term, but which, to the amusement of all the children, disappeared one by one down a drain. He thought about torn trousers, muddy jackets and scraped knees, and he thought about Carina Ahonen, who always got to sit on the teacher's lap and lead the singing in assembly. She was the one who decided that they would draw horses and then all the children drew horses, horses, horses – it was the only thing you were allowed to draw. His were so bad they just had to be displayed, for every-one's entertainment.

He thought about the big green car out on the playground, which held at least six children. Two had to push, and he and Katarina pushed, every single day, in the pious hope that they too would get to sit in that car eventually. The teacher was very particular that everyone should get a turn, but for some reason she always forgot Thomas and Katarina. A few times Thomas managed to be first in the car, but then they threw him out and he had to push again, and this was clearly the way it should be, for the teacher only smiled her usual, sweet preschool teacher's smile.

One time, he remembered, Hans and Ann-Kristin took his cap and threw it to each other, back and forth over his head. Thomas could not get hold of it, but a momentary impulse suddenly gave him the courage to grab Hans's cap and run away with it. Of course, they caught up with him, beat him black and blue, and tore the cap out of his hands. When he got home later, without his cap (as usual), Hans's mother had already phoned Thomas's father to vent her feelings about Thomas tearing her little Hans's cap, whereupon Thomas was sent off to Hans and his mother with ten kronor to beg for forgiveness. For some reason his own missing cap never came up during the conversation.

He was jolted out of his musings when the train stopped and the man he was watching stood up to get off. Thomas, too, got up and followed this shadow from the past.

* * *

The townhouse was only a few minutes' walk from the Enskede Gård metro station. Hans jogged across the

19

street, turned left at the school and turned in among the houses in Trädskolan. Soon he reached a park with unusual bushes and trees, the only memory of the old garden centre that was replaced by new homes in the late 1980s. He turned on to a footpath leading past some shrubbery and up to the play area that was part of the townhouse complex. In the sandpit sat two muddy children in waterproofs; a third child – a one-and-a-half-year-old – stood perched on the top step of a slide.

'Please, Moa, hold on so you don't fall down and hurt yourself,' he called as he dashed over to the slide.

The little girl's face cracked a big smile and she immediately started to climb down. The two bigger children rushed over to their father and he tried as best he could to hug them and keep them at a distance at the same time.

'Hi there!' he said. 'Be careful, I have my work clothes on. Just hug with your face. Come on, let's go find Mum!'

Just then Moa threw herself headlong towards him from the ladder and he was forced to sacrifice his clean jacket, but in return got a big, wet kiss on the chin. In a desperate attempt to spare the jacket further damage, he carried her with his arms outstretched in front of him and, with the two bigger children at his heels, walked up to their front door, where he set her down.

'Hello!' he called as he opened the door. 'Here I come with three dirty pigs; you have to help me! Take off your boots before you go in,' he said to the bigger children as he squatted down and started to undress the smallest.

Pia appeared smiling in the doorway, dressed in jeans and a white blouse tied in the middle, and with her thick, dark hair pulled into a ponytail.

'Hi, honey,' she said, bending down and kissing him on the neck. 'How was your day?'

'Good, but I have to take off in a little while and look at a house. It's here in the neighbourhood, so I'll only be gone an hour or so. Should we feed the kids now, so we can eat when they've gone to bed?'

'Sure. What time are you leaving?'

'In about half an hour. I'll help you with the kids first.'

He finally managed to wriggle the waterproofs off the girl and she rushed in through the door making happy sounds. The other children had taken off their own outdoor clothes and, leaving them scattered all over the hallway, they ran off into the house. He got up and made a resigned attempt to brush the dirt off his jacket, producing no visible improvement. Pia gathered up the boots and outdoor clothes and went in. Hans pulled the door shut after him with a bang that caused the doorknocker to strike.

None of them noticed the man intently observing them through the branches of the bare lilac trees on the other side of the play area.

* * *

Thomas did not know how long he stood there in the darkness, spying, but in his imagination he was inside, in the warm, cosy kitchen that smelled of browned butter and frying meat. At first they all ran back and forth busily between various rooms, but after a while things calmed down, and one by one they sat down at the dinner table.

Thomas could not remember when he had last had a meal with other people. At work he ate in the big cafeteria, with other people around, but always alone. He had no living parents, no siblings, no other relatives that he ever saw, and no friends. It must be nice to have someone to come home to! How marvellous it would be simply to have a friend, just one person to talk to about things, great or small, someone to eat with occasionally. And think how much more fun it would be to cook if you were doing it for someone other than yourself.

Dinner was finished and the kitchen was suddenly just as empty as it had been full of life and motion. The outside door opened and an appreciated and beloved father stepped out of his house and closed the door behind him for the very last time.

* * *

With his hands shoved into his jacket pockets and his collar turned up as protection against the autumn winds, he walked quickly through the neighbourhood. Withered leaves whirled in the light under the street-lamps, and every step made a squishing sound as his shoe lost contact with the pavement. One shoe had a hole in it and his sock was already damp. He should have changed into winter shoes, but he didn't have time to turn back now. It shouldn't take more than fifteen minutes to get to the house he was to look over, and perhaps he would treat himself to a taxi home, given the weather.

He angled across a bigger road and turned on to the street where the property should be. The single-family houses in this neighbourhood were older – most were built in the 1920s and '30s and had mature gardens with fruit trees and arbours. This must be it: an old, pink, wooden house with beautiful bay windows. The garden, much larger than others in the area, sloped from the house down towards the street and was surrounded by a well-tended but overly tall hedge, which did not suit the small house and the garden in general. In the hedge there was an even more out-of-place black iron gate, beyond which a gravel path led up to the house itself. He glanced at the mailbox and confirmed that this was the correct address, Åkerbärsvägen 31, and then pushed open the stubborn gate wide enough to slip through. It closed heavily behind him with a metallic clang.

He hurried up the path without noticing the heavy aroma of soft windfall fruit. Nor did he notice the shadow that, without making a sound, climbed lithely over the large gate behind him and jumped down on to the wet lawn at the side of the gravel path. He stepped up on to the porch and rang the doorbell. An echoing ding-dong sounded from inside the house, but that was all he heard. He waited for a minute or two before he rang again. After a glance at his watch, which confirmed that he was only a few minutes late, he went around the back. The outside lights were on, but only one room of the old house was lit. It was the kitchen; the windows looked out on to the back garden. He couldn't reach all the way to the kitchen window, but he bent over and picked up a small stick, which he threw at the windowpane, still without any reaction from anyone inside. He decided to return to the front and check whether the door was unlocked. To his surprise, he found that it was. Perhaps the person who lived here was old and hard of hearing?

'Hello, anybody home?' he called in a loud voice, but got no answer. 'Hello!' he tried again, this time even louder.

Then he made his decision: he went into the house, carefully drying his shoes on the doormat in the hall and closing the door behind him.

Tuesday Evening

After several weeks in the hospital she could finally go home again. Finally, because she longed to sleep in her own bed, to sit alone in front of her own TV and decide for herself what programme to watch, with her own home-brewed coffee steaming in a cup on the side table. She missed the smell of home, the aroma of her own soap and her own detergent, and the pleasant odour of old preserves that permeated the walls.

On the other hand, it was actually not so wonderful at all. She had difficulty walking after breaking her hip and it would be hard to manage properly by herself. Her interest in food had subsided over the years; it had almost no taste any more. But she did have to eat something and there were practical benefits to being in the hospital, where everything was served to you and you didn't have to worry about shopping, cooking or doing dishes.

The man from the transport service set down her small suitcase outside the door and waited patiently until she got her key ring out of her handbag. She carefully put the key into the lock, which yielded with a click, and the door opened by itself.

'Should I help you in?' he asked kindly.

'No, that's not necessary. I'll be all right now. Thanks very much,' she said, raising her hand in farewell.

'Be careful now and get well soon!' the driver waved, walking backwards down the steps to see that she really did manage to get into the house by herself.

After turning on the ceiling light, Ingrid wiped her shoes on the doormat, set her crutch in the corner inside the door, and took a step over to the coat rack where she wriggled out of her coat while she balanced on her good leg. She reached for a hanger, covered in red velvet with a gold-coloured fringe, and hung up her coat. Then she took a few more steps to a small stool and sank down on it. She pulled off her leather boots and set them symmetrically under the coat rack, reached for her small suitcase and pulled up the zip that ran around the edge. She took a pair of comfortable indoor shoes from the suitcase and let her feet glide into them. She managed to get up again by pushing against the wall.

Supported by the crutch, she limped through the hall, took a quick, displeased glance at herself in the hallway mirror, and continued towards the kitchen. She stopped on the threshold and leaned in to get at the light switch on the wall just inside the door.

As she did so it suddenly struck her that something smelled strange. The usual smells were there, but something unknown was forcing its way into her nostrils through all that was familiar. It smelled of leather. Leather and . . . excrement? Then she turned on the light.

26

First she stopped breathing and stood as if petrified, unable to understand what she was seeing. After a few seconds her brain managed to take in the image of the dead man on the floor and she started to hyperventilate instead. She staggered over to one of the chairs at the dinner table, pulled it out and sat down abruptly. She could not tear her gaze from the bloody mass that had been a face, and she sat there for a long while without thinking anything other than: breathe in, breathe out, breathe in, breathe out . . . It took several minutes for her to calm down. When she finally did, she noticed that everything else was in order, nothing had been touched on the kitchen counter and the kitchen chairs were symmetrically placed around the circular table. Not a trace of any scuffle or drama, only a battered person on the floor. A dead man. Good Lord, who could it be? And why in the world was he there, on her kitchen floor?

With great effort, she got up again and made her way out to the wall-mounted telephone in the hallway. She picked up the receiver and pondered for a moment before she dialled the number for the taxi firm. After ordering a taxi, which according to the dispatcher would arrive in ten to twelve minutes, she undid everything she had done since arriving: off with her shoes, which went back into the suitcase, back with the zip, on with the boots, up and on with her coat, lights off and out, and lock the door. Then she made her way down the path, with her handbag over her shoulder, suitcase in one hand and crutch in the other, and waited on the pavement until the taxi arrived.

'Ingrid!' exclaimed Nurse Margit in surprise. 'I thought you were looking forward to going home!'

Margit Olofsson was a middle-aged woman, tall with ample curves and thick dark-red hair. She was the type of person who radiated motherliness and human concern.

'Nurse Margit, there's something terrible . . .'

'But Ingrid, dear, sit down; you look completely worn out! Has something happened? Are you feeling unwell?'

Margit Olofsson took the older woman under the arm and led her to one of the armchairs in the hospital reception area. Under her white coat a pair of washed-out blue jeans could be seen.

'I didn't know what to do,' said Ingrid imploringly. 'I guess I'm confused, but I couldn't think of anyone other than you . . . It . . . Don't laugh at me now, but . . . there's a dead man lying in my kitchen.'

'Good God! Who is it?'

'I don't know. I've never seen him before. It's not burglars or anything; nothing was touched or taken. He's just lying there. And he's dead.'

'That doesn't make sense. Are you sure he's dead?'

'Absolutely. You can tell. It's . . . completely still.'

'You must have been very frightened.'

'That's true, that's why I came back here.'

'Of course, my dear,' Nurse Margit consoled her, placing her arm around her shoulders. 'You did call the police, didn't you?'

'I . . . No,' admitted Ingrid. 'It seemed so unreal. I couldn't . . .'

Nurse Margit's initial thought was to call the police and social services, but she was suddenly struck by the suspicion that Ingrid Olsson might possibly be not completely lucid. She studied her thoughtfully for a few moments and then took a look at her watch.

'Let's do it this way. I get off in two and a half hours. Then we'll go to your house together and decide what to do. Okay?'

'That will be fine.'

'Do you mind waiting so long?'

'Oh, no, that's not a problem.'

'I'll arrange something for you to eat in the mean-time. And a magazine.'

Then she hurried off, her clogs clip-clopping against the stone floor. She was back again just as quickly, with coffee, a Danish pastry, some biscuits and a stack of *Woman's Weekly*.

'Will you be all right now?'

'Yes. Thank you so much, Nurse Margit!'

'See you later then. Bye for now!'

And there Ingrid remained, sitting by herself but without feeling particularly alone, for she was sure that Nurse Margit would take care of everything.

*

When Nurse Margit finally came back she had changed out of her white hospital coat into a black cotton tunic under an open blue down jacket that fluttered after her as she hurried over to Ingrid. The white clogs had been replaced by a pair of black boots and the clip-clopping by almost soundless steps.

'My car is in the car park,' said Margit, smiling warmly and offering her arm in support as Ingrid got up out of the armchair. 'Has it been terribly boring?'

'Oh, no, not at all. I've been reading the whole time.'

They went out of the hospital entrance side by side and made their way at a snail's pace down a little hill to a stone-paved path, which led through some barberry bushes and on to the enormous car park. After passing several rows of cars they stopped at a white Ford Mondeo. Nurse Margit unlocked the car with a click of the remote control and helped Ingrid into the passenger seat.

'Now you're getting a little exercise too, Ingrid. It's good that you're practising walking. You can look on it as physical therapy.'

Ingrid smiled at her as the friendly nurse got into the driver's seat beside her. She hardly believed herself that there really was a corpse at home. Could she have imagined the whole thing? Perhaps her painkillers were giving her hallucinations? It seemed so unreal that anyone could have been murdered in her kitchen.

The closer they got to Ingrid's house, the more the foundations of artificial security she had been lulled into during her hours of reading *Woman's Weekly* in the hospital reception area were shaken. There was a corpse at home in her kitchen. Full stop. How would that affect her life from now on? The house would probably be invaded by police and crime scene investigators, who would ransack it in search of fingerprints and clues. Who would clean up after them? There would be police tape around the house and neighbours staring. Maybe reporters. Police interrogation.

No, it would doubtless be some time before life really returned to normal. If ever. Would she feel safe again in a house where an unknown murderer had killed a strange man? Well, perhaps it was not very likely to happen again. She would just have to put the whole thing behind her sooner or later, and go on as if nothing had happened. She was not involved in any way; she had just been struck by a little bit of bad luck. People get murdered every day, in Sweden and even more so in other places. You can't worry about that kind of thing, and the only rather unusual aspect of this particular death was that it had happened in her own home. Grit your teeth, forget it and go on, she told herself.

It felt creepy, walking up the path, arm in arm in the dense November darkness. The gravel crunched under their feet, and the only light was the dull yellow glow from a lamp-post at the side of the path and the wall light on the porch. The temperature was close to freezing and the northerly autumn winds caused the bare crowns of the fruit trees to bend agonizingly and the two women to shiver.

As soon as the door opened and she brought her nose into the warm house, Nurse Margit recognized the sickening odour. Ingrid, too, now noticed it immediately. It was strange she hadn't done so the first time she came home. Ingrid turned on the ceiling light and remained standing in the doorway while Nurse Margit nimbly removed her unbuttoned boots and headed resolutely for the kitchen. She stopped on the threshold and fumbled for the light switch. With the light on, she looked around for a few moments before her eyes found what they were searching for. Without hesitation, she rushed up to the lifeless body on the floor. Her fingers searched expertly under the shirt collar for the carotid artery and she quickly verified what she already knew: the man was dead. She got up and went to the phone.

* * *

Detective Chief Inspector Conny Sjöberg was lying on the couch watching a children's show on TV. A boisterous one-year-old was jumping up and down on top of him, trying, despite more-or-less stern reprimands, to tear off Daddy's glasses, which at this point were so dirty with fingerprints he could barely see through them. Another one-year-old marauder was standing by the magazine rack, tossing all the magazines on the floor. Sjöberg observed – for the umpteenth time – that they seriously needed more magazine holders, and made a mental note to buy some tomorrow. On her knees, right in front of the TV, sat four-year-old Maja, totally engrossed in the trials of a zebra, a giraffe, a monkey and two small teddy bears trying to clean a child's room. She seemed completely oblivious to the mayhem going on around her and followed her programme with undivided attention, taking no notice of her twin brothers.

Conny Sjöberg's wife, Åsa, was in the kitchen cleaning up after dinner, assisted by their chatty six-year-old daughter, who loved to do dishes. From his spot on the couch, Sjöberg could hear her light voice over the sound of the TV and the excited voices of the wild toddlers. Their oldest son, eight-year-old Simon, had gone home from school with a friend in the neighbouring building, leaving the family one short.

The Sjöbergs' apartment was a marvel of orderliness, especially considering the size of the family. This was a necessity, however, for the mental well-being of the paterfamilias, and he kept it that way. When all the children were home in the afternoon, and play, baths and dinner preparations were under way, the uninitiated observer might get an impression of total chaos. But by nine o'clock, when all the children were in bed, there was no longer any sign whatsoever of these activities in the apartment.

It was the same in the morning: although seven

people ran around like dazed chickens for a few hours, all traces vanished when the outside door was closed for the last time. Every time new chaos was created, Sjöberg convinced himself that it was best for the children to start from order. In reality, it was mostly because he had a hard time collecting his thoughts if everything was not tidy. With the job he had, as chief inspector of the Violent Crimes Unit, it was important to be able to organize his thoughts in a logical order, and that just didn't work if things were out of place.

The apartment on Skånegatan, right by Nytorget, was large, five rooms with a spacious kitchen, but still too small. The twins shared a room and the girls shared a room. Simon had his own nook, but the girls would also need more privacy in the not-too-distant future. They were also in great need of a second bathroom. Mornings were an endless queue for the facilities. To avoid that, and to be able to sit in peace for a while with the newspaper at the breakfast table, Sjöberg was always the first one up. By five-thirty he was out of bed, shaved and showered, had put on the coffeepot, made two cheese sandwiches and fetched the newspaper. He often had twenty minutes to himself before the rest of the household began to stir, and then a lot had to happen in a short time. Porridge had to be heated and nappies changed, sandwiches made, clothes picked out and put on, hair braided and teeth brushed. And to top it off, there was a constant roar of voices, little feet jumping and running, furniture being moved around, and that damn pedal car that must sound like thunder to the neighbours below. Not an enviable situation perhaps, but Sjöberg truly loved his life with the children, and he and Åsa never regretted their large, noisy family.

Even so, they ought to move somewhere roomier. But a bigger, better apartment in the inner city would be hard to find and certainly much too expensive. A single-family home or townhouse in the suburbs was not particularly appealing. Here they were settled and happy. They were satisfied with the school and nursery, the children had their friends, it was close to work for both Åsa and himself, and close to everything else too: shops, restaurants, and many of their friends. No, it would be hard to find a better place to live.

From the kitchen he heard his oldest daughter, Sara, bellowing, 'Fish pudding, fish pudding, fish pudding, don't give me fish pudding, fish pudding, fish pudding . . .' and wondered to himself why she was singing that – she loved salmon pudding. At the same moment the phone rang and he heard a thud as Sara leaped down from the chair by the kitchen counter to get to the phone first.

'Hello, this is Sara!' she chirped.

'. . .'

'Fine, how are you?'

'. . .'

'No, he's watching *Bolibompa*.'

'. . .'

'Okay, I'll ask. Bye now!'

'Who is that?' asked Åsa.

'It's Sandén!' Sara called, already halfway to the living room at a gallop. 'Daddy, it's Sandén on the phone; he wants to talk to you!'

'Please watch the boys, Sara,' said Sjöberg, removing Christopher from his stomach and setting him down on the floor, and unwillingly peeling himself from the couch.

'Oh, crud,' he moaned when the call was finished.

He could already see the displeased frown on his wife's face, and he understood her all too well. This was not exactly a dream situation, to be left alone with five kids at bedtime.

'What's going on?' she asked.

'An old woman who had been in the hospital came home and found a corpse on her kitchen floor. Unfortunately, I have to go there.'

'Who was it?'

Even if Åsa disliked the situation, she could not help being fascinated by her husband's work. She let him sound off at home, and tried, to the best of her ability, to offer sensible suggestions about the often nasty cases he was working on. Sjöberg frequently used her as a sounding board, and sometimes she gave him guidance and inspiration in complicated investigations.

'That's what's so strange,' Sjöberg answered. 'She has

no idea who it is. He was lying dead in her house, but she'd never seen him before.'

'Dreadful.'

Åsa shivered as she pictured a lifeless body on the first kitchen floor that occurred to her – their own.

'But isn't it most likely that they have met somehow?' she added thoughtfully.

'We'll have to see,' he said, kissing her quickly on the lips. 'This might take all night, I don't know. Take care now.'

'You too, and good luck,' she said, stroking his cheek briefly before he turned to go with a tired sigh.

* * *

The old woman was younger than he had imagined, maybe in her seventies, and she was reclining on a pilled, dark-brown love seat of 1970s vintage. A crutch was leaning against the couch by one of her legs. She sat quietly, looking straight ahead with an inscrutable gaze that revealed nothing of what was going on in her mind. She did not look frightened or sad, and she did not seem particularly curious either about what was happening around her. In the hall outside the living room, Sandén was talking with a middle-aged woman, but the older lady showed no sign of listening to the conversation. Her eyes, behind a pair of gold-rimmed glasses, were grey, and her hair was grey and cut short.

Her legs were thin in a pair of straight, light-blue trousers with sewn creases, and ended in a pair of black shoes. On her upper body she was wearing a grey lambswool turtleneck.

Sjöberg went up to her to say hello, and she turned towards him with a polite but rather uninterested expression. He extended a hand and introduced himself, and she responded with a limp handshake and a nod.

'Can you please wait here for a while, then I'll come and talk to you a bit,' Sjöberg asked politely.

'I'll be sitting right here,' she answered tonelessly, and resumed her study of the air around her.

Sjöberg returned to the hall and Sandén gave him a quick look and nodded towards the kitchen, while he continued his conversation with the younger woman. Sjöberg glanced in passing at the tall, full-figured woman, anywhere between forty-five and fifty-five. Despite her worried frown and serious tone, he thought he detected a lively gleam in her green eyes. Her striking reddish-brown hair fluttered as she turned towards him and met his eyes. For some reason he felt ashamed and immediately turned his face away. A sudden thirst came over him and a shiver ran down his spine.

He approached the doorway between the hall and kitchen and observed the dead body for a few moments, then he looked around the kitchen without entering it. This was his opportunity to take in the discovery site before the photographers, CSI technicians and other police started swarming in. The first impression of a crime scene could be very important, and he took his time before he crossed the threshold.

The kitchen showed no signs of a violent struggle. Everything appeared to be in order, and no furniture was overturned. The work surfaces were clean, and in the middle of the round table was a white lace table cloth on which stood an empty fruit bowl and a brass candleholder. The dead man was lying in front of the refrigerator, dressed in a dark-blue sailing jacket zipped up halfway, khaki trousers and brown leather shoes. His face was badly mauled and a little blood had trickled out from his nose. Otherwise, he looked rather peaceful, lying there on his back on the pinewood floor.

Sjöberg left the kitchen and squeezed past Sandén and the woman in the hall. The agreeable aroma of a not-too-insistent perfume found its way into his nostrils. He went out on to the porch and called to the men. The photographer and technicians already knew what they had to do, but he gave directions to the police officers to set up barricades and look around the garden. He intended to question the owner of the house before he sent her away.

'Is your name Ingrid Olsson?' asked Sjöberg.

'Yes,' Ingrid replied curtly.

'Unfortunately, I must ask you to leave the house for a while. You can't stay here while we conduct the crime scene investigation.'

She looked at him expressionlessly, without answering.

'Do you have anywhere to go for the night?'

'I'll talk with Nurse Margit.'

'Nurse Margit?' Sjöberg asked.

'Yes, I had just been discharged from the hospital and came home and found the body. I didn't know what to do, so I asked Nurse Margit to help me.'

'I understand. Can you please tell me the whole story, from the beginning?'

Ingrid Olsson told her story in a dull voice, but Sjöberg listened attentively, jotting down a few lines in his notebook now and then or asking a question. Her calmness about the whole matter surprised him, but it was probably good that she was not getting too worked up. After all, she would still have to live in the house, and many people in her situation would have decided right then and there to move out. But what type of person, he thought, dismisses a murder in her own home with a shrug? Possibly the type who turns off the news when it's about war and suffering, and turns her face away when she encounters buskers and Save the Children collection boxes. Sjöberg was aware that intuition was an important tool in his occupation but, unwilling to draw hasty conclusions, he was content to assume that Ingrid Olsson was more agitated than she appeared.

'So, you didn't know the dead man?' he continued instead. 'Are you completely sure of that?'

'I've never seen him before,' she answered firmly.

'Do you have any children or relatives who have access to the house?'

'No one has access to the house. No, I have no children.'

'How long have you lived here?'

'For sixteen years. I moved here to be closer to my sister when my husband died.'

'Where did you live before?'

'I grew up in Österåker, and lived there until I moved here.'

'And so your sister lives here in the neighbourhood?'

'She's no longer living.'

'I'm sorry. Who may have known that you were in the hospital? Or more precisely, who might have known that you weren't at home?'

'Well, no one in particular. The neighbours perhaps. The postman. How would I know?'

'Do you have any contact with the neighbours?'

'We say hello.'

'You've never had a break-in before?'

'Never. There's nothing here to steal.'

He silently agreed. What he had seen of the house so far gave no indication that there would be anything of value here, other than possibly the TV, though it seemed pretty old. There were only inexpensive reproductions and framed photographs hanging on the walls, and the furniture was extremely sparse, and all from the 1960s and '70s.

'That's enough for now,' said Sjöberg, closing his

notebook, 'though I'll probably have to speak to you again. We'll make sure that the house is returned to its normal condition when we're done here, so you don't need to worry about that. Thank you very much,' he said, extending his hand in farewell.

A quick smile passed over her lips when their hands met, and she suddenly looked quite sweet.

In the hall he ran into Sandén, who, like him, was on his way to the kitchen.

'Did she have anything to tell?' Sjöberg asked.

'Margit Olofsson? No, nothing other than that she brought the old lady back here from the hospital, confirmed what she said was true, and called the police,' Sandén replied.

Sjöberg tried to quiet Sandén with an index finger to his lips and a nod towards the living room, and continued, half whispering, 'They don't really have any relationship?'

'No, other than that she's a nurse in the ward where the old woman was. The old lady is alone and took a liking to her. Margit Olofsson has nothing to do with the case,' said Sandén quietly.

One of the technicians, Gabriella Hansson, came out to them in the hall, waving a wallet in her gloved hand.

'The identity seems to be established,' she said, pulling out a driver's licence. 'Hans Vannerberg, born in 1962.'

'Anything else of interest?' asked Sjöberg, taking his notebook out of the inside pocket of his jacket and noting the information from the driver's licence.

'A few credit cards, a business card – he appears to be an estate agent – pictures of children, an organ donation card, but it's probably too late for that, I'm afraid. Quite a bit of cash – so probably not a robbery. You'll have the wallet tomorrow.'

'Good. Thanks,' said Sjöberg.

The information about the photographs depressed him. It was bad enough delivering the news of a death, but when there were children involved he had a hard time holding back his tears. Ingrid Olsson came out of the living room, supported by the nurse.

'I guess we'll be leaving now,' said Margit Olofsson to the two police officers. 'I'll make sure that Ingrid has a roof over her head.'

'That's considerate of you. We're sorry about this, but unfortunately there's nothing we can do about it,' said Sjöberg. 'We'll be in touch with both of you.'

He managed to conceal a slight shudder, but now his mouth felt even drier than before.

'Just one last question,' he said, directing it at Ingrid Olsson. 'Hans Vannerberg, in his mid-forties, does that sound familiar?'

'No, not at all,' she answered.

'Think about it,' said Sjöberg. 'Bye now.'

*

'How did she seem?' asked Sandén when the two women were out of the door.

'She gave a somewhat cool impression. Surprisingly uninterested. But she's in shock, of course.'

'She didn't appear to be quite the classic nice old lady. She looked sharp somehow. Poor nurse, getting her around her neck. Do you suppose she's taking the old lady home with her?'

'Presumably,' answered Sjöberg. 'She seemed to be the caretaker type. Now let's go out and check whether they've found anything of interest in the garden.'

A young police assistant, Petra Westman, approached them as they came out on to the porch.

'We've found a number of footprints,' she said before they could ask. 'It's perfect weather for that sort of thing, so we have some really good impressions.'

'Male or female?' asked Sandén.

'I think we have two different pairs of shoes,' Westman replied. 'Both of them seem to be men's.'

'Nothing else?'

'No, not yet.'

She vanished among the shadows again and Sjöberg looked sorrowfully at Sandén.

'You'll have to hold down the fort here while I go to the station and check up on this Vannerberg. He's probably been reported missing. Then I guess I'll have to contact his family,' he said with a sigh. 'Gather the forces for a review at eleven o'clock tomorrow.'

He leaned down to remove the blue shoe protectors

and put them in his jacket pocket. Then he hurried, crouching before the wind, towards the car on the street.

* * *

On his way back to the station he played 'Brothers in Arms' by Dire Straits and phoned Åsa. It was already eleven o'clock, but he assumed she would still be up, enjoying the calm after the usual stormy bedtime for five children.

'Hi, how are things?'

'Fine. They're all asleep and I'm sitting here reading. How's it going?'

'I've looked at the corpse and now I'm on my way back to the station to find out who he was. Then I have to contact his family. It appears that he had children.'

'Oh boy, poor you. And poor them. And the old lady?'

'A little absent. In shock, presumably. She had never seen him before and didn't recognize his name either.'

'Strange. But she probably had some connection anyway, maybe without even knowing it.'

'I'm not so sure.'

'Yes, but otherwise he could just as well have been murdered out in the woods!'

'The house was empty for several weeks while the

old woman was in the hospital. Someone knew that and lured the guy there to murder him. He was an estate agent.'

'But do you really murder someone in a strange person's house, just because it's standing empty?'

Åsa's viewpoint was always worth taking seriously, but Sjöberg was doubtful in this case. Despite everything, this was the reality: the great majority of murders were simply violent acts, without any complicated psychology, advance planning or underlying symbolism.

'Go to bed now,' he said lovingly. 'I don't know if I'll be home at all tonight. See you.'

'Bye now, dear, I'll be thinking of you,' Åsa concluded, and he thanked his lucky stars for this marvellous, positive life partner he was blessed with.

This thought brought him back to Hans Vannerberg and he hoped he had no wife and that the children in his wallet were only nieces and nephews.

The police station was at the end of Östgötagatan by the Hammarby canal, a large, modern office building with a glass façade. At this time of night it was mostly silent and deserted with few lights on inside the transparent walls. He slid his pass card through the reader by the main entrance and entered his code: 'POOP', inspired by his four-year-old's current primary interest. Every time he entered the code it made him feel happy, though he hoped that no one was peeking over his shoulder.

His footsteps on the marble floor in the reception area echoed desolately. Lotten, the receptionist, had gone home hours ago to her equally dog-crazy partner and their Afghans. Sjöberg could not keep from smiling at the thought that Lotten's and Micke the care-taker's dogs actually sent Christmas cards to each other, and birthday cards too. He wondered whether it was dog years or human years that were being celebrated, and decided to ask one of them when he had an opportunity.

He took the stairs up to the second floor in four big bounds and unlocked his door, which six hours ago he thought he had locked for the night. He threw his jacket over one of the visitor chairs before he sat down at his desk. Then he phoned the duty desk at the National Bureau of Investigation, but changed his mind before the call could be connected. Instead, he started looking for Vannerberg in the phone book and found him with no difficulty. He looked up the address in the street register and found to his surprise that it was not far from the crime scene. He decided to call Sandén, who answered almost immediately.

'Hi, Jens. How's it going?'

'No new discoveries so far. The technicians are working away. Hansson thinks he was beaten to death with a kitchen chair, and the discovery site appears to be the scene of the crime, just as we thought.'

'Listen, the local police who were first on the scene, they don't happen to still be there, do they?'

'No, they left while you were talking with Ingrid Olsson.'

'Maybe they know the victim. I have to check on that to be on the safe side. He may have been reported missing to them.'

He got their names and called the local station where they worked. He got a response immediately; one of them was still filing his report. Sjöberg stated his business.

'Yes, the wife was in here this afternoon and reported him missing since yesterday evening, but we haven't had time to do anything about it. It was already five o'clock when she arrived.'

'So why didn't you tell us that? That you already had a missing person with a description like the dead man?'

'Didn't think of it. There didn't seem to be anything dodgy about him.'

'About who, do you mean?' Sjöberg asked, irritated.

'About the man who disappeared, of course. He seemed completely normal, not dodgy in any way. And the wife too.'

'But the corpse was dodgy, you mean?' Sjöberg hissed.

'Well, I guess it's a bit shifty getting murdered like that, in the old lady's house and all . . .'

Sjöberg gave up and asked him to fax over the report immediately. He collected himself and thanked the officer for his help anyway, hung up and went to the copy room to stand and wait by the fax machine. Finally the damned fax arrived and he read it immediately. The date of birth matched, and he had a wife and three children. He worked as an estate agent and, according to his wife, had disappeared about six o'clock the previous evening to do a home visit to a seller in the neighbourhood. He said he would walk there and be back about an hour later, but he never returned.

Sjöberg looked at the clock and saw that it was past midnight. He considered whether now was a good time to visit the family. The wife would surely be beside herself with worry, but he decided to wait until the morning. If the family was sleeping, they could continue doing so. He was in dire need of a few hours of sleep himself, before tackling this difficult task.

* * *

He is standing on a lawn wet with dew, looking down at his bare feet. He is looking down although he feels he ought to look up, but something holds him back. His head feels so heavy that he is barely able to raise it. He gathers all his courage and all his strength to turn his face upwards, but still he dares not open his eyes. He lets the back of his head rest against his neck for a while. Finally, he opens his eyes.

There she stands again in the window, the beautiful woman with the dazzling red hair like sunlight around her head. She takes a few dance steps and her eyes meet his with a look of surprise. He raises his arms towards her but loses his balance and falls backwards.

Conny Sjöberg sat up in bed with a jolt. He pressed his palms hard against his eyes and felt the sweat running down his back. His whole body was shaking, but he was not crying. He was breathing fast through his nose, but without letting out any sound. He could hardly open his mouth – it was completely dry – and he was shivering. He rocked back and forth a few times with his face in his hands before he pulled himself together and went out to the bathroom.

That dream again, that constantly recurring dream. He gulped down two glasses of water before he dared look at himself in the mirror. His body was still shaking, but his breathing was starting to calm down now. The same meaningless dream, over and over. He did not understand why it bothered him so much.

What was new this time, however, was that the woman had a familiar face.

Diary of a Murderer,
November 2006, Tuesday

Never have I felt so exhilarated, so full of energy and
the desire to live as today, the day I committed a murder
for the first time. Even I can hear how absurd that
sounds, like something out of a comedy, but this is no
laughing matter, the whole thing is really very tragic.
Tragic like my shabby life, bounded by loneliness and
humiliation, and tragic like my miserable childhood,
full of violence, rejection and terror. Those children,
they took everything from me: my self-esteem, my joy
in living, my dreams of the future and my self-respect.
They also took something from me that everyone else
seems to have for life: an album of sunny childhood
memories you can dream back to or refer to when you
talk with other people. True, I don't have anyone to talk
to now and never have had, but I don't have any happy
childhood memories either. Not a single light in my
life-long darkness. When you're six years old, a time
span of six years is actually a lifetime. Just as much a
lifetime as a time span of forty-four years when you're
forty-four.

I can put words to it. I can formulate the thought
that it was the children who took everything away from
me, but I can't do anything about it. I just let it happen,

let it overshadow the rest of my life, and became a victim of people's cruelty. I've viewed myself as a victim and lived my life like one. Silent, afraid and alone. But now that's over. I don't feel like a happier person in any way; on the contrary, I feel a kind of gluttony in my own unhappiness and that's what exhilarates me.

I had still not decided what I would do when I stepped out into the light of the kitchen lamp. I didn't intend to hurt him, all I wanted was understanding – some sort of acknowledgement – and an apology. And there he stood, good-looking, prosperous and beloved, with a slightly surprised but friendly smile on his lips.

'Oh, excuse me,' he said apologetically. 'I rang the doorbell several times and threw sticks at the window. I thought maybe you didn't hear so well and since we'd decided on this time –'

'No problem,' I interrupted. I decided to exploit the mental advantage his little estate agent transgression had given me to adopt a haughty, somewhat patronizing tone.

Despite his apologetic attitude and the awkward situation, he stood there with head held high and obviously undisturbed self-confidence. His charming smile and the roguish gleam in his eye gave him a commanding presence. It wasn't possible to think badly of such a person. But it was possible to hate him.

It was enough to travel thirty-seven years back in time and think about the little child lying face down on the asphalt, with a scraped, stinging face in a dirty pool of water. Arms and legs extended like someone being crucified, held fast by other little kids who, sometimes laughing, sometimes struggling with grim faces, obediently carried out the task you had assigned from your clear position as uncrowned king. And there you sat on the small of my back, your legs straddling the sniffling child's back as if on a horse, and jubilantly cut strand after strand of hair with blunt little scissors. Blood and tears – nothing disturbed your undisguised joy.

It's not hard to hate a person who in one miserable year managed to destroy a person's life: mine. It's easy to hate you as you stand there, eager to be rid of me and – so you thought – my house, to return to your beautiful wife and children, and God forbid that they ever have to experience the horrors you subjected me to on a daily basis. Fate willed that evil incarnate – you, Hans – would grow up to be a happy and harmonious, beloved person, with the capacity to love, while I, the victim of evil, only became an insignificant bug, crawling around unnoticed in the dirt and with the capacity only for dark, destructive hatred.

He extended his hand and I took it without revealing my distaste.

'Well, a little guided tour perhaps?' he said politely, but still authoritatively.

'No, I thought we should sit down and talk a little first,' I answered, indicating a chair at the kitchen table with one hand.

I had no plans to sit down myself, but he sat down compliantly on the edge of the chair, with his feet crossed underneath and his hands clasped in front of him on the table. I leaned back against the kitchen counter with my arms crossed and looked at him scornfully as he turned his face up towards me with a friendly, interested expression. Neither he nor I yet had any idea what was about to happen, but I started to feel a certain satisfaction in the situation as it had developed. I was no longer in control of my own actions, there was a higher, stronger power guiding me. Gone was the fear and complaisance – only steely power remained.

'Yes?' he said, after a few moments of silence.

'Yes?' I said, like an echo.

'What did you want to talk about?'

'We are going to discuss you and me and our relationship,' I answered, not recognizing my own voice.

'Relationship?' he asked, not understanding.

He looked uncertain now, with his fingertips nervously drumming against each other.

'Don't you recognize me?'

Of course he didn't. It's not easy to recognize someone you haven't seen since you were a little kid. Unless this someone had left such deep scars in your psyche that you dream about him at night and devote the greater portion of your waking hours to cursing him and what he did. He shook his head.

'Should I?'

'We're old childhood friends,' I answered dryly.

He lit up and exclaimed in relief, 'How nice! When –'
but I interrupted him.

'Yes, I'm quite sure you thought it was. You had a lot
of fun with me. Do you remember when you were all
Indians and I was a cowboy?'

'No –'

I interrupted him again.

'By the bins? I was huddled in a corner, hiding my
head in my hands to keep from going blind when you
shot arrows at me. One arrow stuck in my leg – surely
you remember that – you tore it out and you were so
happy that you got real blood on your arrow.'

'I don't know . . .' he began.

'Sure you do. We played every day. We played that I
wanted to go home from preschool, but you wouldn't
let me. Instead you and Ann-Kristin and Lise-Lott and
whatever their names were first had to hit me or break
something of mine or take my clothes. Once you took
my trousers and I had to go home bare-legged in the
winter. You must remember that, you all thought it was
so funny.'

I spat the words out in disgust at the man in front of
me. He really looked as if he did not understand. Was it
possible that he didn't remember? Could it really be like
that, that these events, of such decisive importance for
me, meant nothing to him? For him, they were not even
childhood memories. Maybe he didn't even remember
an ordinary going-home-from-preschool episode like
that the day after it happened. His puzzled expression

made a mockery of my entire failed existence! I was now boiling with rage inside, but I hid it as best I could. I remained standing, outwardly calm, with my arms crossed. I continued my lecture.

'You do remember the spitting contest though? When you all waited for me outside the gate and then spat on me. Everyone at once. "Ready, set, go!" you said, and then you spat on me, twenty children at once. The one who scored the best hit in the face won, and I'm sure you were the winner, you were so good at it.'

'You must be –'

'There now! You're starting to remember! Do you remember the drowning game in the rain barrel? "We'll count to three and then let you go." Down with my head in the barrel, "One, two, three," and then up. Down again, "One, two, three," and up. "One, two, three," – up. Do you know how waterboarding affects people?'

'But that was just for fun,' he stammered. 'Just kids' way of –'

'Kids' way of what?' I roared now, and I heard my voice breaking.

Even though my intention had been only to hold him accountable and, in the best case, demand an apology from him, and even though I have never been violent by nature, I was in a fury now. Blind with rage at the tyrant's indifference to his actions and the falsetto that revealed my weakness, I aimed a kick against his beautiful face. My foot hit the lower side of his chin and you could hear his jaws slam together with a nasty muffled crack as his head flew back and the chair toppled over. Without thinking, I took hold of the back of the kitchen chair that was closest, raised it over my head and struck. One of the chair legs grazed his forehead, then continued its unmerciful path through his eye down against the cheekbone, which stopped the blow with an unpleasant crunching sound. One more blow with the chair, this one better placed, so that one of the chair legs smacked into the rib cage while the other hit right over the bridge of his nose, which broke with a slight cracking sound. Finally – and this I learned from you, Hans – a well-aimed kick up towards the nose, which, without further resistance, was forced inside.

A little blood was trickling out of the nostrils of the lifeless man on the floor, and in the silence I could hear my own pulse booming in my ears. The fury had already run out of me, and my thoughts now were primarily about how fast it had all happened. In my newly won madness, I did not regret having killed someone, only that I hadn't let him suffer longer. I should have told him about all the injustices he subjected me to. I should have held him accountable for his actions and forced him to beg for forgiveness on his bare knees. Above all, I should have let him suffer a slow, painful death.

Here I sit now – a murderer – studying an old black-and-white photograph from a dark time. The children are looking at me with toothless smiles. The teacher stands furthest back, to the right, with Carina Ahonen beside her. She's wearing a flowered housedress and her hair is pulled up in a massive bun on top of her head. She looks solemnly into the camera as if to show that she takes her work as a preschool teacher extremely seriously. In the very front, in the middle, Hans is on one knee, grinning. He who laughs last . . .

I wish Councillor Göran Meijer luck in his hopeful advances among Katrineholm's insufferable kids, and I truly mean that. But I think he will need a little help getting started.

It already feels much better.

Wednesday Morning

After a few hours of restless sleep, Conny Sjöberg was leafing through the morning paper, not really taking in what he was reading. His thoughts were on what he would say to the new widow. He had a lump in his throat that would not go away. He was also thinking that if Åsa died, he would never be happy again. He would have to keep on living for the sake of the children, but life would be empty and meaningless. Tears welled up in his eyes, and he wondered whether he would be able to get a word out once he was standing there in front of Mrs Vannerberg. Stop, he said to himself, stop thinking about that and concentrate on what has to be said.

Suddenly Åsa was standing there in the doorway. She had slipped in quietly so as to not waken the twins, and stood there watching him. She cried at the same movies as he did, and just hearing about a poignant bit in a book he was reading would bring tears to her eyes. She knew what he was feeling right now, and what he was thinking. She went up to him and gave him a long hug while the tears welled up and ran down his cheeks, dampening the sleeve of her bathrobe.

He finished his cheese sandwich, brushed his teeth, got dressed and went down to the car. Even though it was six-thirty, it was still black as night outside. A lone jogger crossed the playground at Nytorget and went over towards Sofiagatan. Once Sjöberg had eased the car out of the narrow parking spot, he called Sandén to confirm that nothing unforeseen had happened during the night, waking him up.

'I'm on my way to inform the widow,' he said apologetically. 'I just wanted to double-check that it really was Vannerberg.'

'Oh, it's him all right,' Sandén growled.

'He was reported missing by his wife yesterday afternoon, but apparently he disappeared on Monday evening.'

'That sounds right, because the footprints around the house were made in damp soil, and it rained on Monday. Yesterday the weather was clear.'

'That's good, then we have something to go on anyway.'

'Pathology will allow viewing of the body after four o'clock and the technicians should be ready with the contents of his pockets for the eleven o'clock meeting. Hansson will be there.'

'Good. See you then. Excuse me for waking you. Wish me luck.'

'Good luck.'

Twenty minutes later he found himself, still in darkness, at the edge of the townhouse complex in Enskede where the Vannerberg family lived. He parked the car in a visitor's space and made his way to the house. There was a light on in the kitchen window and to his relief he could see that, besides the children, there were also several adults inside. Sjöberg took a deep breath and tried to look amiable and serious at the same time. He struck the doorknocker twice against the brass plate. The door was opened by an older man.

'My name is Conny Sjöberg. I'm a chief inspector with the Hammarby police and would like to speak with Pia Vannerberg.'

'I'm her father. Come in,' said the man, taking a few steps back.

Sjöberg stepped into the hallway and took off his shoes. An older woman nodded politely at him from the kitchen, where she was apparently feeding the three children, but he saw the worry in her eyes. He followed the man into the living room. At one end of a large couch sat Pia Vannerberg, stiff as a board, shaking as if with cold and looking at him with a terrified expression. He sat down carefully in an armchair close to her and her father sat alongside his daughter and placed his arm around her shoulders. No one said anything. Then Sjöberg started talking.

'I'm extremely sorry to have to tell you this, but we have found your husband, and unfortunately he is dead.'

He was squeezing his hands together so tightly that they had turned completely white.

The woman's expression did not change, but a tear ran down her dad's cheek.

'I knew it,' she said in a surprisingly clear voice. 'I knew it all along. He would never just disappear like that.'

'I must also tell you that all indications are that he was murdered.'

Her response to this surprised him, but he would later be struck by the obviousness of what she said, obvious when you really love someone.

'Do you think he suffered?'

'I can't say,' he said calmly, 'because I'm not a doctor. But based on what I saw, it seemed to have happened very quickly, and he looked peaceful.'

'So how did he die?' Pia Vannerberg asked matter-of-factly.

'We're still waiting for the medical examiner's report. It's hard to answer that.'

'Well then, where did he die?' she continued stubbornly.

'He died in a house not far from here. Do you know anything about what he was doing there?'

'He was looking at a property that was for sale. It was somewhere in the vicinity, I don't know exactly where. He walked there anyway.'

Sjöberg felt a sting of bad conscience because he was exploiting the woman's state of shock to ask questions, but it was important to quickly clarify certain details and get the investigation moving.

'What time did he leave home?'

'He left at a quarter to six and said he would be back

about an hour later. We were going to have dinner together . . .'

Her eyes left him for the first time and she looked down at her hands, which were trembling in her lap.

'I'll leave you in peace soon. I just have to ask a few more questions,' Sjöberg said apologetically, without waiting for a response. 'When did you report his disappearance to the police?'

'I called the police about ten o'clock that evening, but they weren't aware that anything had happened and they advised me to wait until the next day. I went to the police station yesterday afternoon, when my parents came here.'

'Did your husband ever feel threatened? Did he have any enemies?'

'No, nothing like that. He is a very respected person. Everyone likes him. Liked . . .'

'Finally, is there anyone I can talk to at his work? Someone who might know who he was going to meet?'

'He runs . . . ran the company along with his partner, Jorma Molin.'

She reached for Sjöberg's pad and paper and quickly wrote down the associate's name and telephone number.

'We would also like you to help us formally establish the victim's identity as soon as possible. This means that a family member has to come and look at the deceased. Can any of you help us with that? Preferably today or tomorrow.'

Pia Vannerberg nodded, hid her face in her hands and disappeared in her father's embrace. Sjöberg got up from the chair, once again expressed his sympathy, and asked if he could come back in a few days with more questions. The father nodded politely in response, even though the tears now had a firm grip on him.

It was getting light when Sjöberg got back in his car and he turned on Radio Stockholm to distract him.

After parking the car in the garage below the police station, he took the lift up to the reception area.

'Good morning, Chief Inspector!' Lotten called before the lift door had closed behind him.

'Good morning, Reception Manager!' Sjöberg replied.

Lotten's cheerful expression could get anyone to forget their worries for a while.

'Any messages for me today?'

'Yes, several reporters have called for you to comment on last night's murder. I don't know what to say to them.'

'That they can call back after four o'clock.'

He went up the stairs and poured himself a cup of coffee on the way to his office, then sat down to call Vannerberg's partner.

'VM Property, Molin.'

The voice sounded courteously welcoming. Sjöberg introduced himself.

'I'm calling about your partner, Hans Vannerberg.'

'Yes, do you know where he is?'

'Unfortunately I have bad news. I'm sorry to say that he's dead.'

'But what the hell −' his voice broke off and there was silence on the line.

'I'm very sorry, but I need to see you. Can I come to your office at once?'

'Yes. Fleminggatan 68.'

'I'm on my way,' said Sjöberg, hanging up.

The man sounded sincerely shaken and his voice had changed during the brief conversation from deferential to anxious and then alarmed. As he put down the receiver, Sjöberg thought he heard a muffled sob. Yet another broken-hearted near and dear one to confront with the devastating news, he thought dejectedly.

It was now nine o'clock and he decided to take the metro to the estate agent's to avoid the frustrating traffic in the inner city. He pulled on his jacket again and gulped down the rest of his coffee standing up.

'I'm going to the victim's office to question his partner,' he called to Lotten as he passed the reception area. 'Tell Sandén when he arrives.'

He raised his hand in farewell and stepped out on to the street.

He used the time on the metro to contemplate the situation − or rather, the little he knew about it. So, Vannerberg left home at a quarter to six on Monday evening to meet a seller at Åkerbärsvägen 31 in Enskede, a fifteen-minute walk from his home. There lives a woman named Ingrid Olsson, who at that time had been in the hospital for three weeks. Had they arranged a meeting that day, or was he lured there by someone who knew that the house stood empty? He went into the house and was beaten to death with a chair in the kitchen, leaving no visible signs of a struggle. Was he let into the house, and if so by whom? Or was the door open? Did someone follow him there? There were footprints of two men in the garden; one of them was presumably Vannerberg. When he did not come home, his wife got worried and phoned the police, but did not make a formal report until Tuesday afternoon. At approximately the same time, Ingrid Olsson came home, found the corpse, went back to the hospital and fetched Margit Olofsson, who went home with her and called the police from there.

He took the notebook from his inside pocket, wrote down his questions and added one more: 'Connection between Hans Vannerberg and Ingrid Olsson?'

The estate agent's office was on the ground floor of a 1920s building, and in the window were letter-sized sheets of paper with descriptions and pictures of apartments and houses for sale, mainly located on Kungsholmen and in the south suburbs – Vannerberg's own surroundings – plus a few summer cottages south of the city. A handmade 'CLOSED' sign was posted inside the glass door, but Sjöberg knocked anyway. Molin opened the door at once and Sjöberg stepped into a small but well-organized office, with two desks and a kitchenette. He extended his hand to a man in his forties with scarred skin and short, dark-brown hair, and got a limp handshake in return.

'Please sit down,' he said, showing Sjöberg to one of the visitor's chairs.

The man himself sat down behind his desk and clasped his hands in front of him.

'Tell me what happened,' he said tiredly, looking at the chief inspector with large, brown sorrowful eyes.

Sjöberg briefly related what he knew, and Molin followed the story without comment, his gaze fluttering between Sjöberg, the window and the desktop.

'Do you know anything about that meeting at Åkerbärsvägen 31?' Sjöberg asked.

'He said he was going to meet a client on Monday evening, but that he was going home first. That's all I know.'

'Perhaps he had a diary where he wrote down scheduled meetings?' Sjöberg suggested.

'Of course he did,' Molin answered, getting up.

Sjöberg followed him over to Vannerberg's desk, trying to avoid the eyes of the children in a framed photograph right next to the large desk diary.

'Let's see now, day before yesterday . . .'

Molin followed Monday's scheduled activities with his index finger and stopped at the last line.

'Åkerbärsvägen 31,' he said. 'That's all it says.'

'Were you close?' asked Sjöberg.

'Yes, we met at college. We were classmates and hung out together even after we graduated. Then we started the firm and we've been here, side by side, for fifteen years. We don't socialize that often any more, we see each other all day anyway and we both have families, but we have a beer sometimes and talk about things.'

'Do you know whether he had any enemies?'

'No, I can't imagine that. He was very kind to everyone. And the ladies were especially fond of him.'

'Which ladies do you mean?'

'All the ladies. Customers, women in bars, waitresses. My wife,' he added, smiling for the first time.

'Did he have anyone on the side, do you think?' asked Sjöberg.

'Not a chance. He had Pia. He didn't need anyone on the side. He was extremely devoted to his family,' Molin said, taking a distressed look at the photograph.

'Nothing from the past that may have haunted him?' Sjöberg suggested.

Molin sat quietly and thought for a few moments, but then shook his head.

'We've known each other since we were in our twenties, and he was never in bother. His mother caused trouble sometimes, but he could handle her.'

'What kind of trouble, for example?'

'She would show up here at the office drunk sometimes and swear and carry on, but he always managed to calm her down. She has problems with alcohol, you might say. And financial problems and emotional problems and every imaginable problem in the world, seems like. But he helped her as much as he could, with money and so on. His upbringing was maybe not the happiest.'

'What do you think it was like?'

'There didn't seem to be any dad in the picture. Hans didn't know who he was anyway. His mum drank a lot and brought home a lot of men. Some stayed for a while and played stepfather, but Hans didn't like them and they probably didn't like him either – or didn't *care* about him anyway. They drank too, I suppose. They moved a lot and Hans was probably pretty unruly as a child. Skipped school, got into fights, and even broke a classmate's arm once. Finally he decided to stay in Norr-köping and get a high-school education, while his mother moved to Malmö. Then he had to take care of himself, and he did too. I think his life went in a differ-ent direction then.'

'I'd like to go through his desk,' said Sjöberg. 'Would you mind giving it a little more thought anyway, and see whether you can come up with anything that might cast a little light on this investigation?'

'Sure, of course,' Molin replied, going back to his seat and looking out over his cluttered desk with a resigned expression.

Sjöberg systematically examined the contents of Vannerberg's desk drawers, but found only various office supplies. He leafed uninspired through a few binders of properties for sale, without finding anything of interest either for the murder investigation or personally. Finally he looked through the whole diary, trying to interpret the dead man's scribbling. It was clear that this diary covered only things that had to do with work, or at least working hours. Sometimes an entry read 'showing', followed by an address, sometimes there were only an address and a name. A few times he found a dental appointment, haircut or car service, but what his eyes seized on at last was an appointment for a showing three months earlier: 'Showing, Åkerbärsvägen 13.'

'Listen,' said Sjöberg. 'What's this? A showing on 15 August at Åkerbärsvägen 13?'

Molin looked perplexed, twirled his chair halfway around and took a binder from the shelf behind him.

'Let's take a look here . . .' he murmured, leafing purposefully through the binder. 'Here it is.'

He stood up with the binder open and took the few steps over to Sjöberg, setting it down on the desk in front of him.

'This is a property that *I* sold,' he said, still hesitant. 'I wonder why that showing was in Hans's diary?'

He looked from the listing to the diary.

'Now I know!' he exclaimed in relief, pointing at the line below. 'Hans was going to look at a summer cottage in Nynäshamn later that afternoon, along with an inspector and a buyer, and he realized he couldn't make it there in time if he took this showing. Normally he takes all the properties in this area, because he lives so close, but I took this one instead.'

'But isn't it a little strange –' said Sjöberg, but was interrupted by Molin.

'Of course, that's what happened. I sold the house at Åkerbärsvägen 13 to a family who moved in a few weeks later. The deal was closed, but the buyer called last week because the seller had taken various fixtures with him, as the buyer saw it: microwave, wall-mounted lamps leaving bare, torn-off cords on the walls, and a large urn that had been in the garden during the showing. He said only a large cement base was left that ruined the view. Whatever, Hans promised to take a look when he was in the neighbourhood to get a sense of the whole thing. That's where he was going on Monday evening, but he evidently had the wrong house number. He couldn't know ... It was my sale, and he had never seen the property.' Molin fell silent, looking distressed.

'What happened? Was he followed by someone, or was there some lunatic inside the house who thought that Hans was a burglar or something? What kind of person does this sort of thing?'

Sjöberg patted him consolingly on the shoulder.

'I'm trying to find that out, I promise you. I have to go now, but I may be in touch again if I have more questions.'

It was ten-thirty by the time he was back on Fleminggatan, hurrying to the metro entrance to get back in time for the meeting. Isolated snowflakes were floating down through the grey November daylight and not a trace of the sun could be seen. In his mind he formulated two more questions to add to his list: who was Vannerberg's father, and who might have been in Ingrid Olsson's house during her hospital stay?

* * *

At eight minutes past eleven, everyone was assembled in the windowless blue oval office where they usually held their meetings. Present, besides Sjöberg, were detective inspectors Jens Sandén and Einar Eriksson, police assistants Jamal Hamad and Petra Westman, the technician Gabriella Hansson, and a representative from the prosecutors' office, Hadar Rosén. Everyone had a coffee cup in front of them except for Westman, who preferred tea. Sjöberg was slightly irritated by the impossibility of getting such a small group to be punctual, but this time it was Prosecutor Rosén who arrived last, and because he had formal responsibility for the investigation, Sjöberg had to swallow his annoyance.

Sjöberg opened the meeting by summarizing what had happened and then reported on his visits to the victim's family and his business partner. Rosén interjected an occasional question and asked now and then for a clarification, but seemed content with the investigation so far. Hansson then reported on the technicians' findings and confirmed that the murder had almost certainly taken place in the kitchen, and that one of the kitchen chairs had blood on it and could be assumed to be the murder weapon. It was, of course, the medical examiner's business to establish the cause and time of death, and the conceivable murder weapon, but the body had not reached him until the small hours and no preliminary report could be given until some time this afternoon at the earliest.

Hansson continued by reporting that there were many fingerprints that had not yet been analysed, as well as impressions from shoes, taken from both inside the house and outside in the garden. The technicians were not finished with those either. Sjöberg noted, as he had so many times before, that Gabriella Hansson was an exceptionally competent crime scene technician: fast, accurate and extremely focused on the job at hand. He reminded her to examine the locks thoroughly too, but she reported that they had already done so and no tampering had occurred. Because the locks were very old, it would be simple for someone to force their way in simply by dragging a steel comb between the door and the doorpost, or by wiggling a steel wire in the lock itself.

'The victim's wife,' Sjöberg continued, 'maintains that Vannerberg was going to meet a *seller*. His partner, Jorma Molin, drew the conclusion that Vannerberg was going to meet a *buyer* at number 13 – not 31, where the murder took place – and that he wrote down the wrong address on his calendar. It sounds like a good explanation, because Ingrid Olsson does not seem to fit into this anywhere. Petra, try to have a few words with Pia Vannerberg – but not until tomorrow – and ask her about this. Also, try to find out as much as you can about Vannerberg and check whether he had a personal diary at home. Take the opportunity to question the in-laws at the same time, see if they have anything to add. Today you can contact the buyer at number 13 and find out what they say about this possible meeting. I also want you to go to Fleminggatan and look on Vannerberg's computer. Look through documents and such, especially private matters, if you find any. Go through all the letters and e-mails sent and received. Sandén, visit the ladies Olofsson and Olsson and question them thoroughly. Ask Ingrid Olsson if she had thought about selling the house and perhaps scheduled a time with an agent. Check whether she has had any unwelcome visitors before. If Vannerberg went there by mistake, he might have been attacked by someone who was taken by surprise – someone who should not have been there. Margit Olofsson seems to be completely outside this, so take her aside and find out what she knows about Ingrid Olsson. What is she really like as an individual and how has she reacted to everything? Maybe she's said something in conversation that might help us. And don't forget to take their fingerprints, the house is probably teeming with them, as you can imagine. Jamal, you go through the house when the technicians are finished. Check for valuables, history, anything that might be of interest to the investigation. Einar, search for Vannerberg in all conceivable registers. See if you can find the guy's father and check on the mother too, perhaps she's run foul of the law. Check on Jorma Molin too, to be on the safe side. I'll try to make contact with Vannerberg's mother and see what she has to say. Does anyone have anything to add?'

'I have the contents of the victim's trouser pockets with me,' said Hansson teasingly, dangling a transparent plastic bag between her thumb and index finger.

'Of course, I'd almost forgotten about that,' said Sjöberg. 'Let's see what you have.'

She opened the plastic bag briskly and emptied the contents on to the table.

'A dummy, some coins – four kronor, fifty öre to be exact – a safety pin, some coupons from the food co-op, a bunch of keys, a tin of snuff and a wallet. In the wallet we found 758 kronor, a co-op card, a Euro-card, driver's licence, membership card for S.A.T.S. Sports Club, a Nordea credit card and a video rental membership card.'

'That's unusually exciting,' said Westman.

'A white-bread kind of guy,' said Sandén.

'No surprises. Thanks, Bella,' said Sjöberg. 'That's all for today.'

Seven chairs scraped against the parquet floor with a deafening noise and everyone left the room. Sandén asked whether they should have a sandwich up at Lisa's Café, and Sjöberg noted that it was high time for lunch.

It was already one o'clock; the exertion of chairing the meeting had made him forget such basic needs as hunger and going to the toilet. After first taking care of one of those needs, he got his jacket from his office and hurried down the stairs to the reception area, where Sandén was waiting for him.

'Any messages, Lotten?' he asked in passing, halfway out of the door.

'Lots!' answered Lotten.

'After lunch!' he called back before the big glass door closed behind him.

Wednesday Afternoon

Lisa's Café was located on Skånegatan, and though it was a little far to walk, it had become their regular place, not just for Sjöberg and his crew but for many of the other officers from the Hammarby police station too. The menu was not extensive, but the bread was home-baked, the atmosphere congenial and the service personal. Lisa herself had the gift of the gab and called all her regulars by name. She had also decorated the walls with their photographs, and Sjöberg, Sandén and Jamal Hamad, who also joined them for lunch, were all pictured on Lisa's wall.

Over homemade meatball sandwiches and a beet-root salad that far surpassed what you could find in a delicatessen, they bantered lightly about the murder, without really getting anywhere. For Sjöberg this was therapy after an intense morning.

'I think he was evil,' said Hamad.

'No, white-bread was the word,' said Sandén.

'He must have done something wrong to get assaulted like that,' Hamad persisted.

'The local police who were first on the scene thought he seemed shifty,' said Sjöberg. 'Found murdered in Ingrid Olsson's kitchen.'

'That's just what I'm saying. It's obvious he was evil.'

'I think it's Ingrid Olsson who's shifty, having a corpse in her kitchen,' said Sandén.

'Maybe both of them are shifty,' Sjöberg suggested. 'No good.'

'I think they are and were good, both of them,' said Sandén, 'although they've had bad luck. They got in the way of a lunatic, to put it simply. Someone they had no connection with.'

'In any case, the wife and children had the worst luck,' said Hamad. 'The old lady seemed unperturbed, and Vannerberg is dead. But the family has to live with the sorrow. And anyway, they're not evil.'

'Don't say that. Children can be pretty wicked. Only Jesus thinks that children are good. Personally, I'm of the opinion that children are evil until their parents take it out of them. That's called upbringing,' Sandén said with conviction.

'Well, Vannerberg himself doesn't seem to have been the world's best child, according to what his business partner had to say,' said Sjöberg. 'But according to what we've seen so far, he seems to have been the world's best grown-up.'

The conversation gradually petered out and Sjöberg went back to the station and his office. A few reporters called, but he was sparing with information. He wanted to wait until he had spoken with the medical examiner, the body was formally identified and the technicians had more concrete facts to present. He phoned Einar Eriksson. True, Eriksson's office was only three doors down, but he didn't feel like getting up again.

'Have you found anything on Vannerberg's mother yet?' he asked, without the slightest hope of an affirmative response.

'No, I've been at lunch and just sat down at the computer,' Eriksson replied as expected.

'Thought so,' said Sjöberg. 'Talk to you later.'

As soon as he put down the receiver the phone rang.

'Conny, you have a visitor,' Lotten giggled. 'A real looker. I'm almost jealous!'

Sjöberg was of the opinion that cheerful co-workers were just what you needed in a job as serious as his was at times, and he never got tired of Lotten's chirping. She did her work flawlessly and was very organized, so the only thing to do was grin and bear it.

'Who is it?' he asked.

'I don't know, your mistress maybe. Her name is Gun, and she's a little tipsy, I think. She's on her way up.'

He put down the receiver and was about to get up to go out and look for his unexpected visitor when the door opened without warning. In swayed an unlikely creature who made him think immediately of Dame Edna Everage, except this was a genuine biological woman. She was probably in her sixties, with a big, bleached-blonde perm, her face almost theatrically made up, big, golden costume jewellery on her ears and around her neck, and black-and-white snakeskin boots with high heels. Under a gigantic, white imitation-fur coat, a pink sequinned dress was visible, cut halfway up the thigh. He thought he was able to conceal his surprise, and courteously extended his hand to her.

'Conny Sjöberg,' he said calmly. 'How can I help you?'

'I am Gun Vannerberg, and I want to look at my son,' the woman answered in a completely normal tone of voice.

He didn't know what he had expected, presumably a hoarse or shrill voice. He pulled out one of the visitor's chairs and helped her sit down.

'I'm extremely sorry about what happened, and you have my sympathy,' said Sjöberg seriously. 'I realize that this is very painful for you, Mrs Vannerberg, and we are still not really clear about what actually happened.'

'I understand,' said the woman faintly, the tears welling up in her eyes.

Suddenly everything that was comical about her appearance was gone, and in Sjöberg's eyes she was just a very small, lonely and desperate person in a big, awful world. He wondered whether she had anyone who also saw her that way and could help and console her.

'I'll call the medical examiner and check whether we can go over there. Perhaps you'd like a cup of coffee, Mrs Vannerberg?'

He felt that he needed one himself. She nodded silently in response and stared vacantly ahead of her. Sjöberg went out in the corridor and over to the coffee machine. Several faces looked curiously at him, but he shook his head reproachfully, took his coffee cups and went back into his office. He closed the door behind him with one foot.

'Thanks very much,' she said quietly, looking intently down into the cup before she took a sip.

'They would prefer that we not come until after four, but I'll ask.'

'Is that so?'

'Perhaps I could ask a few questions about your son, Mrs Vannerberg, since we're sitting here anyway?' he said carefully.

'That's fine.'

'When did you last see him?'

'Last weekend. He came to visit me in Malmö, where I live, with his youngest daughter, Moa.'

'What kind of work do you do?' Sjöberg asked out of pure curiosity.

'I work at a club,' she answered matter-of-factly. 'That's why I have this outfit on. These are my work clothes. I didn't have time to change before I came here. Pia's mum phoned me on my mobile this morning and I took the next train. I was not completely sober and didn't think about bringing along my regular clothes.'

Sjöberg wondered to himself what type of clubs they had in Malmö, but he did not ask.

'What was your relationship like with your son, Mrs Vannerberg?'

'It was very good. Hans was always so kind to me,

and helped me when I needed it. I'm not much to write home about exactly . . .'

Sjöberg thought guiltily that that's exactly what she was.

'He phoned several times every week just to ask how I was doing. They are so nice, all of them.'

'Who do you mean, Mrs Vannerberg?'

'Please call me Gun, otherwise I'll feel embarrassed.'

'Okay. Who do you mean was nice?'

'Well, the children, of course, and Pia and her parents. They're good people, you know, Pia's family. But it's like they don't make a show of it. They talk to me anyway.'

'What was Hans like as a person?'

'Kind. Yes, I already said that. Capable. Good in school, he went to college. And had his own company and that, lots of money. He helped me with the bills if I was short. Charming, he could charm anyone. A favourite with the girls.'

'You moved to Malmö when Hans was starting high school?'

'Yes. We moved a lot, and I guess Hans got tired of that, so he decided to stay put.'

'What other places did you live?'

'There were lots of places. Norrköping, Kumla, Hallsberg, Kungsör, Örebro. Oxelösund.'

'Why did you move so much?'

'Men. Jobs.'

'So, what type of work are we talking about?' Sjöberg

82

asked indirectly, hoping she would explain just what type of men she was referring to.

'I used to do hair during the day,' she answered evasively.

'And in the evening?'

'Sometimes I would dance at clubs . . .'

Sjöberg waited.

'Okay, I stripped. But I don't intend to talk about what kind of clubs.'

'No, you don't have to. But you worked as a hairdresser during the day and stripped in the evenings. It couldn't have been easy to take care of a child too?'

'No, I was not a very good mother. But Hans turned out all right anyway.'

'Hans never had a father?'

'No, I don't know who he was.'

'You must have been very young –'

'Eighteen,' she interrupted. 'I didn't plan to get pregnant. But I've always been kind to Hans,' she added convincingly. 'I'm sure you understand that, otherwise he wouldn't have cared about me the way he did.'

She wiped away a tear with the back of her hand. Sjöberg sighed and reflected for a moment on all the strange human destinies he encountered in his professional life. He thought about his own twin sons, and he wondered how their lives would look today if things had gone differently a year and a half earlier. A female drug addict had been seriously assaulted with a knife in a park. He was responsible for the investigation, and when he had visited her at the hospital after a few days she had been transferred to the obstetrics department – to his, the hospital staff's and not least her own surprise. A few hours later, not one but two well-formed but very small baby boys were miraculously delivered. She had stayed in the hospital for several weeks and he had visited her and the boys regularly during that time. The twins were in incubators and there they stayed for another three months, even after their mother ran away from the hospital. He had become attached to the tiny boys and continued to go to see them even after her disappearance. When she was later found dead from an overdose of heroin in a public toilet, he had taken Åsa up to the hospital. Even though they already had three children and had had no plans for more, neither of them hesitated. The adoption was completed six months later, but by then the children had long since been 'theirs'.

'You don't know whether Hans in some way might have got into bad company, through you, for example? Excuse me for asking, but I'm sure you understand what I mean,' Sjöberg said apologetically.

'No, I never introduced Hans to my . . . friends. Not in recent years,' she added guiltily.

'What was he like as a child?'

'Oh, he was so cute. He was a real rascal, but he had a lot of friends. I guess he was like most boys, fistfights and mischief, but he had a good heart.'

*

Sjöberg concluded the conversation and phoned the medical examiner. Kaj Zetterström, who had devoted half the night and all day to the autopsy of Hans Vannerberg, sounded tired, but he was accommodating and said that it was fine to come over. Sjöberg ordered a taxi himself and then escorted Gun Vannerberg down the stairs, through the reception area and out to the turning area on Östgötagatan and the waiting car.

He held his arm under hers during the brief, agonizing encounter with her dead son, but looked away himself. After the papers were signed he left her, with a twinge of guilt, standing alone on the pavement. It was twenty past three and already dark. The temperature was below freezing and a thin layer of snow was starting to settle over the city.

Thursday Evening

The snow was falling heavily outside his kitchen window and Thomas thought, when he saw the flakes dancing around in the glow of the streetlights and the people moving down on the street with red cheeks and snow in their hair, that it looked cosier outside than it did in his own bare kitchen. Perhaps he should do something about his place after all. He had always thought it served no purpose to make things nice just for himself, but in the past few days everything had felt a little different. He was still slightly exhilarated after what happened on Monday – the adventure. He thought of it as the *adventure*, because he had crossed a boundary for the first time in as long as he could remember. He had done something *forbidden*.

The pan started sizzling and the margarine had already taken on a light-brown colour. He quickly cut open the packaging and tossed the frozen piece of pork schnitzel in the frying pan and the wrapper into the sink. The saucepan of water boiled over and when he dried off the cooker top with a paper towel, a small piece got stuck and the whole kitchen smelled burned. He poured in the noodles and stirred them with the spatula. They were done long before the schnitzel, but when at last it too was ready, it was also burned. He ladled everything on to a plate and wolfed it down in a couple of minutes, even though he was full when he was only halfway through. But there was no point in saving it, and he would rather finish it than throw it away.

Suddenly he made a decision. He got up so quickly that the chair almost tipped over. He walked resolutely out to the hall and fished a ruler out of a box in the cupboard. Then he climbed up on the chair and measured the kitchen window. Tomorrow after work he would go to the fabric shop, choose a nice fabric and have them sew a pair of kitchen curtains for him.

He washed the dishes, wiped off the stove and counter, and made himself a cup of coffee. Then he sat down on the bed with the pillow behind his neck and started thumbing through the tabloid he had bought on his way home from work. Suddenly he froze. A quarter of a page was taken up by a picture of Hans – King Hans – who, according to the article, had been found murdered two days earlier in a house south of the city. The house belonged to a poor old woman by the name of Ingrid Olsson, who said she did not know the victim. It was a summer picture: the wind was fanning his blond hair, he was tanned and he was smiling happily.

'He who laughs last, laughs best,' Thomas mumbled to himself.

The article stated that the family was in a state of

shock, but in his mind Thomas saw something quite different from a grieving wife. It was at that moment he decided to find out how things stood with Ann-Kristin. He felt significant for the first time. He was now a very important person who knew things no one else knew.

Friday Evening

Tracing her was no problem. He called the tax office in Katrineholm and found out that her married name was Widell and that she had moved to Stockholm in 1996. Then he simply looked up Ann-Kristin Widell in the phone book and found someone by that name in Skärholmen. Then he called the relevant tax office and a friendly woman confirmed that she was the person he was looking for.

On Friday afternoon, he did not go home after work. Instead, he took the metro out to Skärholmen. On the local map outside the ticket window he found the address he was looking for almost immediately, and walked there in less than ten minutes. The building was one of several similar massive, white apartment buildings, in a residential area on a hill. The front door opened with an entry code, but after a little while a young mother with a pushchair came out of the building and he held open the door so that she could get the pushchair out more easily. She accepted his assistance without thanking him. As usual he was reduced to nothing.

He took the opportunity to slip in through the open door and scanned the directory until he found what he was looking for: Widell, two floors down – you could also live below street level in these apartment blocks. He went down the steps, his nostrils picking up an odour reminiscent of his childhood apartment building in Katrineholm. It was the floor that smelled – a white floor with black patches, meant to look like stones perhaps – in combination with various cooking odours, especially fish, that escaped through the plain, brown wooden doors of the apartments. He found her door. It said simply 'Widell' on the letter box, but otherwise there was no clue to what kind of person, or people, lived inside. He contemplated going out again to try looking through her window. But the darkness and cold outside were not enticing, and considering the sparse traffic he had seen so far in this stairwell, he did not dare take the chance of not being able to get in again in the near future. Probably she had her curtains drawn to keep passers-by from looking in anyway. Instead, he sat down on the stairs leading up from street level, where he could see anyone coming up from the basement.

Without any real idea of how long he should wait, he sat there thinking about how she might have evolved over the years. Not like Hans, he thought. Not like Hans if she lives here. Only unhappy people live here. No one would actually choose to live here. But how could a person like Ann-Kristin, who had made all the kids dance to her tune, be unhappy?

He remembered how Ann-Kristin had ordered him to go and skip with the girls one day when he was on his way home from preschool. Any other boy would have refused, but not Thomas. He did as he was told, not without some enthusiasm at actually being included. But he couldn't jump; instead he got one foot tangled up in the rope. Ann-Kristin, of course, noticed his predicament, and with lightning speed she tore the skipping rope out of the hand of one of the girls. Then she danced around him, together with the girl holding the other end, turn after turn, until he was completely wrapped in the rope from head to toe, accompanied by the other girls' squeals of delight. Then she knocked him down, so that he was lying on the ground, squirming in his cocoon. Then they dragged him out to the street and there – in the middle of the road – they left him to die.

He remembered the feeling of panic as he saw a truck turn the corner at the far end of the street and head straight towards him. He screamed at the top of his lungs and the girls, crouching behind a parked car, could not conceal their enjoyment. The truck driver spotted him however, put the brakes on and jumped down to where he was lying. 'What kind of damn place is this to play cowboys and Indians!' he swore, untied the skipping rope and gave him a slap. Thomas ran home as fast as he could, with tears streaming down his cheeks, not daring to look over at the car where the girls were giggling. Could that happy, popular Ann-Kristin possibly be living out here in the suburban ghetto, feeling depressed?

* * *

When she woke up it was already dark outside. She looked at the clock on the DVD player and could see it was past six. She turned on the bedside lamp, leaned down and picked up the ashtray from the floor and set it on her stomach. She was almost out of cigarettes. She would have to run down to the corner shop and buy some before seven o'clock. She lit one and took a few deep puffs. There was a half-empty can of beer on the bedside table, and she emptied it in one gulp, regretting it at once. The lukewarm, sticky liquid nauseated her, but by swallowing a few times she was able to minimize the discomfort.

Her eyes wandered across the small room and stopped at the framed photograph of herself and her sisters. It was a happy picture, from summer camp long ago. She was sitting on a little pony with her sisters standing either side. It had been a long time since she had heard from them. At least five years ago, she thought, when their dad died. Marie-Louise, the oldest, had married an American and lived in Ohio on a farm with horses. Viola was wandering around Asia with some idiot, whom Ann-Kristin had only met once, getting high presumably, if she was still alive. Viola always did exactly as she pleased; she'd coasted along, dropped out of school and gone out into the world, without goals and without money.

She was not doing much better herself, but at least she didn't do drugs. She'd had a so-called accident when she was fifteen, but it wasn't an accident. It was Widell, their neighbour in Julita where they were living, who had got off with her at one of her dad's parties. He was drunk, and her dad was drunk, and she was drunk herself and probably didn't really have anything against it. Then he dragged her into the sauna and she didn't like that, but the old guys cheered them on, so she probably didn't resist as much as she should have, being drunk and all. Some time later she moved to the other side of the fence and into the neighbour's house, and after a few years they got married. They had three children in as many years, but they had moved out now, all of them. Widell died when his hand was cut off by a combine harvester ten years earlier, and she'd taken the opportunity to leave that godforsaken hole and move to the capital.

In Stockholm there weren't any jobs for her, but she lived for a while on the money left by Widell. After a few years she started her 'business', as she called it. She figured she might as well get a little money for her trouble after doing it for free for nineteen years with an old lecher like Widell. In the beginning, when she'd still had children to take care of, there hadn't been much left over, but in recent years she had saved piles of money.

Her dream was to move to Ohio and live and work on her sister's farm. She had a long-standing invitation.

She put out the cigarette and set the ashtray on the floor again. After a quick shower, she dried her hair, put on rather heavy make-up, pulled on a pair of jeans and a T-shirt, and rushed down to the corner shop. In her basket she put six cans of beer, Coca-Cola, juice and some bread. At her request, the cashier handed her three packs of cigarettes, then scanned the price tags on the goods and took payment without making eye contact. If there had been condoms in the basket, she wouldn't have been able to keep from staring, Ann-Kristin thought, but that was something she never bought here. She hoped the neighbours couldn't guess what she was doing. That was the big advantage of living two flights down – being the only tenant on the floor, and not having any neighbours pounding on the wall or observing your activities.

After a quick clean of the apartment she changed into more provocative clothes and splashed a little perfume behind her ears and in her cleavage. Then she sat down in front of the TV with a cigarette and a drink in her hand, waiting for the first customer of the evening.

* * *

Thomas was shocked when he saw her for the first time. She had been very pretty as a child, if you overlooked the malicious smile and the calculating look. Now she was fat and bloated, with worn, bleached-blonde hair and heavy make-up that was hardly becoming to a respectable person. When she came jogging up the stairs and out into the November cold dressed only in a T-shirt, he felt nothing but surprise. Pure surprise that the *winner* Ann-Kristin had let her appearance decline to such a degree that she almost resembled a . . . well, he didn't know what. A loser, maybe. Then, when she came back with a cigarette in her mouth and a bag of beer and Coca-Cola in her hands and he saw her from the front, it struck him that maybe she wasn't a respectable person.

A few hours later he *knew* what she was.

* * *

The murder of Hans Vannerberg happened on Monday evening, and though it was already Friday there had basically been no progress in the investigation. Petra Westman was in her office in the police station in Norra Hammarbyhamnen, staring listlessly at the colourful shapes of the screensaver dancing before her eyes. Yesterday's visit with Vannerberg's widow had produced nothing but a sore throat from the effort of holding back the tears. Pia Vannerberg looked pale and emaciated, and perhaps slightly medicated, but it was the sight of the two quiet children that was most depressing. A seemingly inexhaustible grandmother was trying to entertain them with board games while their little sister took a nap, but the children were uninvolved and absent. The following Monday they would go back to school and nursery, and that might divert them for a while, but their childhood was changed for ever.

Petra had spent most of Friday on Hans Vannerberg's work computer, without finding anything of interest. Now it was six o'clock and she was back in her own office. Normally she would work until late in the evening, but she was out of ideas and considered going down to the gym to activate some endorphins.

'Hey, guess what?'

Jamal Hamad was standing in the doorway, looking mischievous. Petra tilted her head to one side and met his eyes encouragingly.

'You don't have to use the default screensaver that comes with the computer. You can even have a slideshow of your own photos to look at while you sit there twiddling your thumbs. If you have any photos, that is. That presumes you have a life. Which you don't have if you don't leave the office when the work day is over. Which you are *allowed* to do. Did you know that?'

'You don't seem to be at a loss for words. What exactly are you trying to say . . . ?'

Jamal and Petra had known each other since their days at the police academy. They were never classmates, but they socialized at times in the same circles and had always had a soft spot for each other. Besides her good qualifications, Petra possibly had Jamal to thank for her job at the Violent Crimes Unit in Hammarby. He had been there a few years longer than her and she imagined that he put in a good word for her when she applied, though she had never asked him about it.

'Forget it,' he said. 'Do you want to go up to Clarion and have a beer?'

'I thought it was Ramadan.'

'Yes, actually, it was. A month ago. Come on.'

The computer emitted a sound indicating that she had been automatically logged out and the screen went dark.

'You see. A sign from God,' said Jamal.

'Allah,' said Petra, getting up from the chair. 'Okay, I'm in.'

After a ten-minute walk along Östgötagatan and up to Ringvägen, they entered the hotel. It was noisy and looked like a construction site; the stairs and passages they walked up and through to reach the bar appeared temporary or perhaps under renovation. There were no vacant tables, but at the bar they managed to get their hands on the only free bar stool. After hanging up her coat and bag on a hook under the counter, Petra convinced Jamal to take the stool and stood beside him.

'I was just thinking about working out when you came and lured me out into bad ways,' she explained. 'I've been sitting all day, so I'm happy to stand for a while. Or does that offend your Arabic manhood somehow?'

'Drop it. What would you like? Something to eat?'

'A beer to start with.'

When they finally got the bartender's attention, they ordered two large beers and peanuts. As it turned out, the kitchen was closed.

'When you're up here and it's dark outside, Johannesbron looks beautiful,' said Petra. 'I guess it's just all the lights that make it seem so cool and urban. Like Manhattan or something.'

The bartender set their beers and a bowl of nuts on the counter in front of them.

'Cheers,' said Jamal, taking a deep gulp.

Petra did the same. As she set the glass down, two young women on Jamal's side got up to leave. She reacted quickly and managed to grab the closer of the two stools as a man in his fifties took the other one. Their eyes met and they exchanged a smile.

'You've got to be on your toes in here,' he said, drawing one hand through his light-blond hair before sitting down on the coveted stool.

Petra dragged the heavy bar stool behind Jamal and over to her own spot, climbed up on it and took another gulp of her beer.

'Are you through exercising now?' Jamal asked.

'Yes,' she answered, clenching her fist in front of his face to reveal her flexed upper arm.

Petra Westman exercised regularly and had nothing

to be ashamed of when it came to biceps. The seams on her shirtsleeve were bulging.

'Thanks for dragging me out. I was stuck anyway.'

'Now let's forget about work for a while and talk about something else.'

'Well said. Let's go for it.'

They toasted each other and drank and she felt the alcohol already making her feel relaxed and a little tipsy. Thinking about it, she had not had time for a real lunch, yet she did not feel particularly hungry. Maybe that was down to the tension of the slow-moving investigation, now in combination with the filling beer.

They discussed Christer Fuglesang's impending journey into outer space and laughed at Swedish television's ongoing parodies of the poor astronaut who never seemed to take off. They ordered another round and Petra wolfed down the last of the peanuts and pushed the empty bowl aside.

'So where's the wife this evening?' she asked.

'She's with the mother-in-law,' Jamal answered, looking down at his glass.

'Yours or hers?'

'Mine, of course.'

'Isn't she comfortable with your big, fat Lebanese family?'

'Sure, but —'

'And you weren't invited to your mother-in-law's?' Petra interrupted. 'Poor you.'

With feigned sympathy she caressed him lightly

on the cheek with the back of her hand, but he recoiled with an irritated frown, so she pulled back her hand.

'What's going on with you?' she asked with surprise.

His reflex movement had embarrassed her. To do something with the rejected hand, she reached again for her glass and took a few substantial gulps.

'Stop flirting or whatever it is you're up to,' said Jamal morosely.

She shifted her gaze over his shoulder and for the second time her eyes met the blond man's. He raised his wineglass to her. He looked friendly, with an open appearance reminiscent of Conny Sjöberg's. This similarity prompted her to respond to his toast, contrary to her usual instincts. Jamal noticed something going on over his head, so he glanced quickly over his shoulder to see whom she was toasting. When he looked back she had put the glass down again and looked him right in the eyes.

'Flirting – what do you mean by that? It felt like an insult.'

'Making toasts with strange men, for example,' said Jamal quietly. 'Don't do that. You seem a little tipsy.'

'Jamal, for one thing, he was the one who toasted me. Secondly, I've had one beer. Thirdly, you said that I was flirting before I . . . before he toasted me.'

'You've had almost two beers. And you haven't eaten a thing. You're working hard, exercising hard and you've had peanuts for dinner. You should expect that to have an effect.'

'You still haven't explained to me this thing about flirting. I think I can touch you without you thinking I'm trying to get you in bed. We've known each other for a hundred years, for Christ's sake. Touched each other for just as long.'

Jamal motioned with his hand to calm her, but this only stirred up more emotions.

'So why did you want to come out with me?' she continued, in a lower voice now. 'I wasn't in the mood, but you were. So you got me to come and here we sit talking and having a nice time and suddenly you get all moody for no reason. Of course I'm hurt, don't you get that?'

Jamal turned his eyes away from her and let them rest for a moment on a vague spot above a security guard who was leaning against the wall behind the bar. Then he turned back towards her and took her hand in his. He looked at her for a while with a dejected look in his eyes before he started talking again.

'Okay, Petra. I take back what I said about flirting. I apologize for that.'

'Seriously?'

She was not sure where this was going, if it would be better or worse, but she did not want to be considered a flirt. Especially not by Jamal, who with his brown velvet eyes, the charming little dimple on his chin and his well-built thirty-year-old policeman's body could have knocked any woman off her feet before he got married.

'Seriously. But you are a little tipsy,' he said, revealing his perfect white teeth in a smile as he let go of her hand. 'That's okay. I guess that's why we're here. You're fine, so don't think any more about that either.'

Jamal sighed and Petra waited attentively for what would come next.

'Now you might think I'm a little sensitive,' he continued, 'but sometimes I get so damn tired of all the allusions to my origins. I know the intentions aren't bad, and I know that in most cases there's no prejudice behind it. But it's just so damn tedious. I am who I am, regardless of my Lebanese roots, which I'm proud of by the way. Sometimes I get the feeling that you all don't see me behind all that Arab stuff you imagine in me. I'm Swedish, damn it! Just like you. I've been living in Sweden since I was six years old, for twenty-four years.'

Petra looked at him with a kind of uncomprehending sympathy in her eyes.

'And I don't like that look either,' Jamal pointed out. 'Don't feel sorry for me. I don't spend my time feeling sorry for you.'

Petra straightened up and tried not to look too sanctimonious. Instead, she gulped down the last of her drink and, without asking Jamal, ordered two more beers. Jamal, too, emptied his glass.

'And where do I fit into the picture?' she asked. 'What was it I said that made you . . . grumpy?'

'It goes on all the time. You don't notice it, because you don't mean anything by it and you know that I

102

know that you like me and respect me. But it's "Ramadan" this and "Mohammed" that, one thing after another. Just little things, but it all adds up . . . What was it you said before . . . ? Something about my "big, fat Lebanese family"? I just get so tired of that.'

Suddenly Petra knew what he meant. She recalled that she had jokingly asked him whether it 'offended his Arabic manhood' that he sat while she stood. She realized how annoying it must be to get such comments about everything you said and did.

'It's as though in every conversation with me you had to insert a little comment about . . . my big ears or something,' said Petra, suddenly feeling that she was blushing.

Jamal's face broke out in a scornful smile. Petra covered her face with her hands and drew up her shoulders.

'I shouldn't have said anything!' She peeped out from behind her hands.

'Now you're flirting, Westman,' said Jamal triumphantly.

'I am not, I really am embarrassed.' Petra looked up at him imploringly. 'I should have made something up, not revealed my sore spot.'

Jamal took her head between his hands and pulled her hair behind her ears with his blunt fingers. Then he said, with a suddenly serious expression, 'I think you have nice ears. Do we understand each other?'

Petra nodded.

'Then I think we should leave this topic of conversation.'

Petra agreed, feeling suddenly stone-cold sober. It was often that way for her. After one beer, when she hadn't had any for a long time, things could really start spinning. After two she felt sober again.

They sat and talked for a while longer. Petra asked what plans Jamal had for the weekend, but he answered evasively and looked at his watch. He asked her about her weekend, but because – as usual – she hadn't planned anything, there was not much to say about that. She ventured to ask what he thought about the war that was once again raging in Lebanon. Jamal sighed and Petra anticipated him.

'I'm asking because I'm interested, not because I want to stir anything up.'

'Yeah, yeah, it's cool. It's just that it's something you can talk about endlessly. Of course I'm against the war. Lebanon was flourishing when the war broke out.'

'Have you been back?'

'A few times. We were there on our honeymoon. It's an amazing country. Was an amazing country.'

'But the war will end sooner or later?' Petra asked.

'I'm not so sure about that. It's all very complicated. And very simple, seen from any particular perspective. Everyone wants what they think they have a right to. And everyone is right in their own way.'

'But who should you support? Who do you support?'

'It isn't a football match, with two teams. You don't even know what teams are playing, do you?'

'Apparently not,' Petra admitted.

'There are more than two teams. The situation in Lebanon is even more complicated than the Israeli–Palestinian conflict. Just as impossible to resolve, but harder to get a sense of. Most people in Lebanon don't even know what it's about.'

'But tell me which side you're on,' Petra tried ingenuously.

'I'm sitting here in Sweden, just hoping for peace. A peaceful solution, with everyone getting their share of the pie. But that's easy to say when you're not in the middle of it. If I was still living in Lebanon, it would be a lot harder to view the conflict from any perspective other than my own.'

'So where in Lebanon did you live?'

'In a village in the south. Then in Beirut. Dad was a schoolteacher.'

'And now? What does he do here in Sweden?'

'He drove a taxi until he retired a year ago. When he came here he was very determined that we would all become Swedes, and that we would not isolate our-selves in some suburb among a lot of other immigrants. That has advantages and disadvantages, of course, but it turned out well for me and my siblings, so we're extremely grateful to our parents. But they have never really managed to be accepted in Swedish society. They live for us.'

'Is your dad happy with your choice of occupation?' Petra continued stubbornly.

'He's very proud of all four of us.'

'What would you have become if you'd stayed in Lebanon, do you think?'

Jamal emptied his glass and glanced at his watch again. It was eight-thirty.

'I've got to go now,' he said, jumping down from the bar stool.

He reached for his leather jacket and put it on without zipping it up. Petra had just started on her third beer, so she decided to stay and enjoy the lively Friday atmosphere around her. Jamal took his wallet from his back pocket and pulled out two hundred-kronor bills, which he placed on the bar in front of her.

'See you,' he said, giving her a quick kiss on the cheek.

'You didn't answer my question,' said Petra.

He looked at her for a few moments, a look that did not reveal what he was thinking.

'Hezbollah,' he answered curtly, and then left.

Petra remained sitting there for a long time with her hands around the beer glass, staring vacantly ahead of her. What could that mean? Hezbollah – wasn't that a terrorist group?

'It sounds like you may need a little refresher on the political situation in Lebanon.'

Petra looked up in surprise. It was the man on the neighbouring bar stool, the man who had raised his glass to her earlier in the evening. He was nicely but casually dressed in a light-blue shirt unbuttoned at the neck, a dark-blue blazer and a pair of well-fitting jeans held in place by a Johan Lindeberg belt. When he smiled the skin around his eyes wrinkled in an attractive way under a lock of hair that tended to fall down over his forehead.

'Yes, that's putting it mildly,' Petra sighed, responding to his smile with a little laugh.

'Please excuse me, I didn't mean to eavesdrop, but I happened to hear fragments of your conversation and I am quite well informed on the subject, so I couldn't help myself. Would you like to talk, or perhaps you'd rather sit by yourself?'

The man gave a genuinely pleasant impression, and the fact that he actually admitted eavesdropping somehow added to his credibility. He had blue eyes and a thick mop of hair that she thought must make any man his age a little jealous.

'No, we can talk a little,' said Petra. 'But I'm heading home soon,' she added to be on the safe side.

'Yes, me too,' said the man. 'I'm working tomorrow, so it will have to be an early evening for me.'

He made no effort to move closer, but continued instead.

'Lebanon is a marvellous country. Did you know that you can swim in the Mediterranean and go skiing in a resort with an amazing lift system all in one afternoon?'

'I think I've heard that, but I didn't know it was so close,' Petra admitted.

'Yes, in Faraya-Mzaar there are something like forty slopes and the view from there is amazing. On one side you have the Bekaa Valley, and if the weather is clear you can see all the way to Beirut.'

'So that's the place to go, if you can't decide between a skiing and a swimming holiday,' Petra laughed.

'Absolutely. But not now. Cheers.'

Petra responded to his toast with a nod and took a sip of her beer.

'So, do you know anything about the war?' said Petra.

He nodded and set his glass down in front of him.

'Then you'll have to brief me. It seems I have a gap in my education.'

'Sure. In the beginning of time – which was not all that long ago . . .'

Petra suddenly realized that they were sitting there shouting at each other at a distance of several metres, and asked him to move closer. The man laughed at the ridiculous situation, took his wineglass and jacket and moved over to the stool where Jamal had just been sitting.

'Peder,' he said, extending his hand. 'Peder Fryhk.'

'Petra,' said Petra.

'Well, both of those trouble spots – Israel and Lebanon – were pet projects for a few European fools in the 1920s who got the idea they should stake a claim to areas with major archaeological value. After the division of the Ottoman Empire, Syria became a French League of Nations mandate.'

'After the First World War?' said Petra.

'After the First World War. The French colonialists took particular care of the Maronites – who were Catholics – in the Lebanon Mountains, the old Phoenician coastland in Syria. Then in the early 1920s, the French drew a few lines on the map and, just like that, Lebanon became a Christian, European country in the middle of all the Muslims. Then, when Lebanon became independent in 1943, political power was divided between Christians and Muslims and a few others. That was a balancing act, but it worked until the Arabs decided to invade the new state of Israel.'

'When was that? 1947? '48?'

'It was 1948. Then Palestinian refugees poured into Lebanon, while hundreds of thousands of Christians fled and made their way to South America. Since then there has been no Christian majority in Lebanon, in fact, quite the opposite.'

'And so the French and Israelis back the Christian minority and the Arab world supports the Muslims?'

'Something like that. Although it's even more complicated than that. You probably can't bear listening to me droning on any more.'

He emptied his wineglass and waved to the bartender.

'Try me,' said Petra.

'Okay. Two glasses of house red, thanks,' he said to

the bartender and then continued his account for Petra, who was doing her best to memorize what he was saying.

Once again she saw the features of Sjöberg in this man. He had really warmed to his subject, and he was so passionate that sparks were flying around him. And the enthusiasm was contagious.

'None of these Palestinian refugees have any rights as citizens in Lebanon, so right there a certain discontent started to grow. Israel, for its part, feared the Arabs who surrounded them in all directions, so they made pacts with any non-Arabs who could be mobilized in the vicinity, including those Maronites in Lebanon. At that time Egypt's President Nasser was promoting Arab nationalism and in the late 1960s he forced the government of Lebanon, which had no say in it, to open up the southern part of the country to the PLO to attack Israel. South Lebanon became a Palestinian enclave. That was when the spiral of violence took off, you might say. And then there was Syria, which had never acknowledged the invention of the French Lebanon as a separate country. So in 1975, when the civil war got going, Syria first helped the Palestinians to kill Christians, and then the Maronites to murder Palestinians. Finally they got what they wanted. With Israel's consent, Syria occupied Lebanon, on the basis that they would keep the PLO in check in South Lebanon. Do you follow?'

'So everyone was dissatisfied and everyone had pretty good reason to be that way too,' said Petra, emptying her beer glass.

Peder Fryhk scooted a wineglass over to her.

'That's just how it was. And it only got worse. Did he say he came from South Lebanon, your friend?'

'Yes, but they moved to Beirut,' Petra confirmed.

'The powers-that-be in Israel got the idea that they should eradicate the Palestinian enclave in South Lebanon, so they invaded, drove the Syrians out of Beirut and installed a Christian regime in Lebanon. Syria then had the new Christian president assassinated, and in turn the Maronites started slaughtering civilian Palestinians in refugee camps. The PLO moved its headquarters to Tunis, but as you might guess, there were foot soldiers still in South Lebanon and they naturally had major support from all the "old" Palestinians in the country, who had been living under a kind of apartheid since 1948. It was then, in the absence of the PLO, that Hezbollah was formed.'

'And that wasn't so strange,' Petra interjected.

'No, not at all. And so now there was a drawn-out war between Hezbollah and Israel playing out in South Lebanon.'

'But the Lebanese in South Lebanon, what did they do?'

'They were peaceful Shia Muslim farmers who tried to keep out of it. Many of them fled to south Beirut, which developed into a Hezbollah enclave, where their sons were trained to be fully-fledged child soldiers ready and willing to sacrifice themselves.'

'Because they had lost what they had and could see no future. Yes, good Lord,' Petra sighed. 'It's never-ending. When was this?'

'Hezbollah was formed in 1982,' said Peder. 'Cheers.'

Petra sipped the wine and suddenly it was clear to her why Jamal's father had taken his family and left Lebanon. And what Jamal meant by what he had said as he was leaving the bar, and why he was unable to explain. And what a badly educated idiot she was. Twice she had been through a course in world history, at primary and secondary school. Neither time had they got further than the First World War. She knew more than she cared to about the Stone Age and the Viking Age, and she knew the list of Sweden's monarchs, but they had never even touched on the conflicts in the Middle East. Or any other trouble spot in the modern world.

Peder continued to explain about the involvement of the United States and the rest of the world in Lebanese politics, Syria's retaking of and later departure from Lebanon, the murder of Rafic Hariri and the current situation. Petra listened with great interest. She hoped that all this useful information would not be completely gone tomorrow, and convinced herself that the essentials would stick in her mind anyway. Two hours later, when yet another glass of wine was put in front of her, it occurred to her that she was in desperate need of a toilet break. She had been so consumed by the sympathetic man's monologue and – she believed and hoped – her newly won knowledge about her colleague and his background, that she had been oblivious to all else.

'How do you happen to be so well-informed about all this?' she asked when she returned.

On her way back from the toilet she had determined that she was not particularly intoxicated, but she decided that it was time to go home after this glass anyway. Three beers and two glasses of wine in five hours was not a problem, but it was more than enough.

'I've worked down there,' Peder answered. 'True, it was a long time ago, but I love that country and so I keep up with what's going on.'

'What did you do there?' Petra asked.

'I worked as a doctor for an organization called Doctors Without Borders.'

Petra laughed at his modesty. 'Are you kidding me, you're a Nobel Prize-winner! Let me congratulate you.'

'I've never looked at it that way, but maybe you're right,' Peder said. 'Let's drink to that.'

They did, and Peder also had a few things to say about the refugee camp in Beirut where he had worked and then revealed, in answer to a direct question from Petra, that he was now working as an anaesthetist at Karolinska Hospital.

'What kind of work do you do?' he then asked.

Petra was in no way ashamed of her choice of occupation, but over the years she had discovered that people's reactions sometimes disappointed her when she answered that question truthfully. For that reason she had a standard response that she gave to people she met off duty and whom she had no intention of seeing again.

'I'm an insurance agent at Folksam,' she replied, absentmindedly fingering her watch.

This answer was so uninteresting there were seldom any follow-up questions, and that was the point of it.

'Then you're close to work anyway,' Peder said.

Petra smiled back and downed the last drops in her glass. She noticed that it was almost midnight and she was starting to feel extremely tired. The week had taken its toll after all, although she had not really accomplished anything. She waved at the bartender and showed him the four hundred kronor piled neatly on the bar. She knew that would be more than enough, tip included.

'Well, I think it's time to move along,' said Petra, getting down from the bar stool.

'I agree,' said Peder, anticipating her attempt to take her coat from the hook under the bar.

He helped her on with her coat and handed her the bag she had set down on the counter, then he put on his own jacket. Petra had spent twenty minutes in the shoe shop trying to decide whether to buy the better-looking boots with a higher heel or the not-as-fashionable but more comfortable ones with a lower heel. In the end she had chosen the trendy boots with the slightly higher heels. Which she regretted now, as one foot folded under her.

'Whoops,' said Petra, with a vague thought going through her mind that had something to do with flirting.

'I'll follow you to your taxi, young lady,' said Peder Fryhk, taking her arm under his.

Diary of a Murderer, November 2006, Saturday

It's eleven-thirty. A man in his sixties, in a leather jacket with a fur collar and checked old-man cap, comes out. The first thing I notice is his hand, and sure enough – there's a ring on it. That's the way to take care of your marriage. Have a lot, want more. I've never had anyone myself. No one to love, no one to talk to, no one to eat with, no one to sleep with. But tonight I'm going to talk to someone. And sleep with someone.

I ring the doorbell. She opens the door and looks at me in surprise, but lets me in right away and closes the door behind us. I'm sure she's worried the other tenants will notice all the comings and goings from her apartment.

'Who are you?' she asks.

'A customer,' I reply.

She studies me up and down suspiciously.

'How did you find me?'

'I've seen you,' I answer truthfully.

'What's your name?'

'John Holmes,' I say disarmingly.

She bursts into laughter and shrugs.

'Well, what the hell!' she says, still laughing. 'So, what do you want?'

'Same as everyone else,' I answer. 'Sex.'

She helps me off with my jacket and hangs it up. I take off my shoes without feeling at all nervous. I feel like I'm finally in my element. The forbidden fifth dimension.

'Is this the first time?' she asks, probably meaning something different from me when I answer, 'Yes, it's the first time.'

'Are you nervous?'

'Yes, I am,' I lie. 'Let's have a little something to drink first.'

She doesn't hesitate to take me up on my suggestion, and I offer her the drink I brought with me, while she provocatively takes off one piece of clothing at a time, until finally she is standing naked in front of me, in all her flabby shame. Then she eases my clothes off, as carefully as if I were made of glass. She kisses me all over my body except on the mouth, which I appreciate. Never will this repugnant creature touch my mouth with her disgusting, sticky lips. But she knows her stuff, I must admit, and as her lips and tongue wander between my legs I cannot hold back the tears. She leads me to the bed where we wallow in our shameless nakedness.

She is lying under me and her movements are languid and slow now. I slide my fingers inside her and she moans quietly as I whisper in her ear, through her worn, bleached hair, 'May I tie you up . . . ?'

And she nods in response, with closed eyes, while her

thighs still arch around my hand. I carefully remove my fingers, retrieve my scissors and twine, and then bind her hands and feet gently but tightly and meticulously, to the bedposts. She is sleeping now, but she wakes with a shriek when I shove my knee into her crotch with all my strength. Her wide-open eyes look at me in stunned terror, but I continue talking in a smooth, almost whispering voice as I straddle her and wave the scissors.

'Now it's time for a haircut . . .'

She screams, but I smother the sound with a corner of the sheet that I force into her mouth. I feel just as gloriously soft and diffuse as when we were having sex, and her quivering body and frightened eyes cannot alter my state of mind. I cut her hair, one lock at a time, and do not neglect to show her the result. All the while I tell her who I am and what she did to me, and she nods energetically to confirm that she knows. I take the sheet out of her mouth and she promises not to scream. Instead she apologizes and she promises and promises to make it up to me, to do anything, while I cut off her eyelashes and finally her eyebrows, although some pieces of flesh come off too.

The blood is running in steady streams down her tear-stained whore's face smeared with make-up, and I ask if it hurts as I cut a little inside her with the scissors. She screams that it hurts and I shove the sheet back in her mouth and tell her that there are many, many different kinds of pain. She shudders convulsively, so I am nice to her and take the sheet out of her mouth again.

She begs and pleads, and so I light a cigarette for her. She thanks me and smiles desperately. I say, 'No problem,' then I put the sheet back and use the cigarette to burn a deep hole on her belly. All the while I am telling her more childhood memories, but eventually the cigarette goes out. I wonder how a little salt in the wound might feel, so I get salt from the kitchen and pour it on the wound but that doesn't seem to feel good at all, and I explain to her what loneliness feels like and self-contempt. I am starting to get tired of the physical violence, because I'm really not a physical person at all, I prefer to stay on the mental plane instead, but I can't think of anything more to say, so for the last time I take the sheet out of her mouth and ask her nicely to really beg me for forgiveness from the bottom of her heart, and then it will be over, and she does that and I strangle her and then it's over.

Now here I go again, not without a little pride, venting my feelings about people's – and my own – evil. I'm no better than they are – never really was – but now the roles are reversed. Now they're the victims and I'm the bully. I have reached a turning point in life and stopped pitying myself. I choose action instead of brooding. The sands of navel-gazing have run out in their hourglass, and the time for retribution has come.

Imagine that Ann-Kristin – pretty, strong, tough, self-assured, unbeatable Ann-Kristin – ended her days as a low-life hooker in an inhuman grey concrete suburb! The thought makes me dizzy. Maybe I did her a favour by putting an end to it all? Then again, she would probably have gladly traded her last half-hour of life for another fifty years in the brothel of this concrete ghetto.

And what have I got out of the events of these last few days? Happiness? Self-respect? Sunny childhood memories and a bright upbringing? No! I couldn't even say that justice was done, because justice would have been for them to suffer for thirty-eight years and for me to have thirty-eight happy years ahead of me. But unfortunately it's too late for either. A broken childhood can never be repaired. Never forgotten, never changed, never got over. It's a kind of chronic pain. What kind of world is it, where happy little children like Hans and Ann-Kristin are allowed to smash other, less fortunate people's lives to pieces?

What I got out of the past few days in my miserable life is revenge. Which in turn has given rise to a new, exciting dimension – insanity. The five dimensions of life: right–left, up–down, in–out, tick-tock and cuckoo. They stole my time, I took theirs – cuckoo; I gave myself the new dimension of insanity.

Saturday Morning

She turned her head carefully and determined that she was alone in the bed. Carefully, she eased herself up into a sitting position and looked around. The lights were off, but a door leading into a bathroom was ajar, emitting enough light for her to form an impression of the room she was in. It was sparsely but fashionably furnished. On the wall to her right was a window with designer venetian blinds. On the windowsill was a large, square pot made of a grey, cement-like material containing a well-tended plant, the name of which she did not know. Straight ahead, large, white custom-built wardrobes covered the wall, and to their left was a closed door. The bathroom was to her left. The large double bed had expensive Egyptian-cotton sheets in shades of beige and brown. On both sides of the bed were small wall-mounted tables. On the one closest to her were two empty beer bottles. Had she had even more to drink? Behind her, a fabric-clad headboard and two wall-mounted lamps. On the ceiling, four built-in speakers and track lighting.

Shit. Her whole body hurt and her heart was racing. Drunk as a skunk, without a clue where she was. Maybe in a hotel room? In that case, a suite. At a very expensive hotel. How could she have been so damn stupid? Why hadn't she left the bar with Jamal? He had told her earlier that she wasn't sober. Why hadn't she listened to him? Instead of staying there to sit and court strange men. Flirting.

But is that what she had been doing? After all, they had just talked. About politics. There hadn't been any flirting. And she wasn't the least bit interested in fifty-year-old men. She was twenty-eight and had never been attracted to older men. She hadn't started last night, either. There had been no vibes like that. He had simply been nice to talk to. True, he was handsome and charming. Educated. But the thought of sleeping with him never crossed her mind.

So how had she ended up here? Wherever that was. Had she been so drunk that she couldn't get home on her own? Maybe she had simply slept here? No, never. The pain she felt in her nether regions spoke for itself. But her bum . . . ? Anal sex was not really her thing. Never had been and never would be. Had she been so drunk that she'd gone along with that? Then she must have been practically unconscious. Would that nice guy – Peder, she recalled – really have exploited her when she was dead drunk? And both front and back besides. Doctors Without Borders . . . she had been into that. So she must have offered it to him. What a slut she was, a drunken slut.

She had a vague recollection that they had got into a taxi together. They were heading in the same direction – that was it. She would drop him off some-where on the way home to Telefonplan, where her apartment was. She had leaned against him as they made their way out of Clarion's bar. Now she remem-bered. She had suddenly felt extremely drunk and had a hard time walking in her new boots. He had helped her, called for the taxi and would ride along part of the way. But after that it was a complete blank. She remembered she had had some difficulty getting into the taxi, but what happened after that . . . it was gone. She should have eaten properly. Had less to drink.

Don't be so hard on yourself, Petra, she thought. No damage done. After a nice evening you go home with a nice man – or to a hotel or wherever the hell she was now – and have a nice night together. A little roll in the hay. He was handsome, smart and well-educated besides. It was just what you needed. Get drunk and get laid. A life, as Jamal called it. Fine.

But what if it wasn't even him she'd ended up in bed with? Peder. Fryhk. Maybe it was the taxi driver or someone else who'd got his hands on her in the miser-able condition she was in. Suddenly she was struck by yet another unpleasant thought. Maybe she'd been robbed. She threw the blanket aside and got out of bed. Hell, how it hurt. In her head and down below. No more sudden movements. There it was. On the floor beside the bed was her handbag, along with her clothes in a pile. And two used condoms, my God. She reached down carefully for her bag and sat on the edge of the bed to investigate its contents. The mobile was there. Her keys. And her wallet too. She opened it and could see that nothing was missing – the money and credit cards were untouched. Her police ID was still behind her driver's licence where it should be, and everything was in order. That was good anyway. And the watch she got from her parents when she got her law enforcement degree was still on her wrist. It was a quarter past four in the morning. What should she do?

She gathered up her clothes and with her thumb and forefinger carefully picked up the two condoms from the floor and slipped into the bathroom. She did not want him to hear her if he was outside. She was not really sure why – he had already seen her naked. She was unsteady on her feet and her vision was blurred, but she managed to make her way into the bathroom and close the door behind her without making too much noise. Looking around, she quickly ascertained that she was in a home, not a hotel. The bathroom was a designer's dream. Large and airy, Italian tile and mosaics, jacuzzi, and a shower with glass doors. Showering was not an option, not here. She wanted to get home as quickly as possible and sleep off the intoxication in her own bed. Wash away everything that had to do with this damned night.

She was about to drop the condoms into the toilet bowl when something made her change her mind. Somewhere in the fog in her head there was a gnawing doubt. Had she been raped after all? However drunk and . . . flirtatious she may have been last night, no one had the right to exploit her in that situation. Sex with an unconscious woman was the same as rape. Even if she mostly blamed herself, no man had the right to do that. Not according to the law, not according to common decency.

She stood for a while, wondering, her gaze fixed on her own mirror image. Tall and slim with straight, ash-blonde hair down to her shoulders, divided by a straight parting almost in the middle. Her eyes were an indefinable colour, between brown and dark grey. Personally, she preferred to call them green. She had thin lips, but her nose was narrow and rather pointed and just the right size, she thought. She refused to look below her face. This bathroom was the wrong place to stand naked in.

Should she take the condoms with her? The man who had used them might wonder where they had gone. On the other hand, her intention had been to flush them down the toilet, wasn't that the most natural thing for her to do? But no, she would not take any risks, did not want to draw suspicion to herself. Didn't she have a packet of condoms in her bag?

She took two out and managed, with fumbling fingers and blurred sight, to pour about half of the unappetizing contents of the condoms into two of her own. The two used ones she sealed with a knot and placed in a little compartment with a zip in her handbag. The new ones she set carefully on the bench by the sink so the contents would not run out. Then she got dressed, picked up the condoms and soundlessly opened the door to the bedroom. She slipped over to the bed and set the new condoms down approximately where she had found the other two. She took the two beer bottles from the bedside table, disrespectfully emptied the last drops on to the bed and then put them in her handbag.

Her head felt clear now, despite a throbbing pain in her temples. But her balance was a different matter. By pure willpower she managed to force her legs to obey her, but more than anything she wanted to go to bed and sleep. She needed to get out of here, and hoped she could avoid meeting the man she had spent the night with.

Carefully she pushed down the door handle, and without a sound the door glided open. Before her was a large room that epitomized the concept of an open floor plan. The ceiling was high: dining room, living room and kitchen all in one, with more square footage than her entire apartment. Everything about the furnishings was in accord with the trends of the time: light wood, large windows with no curtains, and no frills. She was in a villa. She noticed a stairway that led down to the basement level on her right. She had a definite feeling that someone was down there – she seemed to hear faint sounds from below.

At the far end of the large room was a hall and the outside door. She padded off in that direction and caught sight of her boots and her coat, neatly hanging on a hanger, but as she passed the kitchen she stopped. On the glossy black granite countertop, which divided the kitchen from the rest of the huge room, were a number of beer bottles, the same brand as the ones she had put into her handbag. Better safe than sorry, she thought. She wanted to avoid arousing suspicion at any cost, and possibly the fact that the two bottles from the bedroom had disappeared would do just that. She took two bottles from the counter and from her handbag fished out her key ring, which had a bottle opener on it. The problem was how to open the bottles without being heard. She grabbed a hand towel hanging on the cupboard handle under the sink, and held it over the first of the bottles as she opened it. It fizzed, and she imagined the sound could be heard throughout the house.

Suddenly she heard laughter from the lower level. It almost scared her out of her wits, but she seized her opportunity and quickly opened the other bottle too. Then she poured out the contents into the sink. There was no way for her to rinse away the beer smell without being heard. She quickly headed back to the bedroom, passing the stairway with a shudder. She could swear she heard someone moving down there. She entered the bedroom and went straight to the bedside table. She placed the bottles where they should have been. From force of habit she pulled down the bottom edge of her shirt and tucked her hair behind her ears. And there he stood in the doorway. Peder Fryhk.

*

127

He was smiling, with the same friendly eyes as yesterday evening, and just as well-groomed, in a white terry-cloth bathrobe and with slippers on his feet. She felt her heart galloping, but now it was only a matter of steeling herself and playing this scene to its end.

'Are you awake?' he said in a voice showing both consideration and surprise.

He held his arms out towards her, but she was not capable of taking a step in his direction. This was not necessary, though, for he immediately came up to her and gave her a gentle, careful hug, as if she were fragile. Which she was, just not around the shoulders. A shudder passed through her, but she managed to conceal it with a movement. To her own surprise she responded to his embrace and she took a deep breath while she collected herself. He held her head in his hands and gently pushed her back so that he could look her in the eyes.

'I didn't think you'd wake up before lunch,' he said with a smile that caused all the laughter lines to pull together. 'You were a bit on the tipsy side last night.'

'I know,' said Petra. 'I . . . I shouldn't have had that last glass. I hadn't eaten much either. I usually don't . . . I'm sorry.'

'No, no, no, it was nothing. You were incredibly charming.'

He gave her a light kiss on the cheek. She felt like vomiting, but heard herself saying, 'Thanks for last night. It was really nice.'

The pain in her private parts was throbbing in time with her pulse. He drew her to him again and said, almost whispering, 'Thank you. It was marvellous. You were marvellous.'

That would have to be enough for now. She had to get out of here. Quickly. She placed her hands on his, which were resting on her hips, and lifted them away with a gentle movement.

'I have to go now,' she said in her most soothing voice, looking him right in the eyes.

'Are you sure you don't want to stay a little while longer?' he asked with a wink.

'No, I can't. I'm sorry. You have no idea what a headache I have.' Petra managed to produce a little laugh and shook her head in an attempt to appear ironic at her own expense.

'You can have a couple of aspirin if you want. I have some in the bathroom.'

He started to go and get them for her, but she stopped him.

'No, thanks, it's fine. I usually try to avoid medicine. You reap what you sow, I always say.'

She bit her tongue. That was probably the dumbest thing she had ever said. But he laughed and put his arm around her, escorting her out of the bedroom and through the beautiful main room.

'Do you want me to call a taxi for you?' he asked.

'I think I could use the walk,' Petra replied.

He helped her put her coat on. She had to sit on a

stool as she pulled on her boots so as not to lose her balance. He helped her up and Petra realized that she would have to suffer through another embrace before she could leave.

'Do you want to see me again?' he asked during the farewell hug.

Why don't things like this ever happen for real, thought Petra.

'I'll be in touch,' she said, leaving him with a smile.

At five-thirty on Saturday morning Petra Westman was outside a house at Lusthusbacken 6 in Ålsten, where she had gone by taxi from the southern suburbs.

The trip there had been preceded by certain steps, the rhyme or reason of which she was still unable to judge in her clouded condition. She was following her instincts. When she left Peder Fryhk in his beautiful mid-century house, she made a note of the street number. It was enough to look at his mailbox, where she also saw how his surname was spelled. At the closest intersection she found the name of the street and made a note on her phone: 'Peder Fryhk, Båtviksvägen 12.' Further down the street she met an older woman with a bull terrier, who showed her the way to the nearest metro station. She added 'Mälarhöjden' to her phone notes.

Then she called the commander on duty at the Hammarby Police Department. She knew him, and for that reason he finally yielded and gave her the phone number for the after-hours doctor.

'But Westman, when did you start in traffic?' he asked with some surprise.

'I just need to get in touch with the doctor. Don't be so nosy,' she replied, with a feigned gleam in her eye that she hoped would be conveyed over the phone.

'I'm the one who calls the doctor here,' he tried, but Petra convinced him that it would be fine her way too.

He was content with that and so she had got the name and number of a certain Dr Astrid Egnell, whose address she found through directory enquiries, and now she was there.

Petra decided to phone first before knocking on the doctor's door, in case she was still asleep. As expected, the doctor herself answered.

'This is Police Assistant Petra Westman at the Hammarby Police Department,' she began, trying to speak as clearly as possible, although it was still easier to slur. 'I understand you're on call.'

'Yes, that is right.'

'I need help with a drug test.'

'I'll be there in half an hour,' Egnell replied.

'I thought I could spare you the trouble,' said Petra. 'I'm standing out here on the street and wonder if we could do the test at your house instead.'

'I do not let drunk drivers into my home,' the doctor answered curtly.

'I know this is probably against regulations, but the fact is I'm the one who needs to be tested,' Petra offered.

She saw a curtain on the upper level being pulled to one side and she waved in embarrassment up at the doctor. There was silence on the line.

'I suspect I've been drugged and it's very important to me to find out what's going on,' Petra explained. 'I can show you my ID and I'm not violent, so you don't need to worry.'

There was still silence on the other end. Petra searched for her wallet in her handbag among the beer bottles, managed to wriggle out her police ID and held it up in the direction of the window. It was, of course, impossible for the after-hours doctor to see what she was waving, but she hoped the card would function as a sort of white flag.

'Are you under the influence, officer?' she asked.

'I believe so,' answered Petra. 'That's why I'm here.'

Having promised not to make any noise and wake the sleeping family, Petra was let into Astrid Egnell's kitchen where she dutifully sat on a chair.

'What is this all about?' enquired the doctor, who was dressed only in a bathrobe.

'I would rather not go into details, but I'd like to find out how much alcohol I have in my blood and if I have any other drugs in my system.'

'And how should I register this, did you think about that?'

Astrid Egnell actually seemed very nice, despite her

stern tone, but Petra had no problem understanding her scepticism about the whole thing.

'I would prefer it if you didn't enter it at all . . . if we could settle this between us. I'm prepared to pay for it, if you'll just do the tests.'

'But I'm not the one who analyses the samples,' said Astrid Egnell, her tone somewhat friendlier now. 'They have to be sent to the lab at Linköping and it may take several weeks before we get the test results.'

Petra had not thought about these complications, but suddenly she had an idea, which she kept to herself.

'I'll take care of it,' she said calmly. 'You're a doctor, you do the tests. I'll take the samples and arrange the rest myself. You'll be rid of me as soon as the samples are taken.'

Astrid Egnell studied her with a surprised expression.

'Does it hurt anywhere?' she asked unexpectedly.

'Yes, my head.'

'Do you have memory lapses? Difficulty walking?'

Petra nodded in agreement.

'For more than one reason perhaps,' said the doctor, opening the bag on the kitchen table without looking her in the eyes.

Petra did not reply.

'Clench your fist,' said the doctor, snapping a rubber band around her upper arm.

'For more than one reason perhaps,' said Petra, giggling.

The doctor looked at her with amusement and stuck the needle into the crook of her arm.

'I know, I'm not sober,' said Petra.

She felt the tension begin to subside now, but she could not relax. She had a long day ahead of her and she had put aside any thought of going home to bed.

'You have to give a urine sample too. Try to be quiet.'

She handed Petra a jar and showed her to a bathroom by the front door. Petra did as directed and gave the jar to the doctor, who put it in a plastic bag that she then tied shut. Then she put the tube of blood and the jar of urine in a plastic grocery bag, along with some papers that would guide the laboratory. Petra tried to pay, but Astrid Egnell refused to take her money.

'Next train to Linköping leaves at eight. I suggest you go home and shower before you leave, because you don't look sober. Take care of yourself,' she said, closing the front door.

At 10:40 a.m., about twenty minutes late, Petra Westman got off the train at the central station in Linköping. Her only luggage was a grocery bag containing two beer bottles, a sample tube of blood, a jar of urine, two condoms and her own used toothbrush. On the platform she was met by a certain Håkan Carlberg, whom she had met twice before: the first time at a cousin's wedding and the second time at another cousin's wedding. Both times they had been seated next to each other at dinner – the second time apparently because the seating arrangement had turned out so well the first time. Håkan Carlberg was a rather well-built local in his forties, with dark-blond, close-cropped hair. He had a cheerful, pleasant manner and a gleam in his eye, at least when he was at a party, and Petra hoped he would not be too different on an everyday basis.

It was not because of these qualities, however, that Petra had called and woken him up at seven-thirty on a Saturday morning and asked to see him. Håkan Carlberg worked as a technician at SKL, the national crime laboratory, and was in possession of certain expertise and equipment that Petra was in need of on this gloomy November morning.

Today he was unshaven and dressed for the weekend in a pair of washed-out jeans and a bright-blue, long-sleeved T-shirt under a navy-blue down jacket. Petra was uncertain of the most appropriate way to greet him, so she extended her hand so as not to appear forward. He ignored that and gave her a big hug, which made her feel even more idiotic, but it did give her hope for their immediate future together.

'Shall we get a bite to eat?' Håkan suggested. 'I haven't had any breakfast.'

'Me neither,' Petra admitted, and they headed for the station building and the restaurant there.

'Now I'm getting a bit curious as to what this is all about,' said Håkan, when they were sitting at a table by a window facing the street.

Petra had a liver-sausage sandwich and a mineral water in front of her and Håkan had the same, supplemented by a cup of coffee. Petra insisted on paying for breakfast and was allowed to, after initial objection from Håkan.

'I have a few odds and ends with me I'd like you to take a look at,' said Petra. 'Off the record, so to speak, but according to all the rules of the art.'

'Goodness. Is this private detective work?'

'I wouldn't say that.'

'Is your boyfriend having an affair?' Håkan said jokingly.

'If only it were that simple,' sighed Petra. 'No, it's nothing inappropriate. Not like that, anyway.'

'What kind of odds and ends then?'

'For one thing, there are a couple of beer bottles I would like you to check for fingerprints.'

'I'll be glad to do that for you. But did you have to come all the way to Linköping to get help with that? I would think you have your own lab for such things.'

'Yes, I know,' sighed Petra. 'But there's more.'

'Shoot.'

'I have blood and urine that I would like to have tested for alcohol and drugs. And I have semen that I would like to have DNA tested.'

Petra looked at Håkan Carlberg with an embarrassed smile. She knew this was a lot to ask.

'You must be joking,' he said seriously. '"Off the

record"? Do you know what it costs to do DNA analysis?'

'I know,' said Petra, who had no idea, although she was well aware that it was expensive.

'What would be the point of a DNA analysis without something to compare it to? Is it a pretty diagram to hang up on the wall you're after, or what?'

'I know who the DNA belongs to. When we arrest him we'll have this to compare to.'

'Well, why don't we run the DNA analysis at that time instead? When we have a case? I suppose you're going to arrest the owner of this sperm sample?'

'Sooner or later. I'll see to that.'

'So why don't we already have an ongoing investigation? You have to explain what you're up to, otherwise I'm not interested.'

Petra sighed heavily and ate for a few minutes in silence. Her headache made itself apparent again, and she drank half the bottle of mineral water in one gulp. Håkan ate too, and his gaze wandered thoughtfully between Petra and what was going on outside the window, which was basically nothing.

'Come on now, Petra,' he said at last. 'Tell me about it. Even if I decide not to help you, I'm not going to tell anyone. I swear to that. Except possibly Helena. And maybe Anna.'

Her cousins. Petra looked up at him in terror. He met her eyes with a loud laugh.

'I'll keep my mouth shut,' he said, suddenly serious again. 'I think I understand what's happened.'

He reached across the table and placed his hand over hers.

'Were you raped?' he asked gently.

Petra felt suddenly that she was extremely close to tears, but she straightened up and drank a little mineral water to shake it off. Just like with the on-call doctor this morning, there was some relief in being met with understanding.

'I don't know,' Petra said frankly. 'But I think that must be what happened.'

And then the whole story bubbled out of her. Håkan Carlberg listened attentively, interrupting her occasionally with a question or to clarify something.

'How do you feel now?' he asked when she had finished her story. 'Purely physically, I mean. Mentally you seem to be on top form, occupied with private investigations and other exciting stuff.'

His joking tone dissolved the heavy atmosphere at the table and Petra smiled for the first time in many hours.

'I have an excruciating headache, pain in my belly and arsehole, and poor control of my extremities. But I feel a lot less clumsy now. This morning I was seeing fuzzy too, but that's passed.'

Once everything had been explained, it was much easier to talk about. The whole event was reduced to a narrative, something that had taken place but could now be looked at clinically. She hoped it would stay that way.

'And why don't you report the whole story to the police?' Håkan wanted to know.

'I *am* the police, damn it.'

'You know what I mean.'

'Would you want your colleagues to do an investigation of you? Analyse your sperm and . . . take blood samples and fingerprints?'

Petra could hear how dumb that sounded, and Håkan looked amused as he listened to her perhaps not-so-well-thought-out comparison.

'Well, that part about fingerprints does sound really terrible,' he laughed. 'But I understand what you mean. Being examined by the police doctor in a gynaecology chair, while your buddies in the department sit alongside with pen and pad. Being perceived as a victim instead of hunting the perpetrator. That doesn't sound like a very comfortable situation. You don't think you have any injuries?'

'I'm sure I do,' said Petra, 'but nothing that won't heal on its own. I'm grateful in any event that he used a condom. Imagine if I got pregnant on top of everything else. Or worse.'

'Don't you think he'll be worried you might send him to jail? Being a police officer and all.'

'He doesn't know I'm a police officer. I told him I work at an insurance company.'

'But wasn't your police badge in your wallet?'

Petra sat quietly for a moment.

'I keep it hidden behind my driver's licence. I don't think he went through my wallet and —'

'Of course he did,' Håkan interrupted. 'He'd want to know who he was dealing with. Your name. Where you live.'

'If he did, I don't think he found my police ID anyway.'

'And if he did find your ID, he might very well think the experience was even more exciting. But maybe he'll also have more reason to be suspicious.'

'Are you trying to scare me?'

'I just want you to be careful.'

'I took the used condoms and replaced them with two unused ones. With contents. I took the beer bottles and put two others back instead. I also apologized for getting so drunk and then played a tender farewell scene that would have won an Oscar. There's no reason to worry.'

'I hope you're right. That was an ingenious rape procedure, I must say.'

'If it was a rape,' Petra sighed. 'Maybe I was just drunk and horny after all. But I've never done anything like that before. And I'm never going to again, heaven help me.'

'From your description, he sounds awfully cunning,' said Håkan, rubbing his unshaven cheeks. 'No moves during the evening in the bar. No groping, no shameless proposals. Just cultivated conversation.'

'Handsome, charming and intelligent. He shouldn't have any problem at all attracting women.'

'Which makes him truly perverse,' Håkan interjected. 'He prefers unconscious women to willing ones.'

'You should have seen how he treated me in the morning,' said Petra. 'Like a porcelain doll. Those kinds of guys don't grow on trees in real life.'

'What a charade you played for each other. He played tender and loving and grateful for your little dalliance, and you did the same. Both of you knew he had raped you, but neither of you let on. But it's one–nil to you, Petra. He thinks he knows something you don't, but in reality it's the other way round.'

'He's going to jail sooner or later,' said Petra with conviction. 'He's done this before, and he's going to do it again. I hope my bodily fluids won't have to be used as evidence, but if that's what's required, then that's how it will have to be.'

Petra handed the grocery bag across the table.

'Take good care of them,' said Petra.

'I'll see what I can do,' said forensic laboratory technician Håkan Carlberg, taking the bag with a wink.

Saturday Evening

Åsa was with Christoffer and Jonathan at a two-year-old's birthday party. Conny Sjöberg had been Christmas shopping with the older children, though it was still only November. If Christmas shopping seemed stressful now, it was disastrous to wait until December rolled around. Besides, it was pure delight to sit at home in an armchair, sipping mulled wine in December, knowing that almost everyone else in Stockholm was either slogging through crowded department stores or tormented by anxiety at the prospect of doing so. That Åsa was one of the last-minute shoppers did not make it any less enjoyable.

Now he had hidden all the Christmas presents, wrapped and ready, in a cupboard to which, by tradition, Åsa and the children did not have access during the last two months of the year. The cooking patrol were gathered around the kitchen table, drawing up the guidelines for the regular Saturday dinner project.

'Sara will get out all the ingredients for the tapenade,' said Sjöberg, pointing to a recipe in a cooking magazine. 'Then you'll try to measure the exact amount it says, and put it in the blender. I'll help you crush the garlic. Do you know what this means: "tbs"?'

Sara shook her head.

'It means "tablespoon",' said Sjöberg. 'I'll show you which one it is. Maja will roll the dough out into thin squares and then you'll both help spread the tapenade on the dough when you're ready. Okay?'

'Okay,' said the girls in unison.

'Simon will make the salmon salad here, but it's in the same magazine, so you'll have to share. You'll manage by yourself, won't you?'

'You bet,' said Simon. 'But the salmon has to marinate for three hours, so we'll never get anything to eat!'

'Ha, ha,' Sjöberg gloated, 'I've already marinated it! But take care of everything else first, and we'll add the salmon last. I'll peel the potatoes for the turbot and grate the horseradish.'

'I don't like horseradish,' said Maja sullenly.

'No, it is a bit strong, but we're having peas too, and melted butter, so I'm sure you'll be fine. Let's get going!'

'Stop!' said Maja. 'We've got to have a cooking beer too!'

'Of course, I completely forgot about that. Can you bring it in from the balcony? Simon, help her open the door.'

The project was in progress, and this was truly the high point of the week for everyone involved. Sjöberg put on his apron and reminded himself that he was going to get an appropriate size apron for each of the children as a Christmas present. Maja came in twice with three soft drinks and a beer, and Simon opened them with a practised hand. Sjöberg set the potatoes in the sink and started to peel them. The kids were concentrating on their tasks and he wondered what the mood was like among Vannerberg's children this Saturday afternoon. Poor things, he sighed to himself. Hans Vannerberg's façade undeniably seemed spotless, but had there been a crack somewhere after all?

The investigation was at a standstill and nothing new had emerged as the week came to an end. Ingrid Olsson had never planned to sell her house, so she hadn't spoken to Vannerberg or any other estate agent about it. True, Pia Vannerberg was certain her husband had said he was going to meet a seller that evening, but could you rely on that? She might have misheard or misinterpreted him, or he might have misspoken. Unless the murder was premeditated. That would mean someone had arranged a meeting with Vannerberg in Ingrid Olsson's house, perhaps for the purpose of murdering him. In that case, what relationship did this person have to Olsson? No, that seemed too far-fetched. The guy had an irreproachable past, he had stable finances, no unpaid debts, no unusual transactions, and he was not in any of the crime registers. He was unlikely to be having an affair, had no enemies and no shady contacts.

On the other hand, the buyer at Åkerbärsvägen 13 maintained that they had not agreed to meet that particular Monday, but that Vannerberg would stop by when he was 'in the neighbourhood'. It was most likely that he decided to stop by that very evening, to get it over with, but then wouldn't he have called first? He was home, after all, and it would take a little while to walk there. And if it was number 13 Vannerberg was going to, what kind of lunatic had taken up lodgings at 31? Or had he been followed by someone who took the opportunity to kill him in the empty house, and in that case, how had Vannerberg got in? Had the old lady forgotten to lock the door? That didn't seem very likely. No, this was truly a mystery.

The only remarkable thing about Vannerberg was that he lacked a father. And that he had a mother who was in the striptease business, but that could not be held against him. After Petra Westman got hold of Vannerberg's personal diary, the investigation team had mapped out his final weeks, but nothing interesting had emerged. On his computer at VM Property nothing of interest had been found either. He had nothing personal at all on the computer, and his e-mail communication was limited to a few messages a week; nothing concerning his possible meeting with the mysterious seller at Åkerbärsvägen 31. Jorma Molin had nothing to hide either, apart from a few speeding tickets and an old overdue payment notice.

As far as Ingrid Olsson was concerned, Sandén relayed that Margit Olofsson had nothing to say about her other than that she was a person who rarely smiled. Olofsson took pity on her because she was old, sick and, above all, alone, and because she had asked her for help. According to Olofsson, Olsson had a rather indifferent attitude about the murder, which was somewhat surprising. But indifference was not a crime.

Nothing had been stolen from the house either. The jewellery box, which proved to contain the only things of value that Ingrid Olsson owned, was untouched, and the technicians, with the meticulous Bella Hansson in the lead, had not found any traces of anyone other than the owner herself elsewhere in the house – only in the kitchen, hall and living room. Margit Olofsson's fingerprints were found here and there. Vannerberg's fingerprints were in the kitchen and on the outside door handle, which might suggest that he opened the door and entered the house on his own, if it had been unlocked. On the kitchen chair, the probable murder weapon, there was another, unidentified set of fingerprints, not found anywhere else in the house.

His musings were interrupted by the six-year-old's happy voice.

'Daddy, you were going to show me the "tbs",' said Sara enthusiastically.

'Of course, the "tbs",' said Sjöberg.

He took the measuring spoons from one of the kitchen drawers.

'Look here, this is the tablespoon measure.'

'Which one is the "dl"?' Sara asked.

'That's this one,' Sjöberg answered. 'It's called "decilitre". What's measured in decilitres?'

'The olives.'

'Look, Daddy, look how nicely I'm making this!' said Maja, showing him the slabs of dough she was rolling out.

'Yes, look how clever you are. Now I'll get out the baking tray and put some greaseproof paper on it, then we'll put the spirals on there.'

Simon was busy cutting green peppers, cherry tomatoes and chillies into small pieces, and Sjöberg placed a hand on his shoulder.

'That looks really nice.'

'I know,' the eight-year-old answered self-assuredly.

The sound of the outside door being opened and Åsa's breathless voice was heard from the hall. Maja let go of the rolling pin and rushed out to her. Sjöberg followed and greeted her happily, then he lifted the twins out of the pushchair in the stairwell, closed the outer door, set one on the floor and sat down with the other one on his lap. There was a lot of clothing to take off and put on at this time of year.

'We've done our Christmas shopping,' Sjöberg said proudly, and Åsa gave him a stern look.

'It's only November,' she muttered.

'Yes, exactly, and that's the best time to do it. Isn't it, Maja?'

'Yes, yes, yes,' Maja agreed.

He put undressed son number one on the floor and attended to number two.

'How was the party?'

'It was really nice. Eight wild children running around, and some nice parents having coffee. Caroline is going to have a little brother.'

'I see, they know that already?'

'Yes. The boys are all done in. Let's put them to bed at once. They won't need any food after everything they've been stuffing themselves with. What kind of good things are you cooking?'

'Mummy, Sara and I are making tapenade spirals,' said Maja. 'Come and look!'

They all went into the kitchen and Åsa seemed suitably impressed by the good food that was being prepared.

'I'll put the twins to bed while you make dinner,' said Åsa.

Jonathan and Christoffer were both standing next to Simon, whining imploringly and pointing. He gave them a cherry tomato each, and they fell silent at once. With some prodding, Åsa managed to herd them into the bathroom, and Sjöberg finished his potato peeling and put the saucepan on the stove. He assembled the food processor and poured in Sara's black olives, anchovies, capers and oil, and added some crushed garlic cloves that she had prepared. They mixed the ingredients to an evenly blended black paste, and the girls then helped spread the tapenade on Maja's rolled-out squares of dough. Sjöberg cut three-inch-long strings out of the dough, which the girls twisted into neat spirals and put on the tray.

Meanwhile Simon rinsed the marinated fish in a colander. Then he carefully stirred the salmon cubes into the chopped vegetables and a little coconut milk in a bowl, adding cut chives and spices.

The dishes were ready at the same time, but Simon had prepared his dish himself, while Sjöberg and the girls were a team of three on theirs, so in his personal opinion, he was the best. Which, of course, annoyed the girls. Sjöberg pointed out that actually he had marinated the salmon and therefore they were all equally good, after which Simon retreated with a snarl and peace was restored.

After ten minutes in the oven the dough was crisp, and the little boys had been cleaned up, put to bed and were already asleep. Åsa uncorked a bottle of white wine and a big bottle of fizzy passion-fruit juice, and the wakeful part of the family sat around the table, each with a glass and a bread basket full of tapenade spirals, waiting for the potatoes to be ready.

The children noisily told first one story, then another: mostly episodes from school, the playground and nursery. Sjöberg leaned back contentedly, enjoying these stories from the uncomplicated side of real life that he so rarely came in contact with in his job.

The starter was an unqualified success, as were the tapenade spirals, and Åsa was very impressed by her children's cooking talents. Both Sara and Maja were already so full they couldn't eat any of the main dish, and were excused to watch a children's programme instead. After the turbot, Simon, too, disappeared from the table and adult conversation took over.

'I want to try something out on you, Conny,' said Åsa. 'One of the psychology teachers at school tried an amusing test out on us in the staff room.'

Åsa taught the unusual combination of mathematics and physical education at Frans Schartau High School.

'It's an ethics test. I'll start by telling you a story. Then you rank all the individuals in the story by how well you think they behave, in purely ethical terms. Do you follow me?'

'Yep,' Sjöberg answered enthusiastically.

He loved games, play, the romance quizzes in the tabloids – all that sort of thing.

'Stina lives in a cottage on one side of the river. On the other side lives Per in his cottage, and they are in love. The problem is that the bridge over the river has collapsed and the river is full of crocodiles, so it's not possible to swim across. Stina longs to see her Per so much that her heart is almost bursting. So she goes to her neighbour Sven, who has a boat, and asks to borrow it. He just laughs and says that of course she can, but she has to sleep with him first.'

Sjöberg grinned and Åsa continued.

'Stina is desperate and goes to her other neighbour Ivar, who is the strongest, most authoritative person in the village. Everyone respects him and does what he says. She tells him about her desperation and asks him to make Sven see reason, but he just says that he doesn't care. Sven can exploit the situation any way he wants, Ivar does not intend to get involved. Stina is now completely exasperated and tells herself that Per, who loves her so much, will surely understand and forgive her, so she goes to Sven and sleeps with him and gets to borrow the boat. When Stina makes it across the river, she does not spare her beloved the painful truth, and tells Per at once about the terrible thing she had to do and asks him to forgive her. Per is furious and kicks Stina out and makes it clear that he never wants to see her again. Stina then goes to Per's neighbour Gustav, who is a reliable person, and cries her heart out. He consoles her and gets so angry when he hears how Per has treated her that he goes over to Per and punches him on the nose.'

Sjöberg laughed and shook his head.

'Well,' said Åsa, 'now you have to rank these people according to what you think of their ethics. Not the law, remember that. One is best and five is worst.'

'Well, that little floozy, Stina . . .' said Sjöberg with a grin.

'Conny, be serious now!' Åsa interrupted.

'I'm just joking. I have to think a bit.'

'I've already decided what I think,' said Åsa. 'It will be interesting to see if we think the same way. Then we can discuss it.'

He loved her habit of planning how the conversation would proceed. He loved her enthusiasm and her way of letting it rub off on others. He loved Åsa, to put it simply, the whole Åsa. Though I don't think I'd be too happy if she went to bed with Sandén, just to see me, Sjöberg thought.

'So, we have Stina, who is honest and good-hearted, but a little dense,' Sjöberg summarized. 'She lives in the present, with no concern for the consequences of her actions. We have Per, who is selfish and unforgiving. Gustav has a good heart; he has empathy and stands up for his opinions but uses his fists and sets himself up as a judge over others. Sven is unhelpful, scornful and undependable and takes advantage of the misfortunes of others. Ivan is indifferent and lacks empathy. I say that Per is the most ethical, then Stina, Ivar, Gustav, and Sven last.'

'But surely you can't mean that Ivar is better than Gustav!' Åsa exclaimed. 'He could easily have told Sven what to do and solved Stina's problem!'

'Yes, I guess Gustav is somehow the most ethical, but he's really the only one who commits a crime here. You can't just attack people willy-nilly. And indifference is not a crime,' Sjöberg added, suddenly struck by a feeling of déjà vu.

'But how can you put Per before Stina? There's nothing bad about Stina, is there?'

'Per didn't like Stina's actions and simply broke up with her. He has the right to do that. It's like he's not involved. Stina actually behaved really stupidly, I think anyway.'

'But it was for a good cause. Although you're right,

in principle, that you wouldn't have done the same thing yourself. Well, purely in terms of goodness, I think that Gustav is best. I like people who stand up for what they think and take an active part in what is happening around them. Ivar is a real jerk. I can agree that Sven is the very worst, but Ivar is almost as bad. And Stina is two and Per three.'

They cleared the dinner things off the table and Åsa went out to the children. It was almost their bedtime. Sjöberg cleaned up in the kitchen. His musings about indifference stayed with him. It was certainly no crime. No one could get involved in all the problems of humankind. You chose certain people and certain wars and certain natural disasters to care about more than others. Then there were those people who did not choose anything at all. It was undeniably simpler to live like that. Then it struck him that indifference was actually a deadly sin, that some philosopher had actually thought it was among the worst crimes a human could commit. He dug in his memory for the other deadly sins. Gluttony, lust, pride, wrath, greed and envy. In purely legal terms, Gustav was the only one who committed a crime, but according to the medieval understanding of morality, Ivar was guilty of indifference, Gustav of anger, Stina of fornication, Sven of greed and fornication, and Per perhaps of anger, perhaps pride. They were all cut from the same cloth.

In the Sjöberg family, elements of gluttony, wrath, greed and envy all appeared. Life is hard. He happened

153

to think about those poor teachers in Landskrona who lost several children in the waves at the beach. What was their crime? Indifference to danger? What about the racist murder of John Hron? That third guy, was he guilty because he hadn't called for help on his mobile? Perhaps indifference was a crime, after all. In the eyes of some, indifference was undeniably a crime in certain situations. You could say that. In the eyes of some, perhaps Ingrid Olsson was a criminal.

When the kids were in bed, he mixed drinks for himself and Åsa. He had a rum and Coke, but Åsa preferred a vodka and Red Bull, with a little squeezed lime. It was his brother-in-law Lasse's invention, and it was surprisingly good. According to some sources, however, the combination of alcohol and energy drink was considered unhealthy, about which Sjöberg did not miss an opportunity to remind his wife. They sat down in front of the TV to watch the news. A forty-four-year-old prostitute and mother of three had been found tortured and murdered in her apartment in Skärholmen. No suspects. The police were looking for witnesses. It was not a good week for forty-four-year-olds, Sjöberg thought absentmindedly. After the news they played cards and had another drink. Then they went to bed.

Monday Morning

The water was running in the bath and she was standing by the bedroom window, looking out over the courtyard. Some kids were sitting in the sandpit, making a mess in the wet sand. They had warm caps and waterproofs on and didn't seem to notice the biting wind and bleak sky. Their mothers sat shivering on a bench, hands in their jacket pockets and collars turned up. Otherwise the courtyard was empty, at this time of day. The bigger kids were at school or nursery.

She had lived here her whole life and never felt any longing to leave. She grew up in one of the buildings on the other side of the courtyard, where her parents still lived. When she and Jörgen moved in together, it never occurred to her to move to a different part of town, and when an apartment became available on the block, they seized the opportunity without hesitation. Being so close to her parents also meant that childcare had never been a problem.

The hours before noon were nice, when she could be by herself and just sit at home and take it easy. Therese, their fourteen-year-old, was in school and Tobias, who was seventeen, worked as a postman and did not come home until after lunch, if he came home at all. Jörgen was at his job in the ball-bearing factory, and she did not have to leave to clean before two o'clock.

She had taken early retirement a few years ago because of chronic pain in her back and arms from her low-paid cleaning job at the hospital. She went to the doctor and was granted extended sick leave, and a few years later she was allowed so-called sickness benefits, without any further discussion. It did not hurt so badly that she couldn't clean at all, so now she cleaned people's homes cash in hand in the afternoons and collected a pension too. That way she brought in considerably more money to the household treasury than Jörgen did, even though he worked full-time. They sometimes discussed whether he should do the same thing, but he was not keen on taking cleaning jobs. That was women's work, he thought.

She went into the bathroom and turned off the tap, brought out the tub of water and set it on the wall-to-wall carpet in the living room. She sank down in the armchair, carefully lowered her feet into the hot water and lit a cigarette. Ricki Lake and a dozen obese Americans were trying to make themselves heard on the topic 'My partner is unfaithful with my best friend – the lie detector can prove it'. She had never been unfaithful herself, not since she and Jörgen got married anyway, and that was more than twenty years ago. She could well imagine Jörgen having had a fling or two, but, if he had, she didn't care all that much about it.

They lived under the same roof, but that was about it. They didn't talk much. He had his interests and she had hers. He had the guys, bandy and football, and she had TV and the kids. Sometimes she went to The Sapphire and danced with a girlfriend, but otherwise it was mostly soap operas, the cleaning job and housekeeping for the rest of the family that occupied her time. Pretty thin gruel, you might say, but she did not complain.

The doorbell rang and she cursed to herself because, as usual, she had forgotten to bring the towel with her from the bathroom. The door was open anyway, so she didn't have to get up.

'It's just me! What are you doing?'

'Mum, will you get my towel from the bathroom? I'm taking a footbath.'

Her mother was a somewhat overweight woman, about sixty-five, but her dark-brown hair had only minimal streaks of grey. She had just had a perm and looked quite stylish.

'Your hair looks really nice,' said Lise-Lott.

'I just came from the hairdresser. Do you think it turned out okay?'

Her mother handed over the towel and sat down on the couch.

'I said your hair looks really nice.'

Lise-Lott stubbed out her cigarette and lit another.

'Would you like one?' she asked, tossing the pack on to the coffee table, in front of her mother.

'I'll put the coffee on,' her mother said, getting up and disappearing into the kitchen.

The audience was booing and Ricki Lake was shaking

her head, gasping in surprise at the evidence of the lie detector. Shaquil looked relaxed in his chair, but he was shaking his head too, and stubbornly maintained that the lie detector was lying, while Cheyenne was jumping up and down in fury, screaming a lot of things that had to be bleeped out. Her best friend, Sarah-O, just sat and smiled in embarrassment, rolling her eyes.

Her mother came in with two cups of coffee and sat back down on the sofa, took a cigarette from the pack on the table and got involved in the programme. They watched a while in silence, until there was an ad break.

'Was Jörgen at the match yesterday?' her mother asked.

'Yes.'

'Don't you ever go along?'

'Why would I?'

'Irene asked if I wanted to go to the theatre on Sunday. There's a play at Cosmos.'

'So, are you going?'

'Are you nuts? She thinks she's something, Irene, that's what I say.'

'What makes you say that?'

'I guess it's 'cause of her kid. He's at college. Whatever good that will do.'

'What's Dad up to?'

'He's watching *Oprah*. I think this is more interesting. I bought a chemise for Therese.'

'Really? Where?'

'At Åhlén's, on sale. It only cost a hundred kronor.'

'Do you think she'll like it?'

'Sure, all the girls have them. White, you know, with thin shoulder straps.'

'Sounds cute. I can take it instead.'

'You can fight over it,' her mother laughed and puffed out a large smoke ring that slowly dispersed on its way up to the ceiling.

'I think she's the one who's lying, not him,' said Lise-Lott about a girl on the TV. 'I'm sure she's a lesbian too. There was one on before.'

'You don't say.'

'Yeah, she slept with her boyfriend's sister.'

'They're out of their minds in America.'

'Yeah.'

'Dad says that guy in number 10 is a homo. Niklas, you know.'

'What makes him say that?' Lise-Lott asked.

'I don't know. You can tell by his looks, he says. I don't think there are any homos in Katrineholm.'

'There must be homos everywhere.'

'No, I don't think so. They all live in Stockholm.'

'Therese is going to Stockholm.'

'She is? Why?'

'Clothes shopping.'

'Are you letting her do that?'

'Depends on what you mean by letting her. She pretty much does what she wants anyway. The other girls are going.'

'Maybe you and I should go to Stockholm and do some shopping.'

'It's pretty expensive. You can find good clothes here.'

'We could go to Norrköping.'

'Why?'

'Just to do something.'

'We could do that. Then we'll go to McDonald's,' Lise-Lott suggested.

'I don't like hamburgers.'

'So what do you like?'

'Whatever. Chinese food.'

'You can just as well have that here in town.'

'But we never do.'

'Why not?'

'It's expensive.'

'Do you think it's cheaper in Norrköping?'

'Now just give it up! You think we should take the camping stove and make our own food?'

'You were the one who didn't want to go to McDonald's.'

'I never said that! I just said I don't like hamburgers.'

'It's the same thing.'

'No, it isn't. They have other things.'

'Like what?'

'I don't know! You're the one who wanted to go to McDonald's!'

'Don't you want to go there?'

'Sure. We'll just have to see what they have.'

'I'm sure they have the same things they have here in town.'

'Probably.'

The conversation died out and they finished watching the programme. Her mother got up.

'Well, I have to get home to Dad. He'll probably want coffee.'

'See you. Say hi.'

'Thanks for the coffee. Bye now, love.'

TV-Shop started and she remained sitting in front of two idiots cheering over a set of frying pans. She wondered whether they were genuinely enthused that the frying pans produced such splendid results or whether they were paid actors. In that case they were almost unbelievably skilful. And the whole audience too, standing up and applauding the great food. She decided they were probably for real, but that there was some trickery with the frying pans. She had never seen such impressive results in real life, either for herself or anywhere else.

She lit a cigarette and switched to another channel, where her favourite British soap opera was just about to start. There was a rustling at the letter box and a dull thud was heard on the hall floor when the post arrived. She remembered that it was Monday and hoped that *OK!* magazine was waiting for her out there. But first she would see how things were going for the Dingles in *Emmerdale*.

She never found out. Twenty minutes later she was dead.

Diary of a Murderer,
November 2006, Monday

I never imagined that it would be so simple! You just step into people's lives for a few minutes and then out again. As if nothing has happened. Easy as pie. That's the advantage of being an invisible person like me. It's true you don't get noticed when you want to, but when you don't want to be noticed, it's excellent.

I'm one of the invisible people. The invisible people who cower through life, regardless of weather and business cycles. For us it's always a recession, always fog. We always cower for fear of a fist in the face or a kick in the guts. For no good reason – nobody sees us anyway.

Nobody looks at me and thinks, 'Nice hairdo. I think I'll get my hair cut that way too.' Nobody looks at me and thinks, 'Yuck, what a terrible jacket! That's been out of style for years!' Nobody looks at me at all. Not if I'm standing in the way, not if I'm holding open the door, not if I offer someone my seat on the metro, and not if I don't. Not any more. I was visible as a child. To children. Not to grown-ups. It was as if, as a child, I carried a big, yellow sign that said, 'Look at me! I'm ugly and ridiculous! I wear strange clothes and say weird things! Hit me, mock me! Do it, do it – hurt me! Beat the abnormality out of me so I can become a normal person!' But they didn't succeed. 'Cause I became a grown-up, but not normal.

Nobody saw me when I bought the train ticket to Katrineholm. Nobody saw me as I looked out of the window at the landscape of my childhood. The oak hills and lakes of Södermanland, enchanted forests and pastures.

I take the short cut to my childhood street – and Lise-Lott's. From the train station I simply follow Storgatan for a while, which then turns into Stockholms-vägen. Take a left towards East School and you're there. She still lives here, after all these years, in this godforsaken place. If I'd stayed here I would have been dead a long time ago. But I'm alive and it's Lise-Lott who's dead.

But let's not get ahead of ourselves. I'm walking between the apartment buildings, into the courtyard. Same courtyard, new equipment for the children. A few kids are playing in the sandpit and their mothers are sitting on a bench watching, otherwise the court-yard is deserted. The bushes with the big white berries that pop when you step on them are still there along-side the buildings. The bushes were so big you could walk around inside them, play hide-and-seek and make forts. Now they look rather unassuming.

That was where Lise-Lott and a few others – her sister and friends from the estate – tore off all my clothes and smeared mud all over me. They hung my clothes over the climbing frame and when the game was over I had to choose between going naked out on to the courtyard and taking down the clothes, in full view of everyone, or sneaking into the basement. I chose the latter, and when the children scattered and I dared go back to the courtyard to fetch my clothes, they were gone. The kids and the clothes.

The climbing frame. It's been replaced by a new, more modern version, with a climbing wall and ropes and a built-in slide. You could crawl inside the old one – a big sphere of air encased by red steel bars – and climb up and hang by your knees. I spent an afternoon there, tormented by Lise-Lott and her like-minded gang. I sat on the top, my legs dangling, sweaty with the fear of what would happen if I came down. They threw clods of dirt at me, and snowballs. A few times they tried to drag me down by pulling on my feet, but I held on for dear life. They screamed at me and insulted me – shouted how ugly and stupid I was – and sometimes they retreated a little, to lure me into venturing down. When I did, they came rushing back again. The whole thing ended when Lise-Lott packed some pieces of glass into a snowball and threw it at me. One piece cut a deep gash in my neck, the pain caused me to release my desperate hold and I fell to the ground. I got a concussion in the process. I vomited, to the children's delight, but when they saw the blood they ran away. I staggered home, had to go to the hospital and get stitches, and then stay in bed for a few days. One good thing came out of it anyway.

Lise-Lott's dad locked me in the basement once, because I told Lise-Lott that my dad was a cop, which, of course, was something I had made up. True, Lise-Lott's dad wasn't a cop either, although she said he was on a daily basis – so you wouldn't dare talk back, I guess – but he clearly had the authority to lock people up anyway. If I remember rightly, he worked as an assistant at Karsudden, a mental hospital for criminals. Of course, he must have learned that trick there. It worked: I never lied about my dad again, but Lise-Lott carried on as usual. At home it was not considered a good idea to lock people in the basement, so we never tried it on Lise-Lott, despite dogged attempts at persuasion on my part.

After pondering my miserable childhood for a while, I make my way via the basement into Lise-Lott's current building. In the stairwell I run into her mum, who is on her way out of the apartment. So Lise-Lott is at home and I can both see and hear that the door is unlocked, which makes the whole thing even simpler. The mother is her usual self. She's put on a bit of weight, but she has the same matronly perm, the same ruminating chewing gum, and the same surly, arrogant expression. Of course she doesn't see me, even though we brush against each other in passing. I hear muted TV voices from inside the apartment before the door closes. Then I know where to find her.

I go up a few more flights and wait for several minutes by a window that faces on to the street. The outside door slams shut and someone comes running up the stairs. The postman rushes by, taking no notice of the insignificant figure he passes, and then he's back again, on his way down through the building with the mail. He takes no notice of me this time either.

When he is gone I go down to Lise-Lott's apartment, carefully open the door, sneak into the dark hallway, soundlessly close the door behind me and lock it.

She is sitting taking a footbath with a cigarette in her hand, while some idiotic soap opera plays out on the TV in front of her. I think that reality often surpasses fiction, and then I step out into the light. She does not even look surprised, but instead just gives me a dull, furtive look and asks what this is about. I tell her what this is about, while her gaze wanders between me and the TV with no noticeable reaction.

'I have no memory of that,' she says simply, taking a few deep puffs on her cigarette before she returns to her TV-watching.

I take a few steps forward and grab hold of her neck with one hand.

'Try to remember then,' I say threateningly, but she only stares at me in surprise.

'What the hell are you doing?' she says calmly. 'Are you out of your mind?'

'Maybe,' I answer.

'Let go of me!' she says angrily.

'Then remember,' I say, pressing my fingers hard against her neck. 'Remember what you did to my neck.'

I try to get her to remember. I tell her, but she just stares back stupidly. Then I throw her down on to the floor in a kneeling position – keeping a firm grip on her neck – and force her head into the basin of water. I hold her under the water's surface for a little while and she flails her arms and legs, without letting go of the cigarette between her index and middle finger. When I finally let her up again, she's livened up. She snorts and blinks to get the water out of her eyes and to see me clearly.

'What do you want from me?' she moans at last, when her breathing has recovered enough.

'I want you to remember,' I say, still grasping her neck. 'Remember, understand and ask for forgiveness.'

'But I don't remember! I can't help –'

'You have to remember,' I interrupt. 'You have to remember how you tortured me for days on end. You have to understand that you can't abuse a person the way you and your friends did, without leaving marks. Lasting impressions, incurable wounds. Don't you understand that? Don't you understand that it could be your child lying out there in the mud, with a

167

beaten-up face and their clothes in rags? How would that feel?'

'That ... that would feel horrible,' she whimpers, and tears well up in her eyes, run down and mix with the streams of water on her cheeks.

'So why did you do it?'

'I don't even know if I did!' she cries desperately. 'We were just kids, I can't believe . . .'

I am getting tired of her talk and her bad memory, so I press her down under the water again – for longer this time. I see the cigarette burning down to her fingers, and she finally lets it go when it burns her. When I decide to let her up again, she is completely done in and can no longer hold herself up, so I have to release my grip on her neck and lift her head by the hair. I throw her head back and forth and she coughs and puffs for several minutes, not able to get a word out. During that time I tell her about crushed dreams, about a childhood without sunlight, about a life in loneliness, about a naked, withered soul. When she regains her ability to speak, she hisses out, 'I'm sorry.' I don't believe her, but that doesn't matter; she's going to die anyway.

'Your suffering is too short,' I say. 'Mine has lasted for thirty-eight years. But my arms are getting tired. Bye-bye, Lise-Lott.'

I press her head down into the footbath for the last time, but she has already given up. She struggles involuntarily a little and then she is quiet. I leave her where she is, on her knees, bent over the basin, but I can't resist putting the burned-out cigarette back between her fingers before I get up.

On the TV they are arguing and someone rushes out of a room and slams the door. I leave calmly and carefully close the door on Lise-Lott.

Tuesday

As usual Petra Westman tackled the work assigned to her energetically, but for once she didn't take on any new initiatives of her own. Instead, she devoted the downtime between her allotted tasks to digging for information regarding a certain Peder Fryhk.

Peder Fryhk was fifty-three years old and originally from Hudiksvall. He qualified for college with high scores in 1972, then did his military service as a commando at KA1 on Rindö in 1972 and 1973. In 1973 he started his medical training at the university in Lund and got married. In 1974 a daughter was born, but for the years between 1975 and 1980 information was lacking. His wife and child were in Hudiksvall during this period, where they were both still registered today. In 1980 he showed up again, resumed his studies in the autumn and got a divorce. In 1984 he received his medical degree, after which he worked at various hospitals in the Stockholm area and he was now a senior anaesthetist at Karolinska.

A colleague in the economic crimes unit helped her to gather information on Fryhk's financial dealings. There were no irregularities here. He was single with a good income and living expenses to match. Nothing strange. Petra confirmed that he had no criminal record with a search in the register. Searches in ISP – the police department's internal register of descriptions – produced nothing. Nor was there any information to be found in ASP – another of the police department's internal registers, where you could search for individual names among comments entered in connection with crimes. He seemed to have a blemish-free past.

From a telephone call to Doctors Without Borders, Petra discovered that the organization had done work in Lebanon only during 1975. Peder Fryhk was twenty-two years old then and had finished only two years of pre-clinical studies. So he could not have worked as a doctor in Lebanon in 1975. He was not found on any of their lists. At the very least, she had caught him in a lie.

But how could she go further? Under no circumstances did she want Fryhk to find out about her investigations. For that reason she could not contact his mother, who was still alive, his neighbours, colleagues or employer. Nor did she dare contact his daughter. But the ex-wife seemed like a fairly safe bet. He had left her and his newborn daughter for a five-year stay abroad and then divorced her as soon as he came home. Presumably she did not speak to him very often, if at all.

After repeated attempts, she managed to reach the ex-wife at work late that evening. She was an operating-room nurse at Hudiksvall Hospital.

'I'm looking for Peder Fryhk,' Petra lied.

There was total silence on the line and she hoped this was a good sign.

'Hello?'

'I haven't had any contact with him for years. You'll have to look elsewhere. Who's asking?'

Petra had deliberately avoided introducing herself. After careful consideration, she had decided not to lie about her identity to this woman. Conversely, she had considered ending the conversation at this point – without introducing herself – if the answer had been different.

'My name is Westman and I'm a police officer,' said Petra. 'He appears in an investigation I'm working on.'

'Then you know you won't be able to find him through me,' said the woman, whose name was Mona Friberg.

She obviously had her head on straight.

'Actually you're the one I wanted to talk to,' Petra admitted, quickly trying to regain control of the conversation. 'When did you last speak to him?'

'In 1980,' the woman replied curtly.

'In connection with the divorce?'

'That's right.'

'So you've had no contact with him whatsoever since then?'

'As I said.'

'And your daughter?'

'Not her either, as far as I know.'

'May I ask why?'

Mona Friberg hesitated for a few seconds before answering.

'His involvement with his daughter has been non-existent. Neither she nor I have the slightest interest in having any contact.'

'Please forgive me if I seem a bit forward,' Petra said, 'but why did you marry him in the first place?'

She was aware that she had now given the woman a reason to end the conversation, but something told her she would not.

'The classic. I got pregnant.'

'And he took responsibility?'

After a moment's hesitation she replied, 'On the surface. In reality, we never saw each other for the most part. He moved to Lund and then he went abroad and was gone for several years.'

'And when he came home he asked for a divorce?'

'Yes. Without seeing me. I haven't seen him in person since 1975.'

Mona Friberg's voice revealed no bitterness. She gave brief, factual answers to the questions she was asked. Nonetheless, Petra seemed to detect some ambiguity in her attitude to it all. What she was saying was anything but flattering to Fryhk, yet she had her guard up. While the conversation was going on, Petra could not put her finger on it, but afterwards she decided that Mona Friberg was holding back part of the truth about Peder Fryhk.

'Has he paid child support?' asked Petra, even though she already knew the answer.

'No, and I never asked for any either. My finances are good.'

'That might also be interpreted as you having strong reasons not to want to have anything to do with Peder Fryhk,' Petra attempted.

'I prefer to be independent,' replied Mona Friberg without so much as a quiver in her voice to show that this might be untrue.

'Have you any idea where he was during that stay abroad between 1975 and 1980?' Petra enquired.

'No. And no one else does either, that I know of.'

'What is he like as a person?' Petra ventured to ask.

'Intelligent and goal-oriented. Selfish. Extroverted.'

In the midst of the positive judgements she had slipped in a negative one. She supplied facts and appeared to be completely objective. But what was it she wasn't saying? She said extroverted, not pleasant. And goal-oriented, was that necessarily positive? No, not when it was followed by selfish. Petra did not have time to complete the thought.

'Interested in war,' said Mona Friberg. 'Extremely interested in war. I must get back to work now.'

That ended the conversation.

Wednesday Evening

The mood in the investigation team was subdued. It was already Wednesday and there had been no new developments in the case. The fingerprints from the chair in Ingrid Olsson's kitchen had been run against the register of known criminals, with no match. They did not belong to anyone else who figured in the investigation either. Nothing new had come up in the extended questioning of Vannerberg's family and business partner.

The medical examiner Zetterström's report was complete, but contained no information that led anywhere. The death had occurred between four o'clock and eight o'clock on Monday evening, which is what they had assumed all along. The cause of death was also as expected: cerebral haemorrhage caused by blows with a blunt instrument to the head and face.

Questioning the neighbours in the area had produced the following information: Lennart Josefsson, living in a house across from Olsson's, saw two men pass by outside his window a short interval apart about the time of the murder. Because it had been dark he could not provide a description, but he could not rule out that Vannerberg had been one of them. A family on another street had had their garage broken into during the summer holiday. Several families in the area had been visited by a female Polish picture-seller during the month of November. Several times an older couple had noticed an unknown woman with a 'Swedish appearance' walking on Åkerbärsvägen. Some of the neighbours had noticed a male jogger in a light-blue tracksuit passing by on the street. He proved to be a resident of Olvonbacken, a cross-street to Åkerbärsvägen. A male cyclist in his thirties or forties, presumably drunk, had been seen wobbling around the streets on the Saturday evening before the murder. Finally, nine families in the area had been visited by a shifty-looking twenty-something with a Swedish appearance selling toilet paper emblazoned with the badge of the local tennis club. Three individuals in the immediate neighbourhood had witnessed Ingrid Olsson being picked up by ambulance after she broke her hip.

The team was working along several lines of enquiry, but agreed on the main hypothesis that Hans Vannerberg, intending to visit the new family at Åkerbärsvägen number 13, had left home on Monday evening and by mistake ended up at number 31, where he met his killer, who had followed him there for reasons so far unknown.

The prosecutor, the long-limbed Hadar Rosén, was starting to get impatient and proposed that they investigate whether there were any similar cases in Stockholm or elsewhere. Einar Eriksson had researched this and found no direct parallels anywhere, in terms of the murder method or crime scene. After all, most murders were the result of either family tragedies or drunkenness.

When Sjöberg went home that evening it was pouring with rain and, as usual, he had no umbrella. If he brought an umbrella with him to work, he left it there and didn't need it until he got home, but if he left the umbrella at home, it rained just as he was leaving work. He made a snap decision to go a few blocks in the opposite direction to a shop that sold handbags, hoping they would have umbrellas, which proved to be the case. This didn't help, however, for the shop had just closed and he had to trudge those three blocks back.

On the way home he passed a stationery shop, which he entered without really knowing why. He had a definite feeling that there was something he needed in there, but he came out a little later with a pencil case for each of the girls, wrapped in Christmas paper, and a sense of dissatisfaction at not being able to remember what it was he really should have bought.

Finally at home, he was showered with sympathy for his soaked appearance and as he lay down on the couch to keep the children company in front of the TV, it suddenly occurred to him what his errand in the stationery shop had really been. Christoffer and

Jonathan had teamed up and managed to throw fifty or so magazines on the floor, of which at least three were completely shredded.

When the four youngest children were in bed, and Simon was sitting in front of the computer playing games, Sjöberg sat down at the kitchen table to eat the warmed-up leftovers from the children's dinner. Åsa had eaten with them earlier in the evening but she kept him company anyway. She asked about the murder investigation and, between bites of hot dog, he recounted the developments of the last few days.

'One thing strikes me,' said Åsa. 'They seemed to have a good relationship, the Vannerbergs, didn't they?'

'Seems like it,' answered Sjöberg.

'More or less like you and me?'

'Yes, maybe.'

'Two reasonable people who talk to each other?'

'Apparently.'

'Say you have an appointment this evening and have to go out. Suppose you have to question a witness. Then you'd say to me, "I have to leave for a while and question a witness," wouldn't you?'

'Something like that.'

'You wouldn't say you were going to question a suspect. Later on, I wouldn't recall that you said "a suspect", although you actually said "a witness".'

'I think you're on to something.'

'Besides – and I'm not sure about this – I don't think

you'd come home first to be with the family, and then "have to" leave and meet someone you hadn't set up a meeting with. Vannerberg could have gone there first, straight from work.'

'Maybe they weren't home until after six, maybe he knew that.'

'Then check that out. If that was the case, he should have called first, because he really wasn't just passing by. Maybe they weren't at home.'

'But they were.'

'He couldn't know that, because he hadn't called and asked.'

'You're right. And that puts us –'

'That puts us in a situation where Vannerberg was lured to a deserted house by someone who planned to murder him there,' Åsa interrupted.

'Someone who knew that Ingrid Olsson wasn't at home,' Sjöberg filled in. 'Someone who either wanted to get at her too, or simply chose her house because it was empty.'

'So, someone with a connection to both Ingrid Olsson and Hans Vannerberg. Find that connection and the mystery is solved,' Åsa declared contentedly, putting her hands behind her neck.

'You're damn right about that,' said Sjöberg with a preoccupied expression. 'I'll go call that buyer.'

He got up from the table, leaving the dirty dish behind for his proudly humming wife.

He started by calling Petra Westman, who had been

in contact with the buyer previously. She was still at work and, with some surprise, gave him the telephone number for the family at Åkerbärsvägen 13.

'I'll tell you tomorrow if I get anywhere,' Sjöberg said mysteriously, thanking Westman for her help and ending the call.

Then he called the buyers, and the husband answered. He was the one who'd had contact with the estate agent regarding the complaints about the seller.

'Excuse me for calling so late. This is Conny Sjöberg, chief inspector with the Violent Crimes Unit, Hammarby Police Department. I'm leading the investigation regarding the murder of Hans Vannerberg.'

'No problem. How can I help you?' the man asked readily.

'I wonder if you ever spoke to Hans Vannerberg in person.'

'No, I didn't. I only talked to Molin.'

'Did you ever talk to Molin about suitable times for Vannerberg to come over and look at those things you were unhappy about?' asked Sjöberg.

'I said that any time was fine. My wife is home with the children.'

'Wouldn't Vannerberg have called first? Perhaps your wife isn't home all day?'

'Sure, of course that would have been reasonable. If he hadn't just been passing by . . .'

'Thanks very much,' said Sjöberg, 'and I beg your pardon once again.'

Åsa smiled triumphantly at him. He hugged her and gave her a kiss on the forehead.

'Where would I be without you, darling?' he laughed. 'Now it's time for Simon to go to bed, I think.'

Åsa was reading a book and Sjöberg watched the TV news distractedly, while his brain worked over what might be a new direction for the investigation. He decided to contact Ingrid Olsson tomorrow and go through the house himself, in pursuit of something – but he didn't quite know what. Hopefully he would recognize it if he saw it, but he felt by no means sure of that.

The reporter went on and on about Hamas, suicide bombings in Iraq and the poisoning of the Russian ex-spy Litvinenko, but Sjöberg was having a hard time concentrating on the news. One story, though, caught his interest. Some uniformed policemen were shown conversing with one another on the screen while the TV anchor summarized the event:

'In Katrineholm a forty-four-year-old mother of two was found yesterday, murdered in her apartment. The woman was discovered by her seventeen-year-old son at lunchtime and is believed to have been drowned in a washtub some time in the morning. The police do not yet have a suspect.'

This has truly not been a good week for forty-four-year-olds, thought Sjöberg. Three murders in nine days, this just doesn't make sense. A colleague from the Katrineholm Police Department was interviewed about the murder by a female reporter, while the camera swept across a muddy play area and a group of people crowding at the barricade around a basement stairway.

'The forensic investigation is not finished, but all indications are that the woman's life was taken by one or more unknown assailants,' said the police commissioner.

'We have information that she was drowned,' coaxed the reporter.

'Is that so?' asked the police officer. Suddenly something clicked in Sjöberg's head, though he couldn't immediately pinpoint what it was he had reacted to.

'Yes, this much I guess I can say,' the police officer admitted after a moment's hesitation, 'drowning is a probable scenario we are working on. I can't say more than that right now, but we expect the forensic investigation to be finished over the weekend and then we will know more.'

'Weekend,' Sjöberg muttered to himself. 'Funny pronunciation, very different from ours. "Is that so,"' he mused, in an affected, whining tone of voice. 'Meaning "I see."'

There was something familiar about those dialect expressions and the whining tone, but he could not for the life of him think where he had heard them before. At last he reluctantly pushed the thought away and turned his attention back to the report on the consequences of the major snowstorm at the beginning of November.

* * *

Thomas shuddered when he opened the jar of lingonberry jam and saw that the surface was covered with greyish, furry mould. He quickly screwed the lid back on and threw the jar in the bin bag hanging on the knob of the cupboard under the kitchen sink. He sat down at the table and attacked the black pudding, not without a certain disappointment.

The kitchen window still gaped vacantly, except for the old transistor radio that had been there since the days of Uncle Gunnar. But the kitchen curtains were ordered. Last Monday after work he had ventured into the fabric shop down at the corner. There was a sign in the window offering to sew curtains for free, if you bought the material there. The fabric he decided on was warm yellow with a thin, blue check that would probably go well in a kitchen. Actually, it was the woman in the shop who finally got impatient and firmly recommended that he choose it. Thomas gratefully accepted the suggestion and overlooked her irritated facial expression and angrily exaggerated motions. He left it up to her to decide on the type of curtain; they had not even discussed the different options. The workmanship on the curtains would

183

have to be a surprise and he had not dared ask what it would all cost either. He could pick them up next week.

His gaze landed on the old radio and in his mind he saw Uncle Gunnar, his grandmother's brother, sitting at the same kitchen table where he was sitting now. On weekdays he listened to 'Let's Celebrate' with his morning coffee, and on Saturdays they would try to solve the melody crossword together. Thomas did not make much of a contribution, but they were together and had a nice time and Uncle Gunnar was quite good at it.

Uncle Gunnar had not been a man for grand gestures. He was somewhat taciturn, and they did not exchange many words during the course of a day, but it was a companionable silence. He accepted Thomas as he was and neither criticized nor was irritated by him. Thomas, for his part, overlooked the old man's lack of personal hygiene and felt relieved at finally having left the narrow-mindedness of the small town for the anonymity of the big city.

He thought about his last days in Katrineholm and working with the old couple in the haberdasher's. They had assumed he was basically a delinquent – reasonably, perhaps, since he had dropped out of school – and treated him with great suspicion the whole time. They never dared leave him alone in the shop, and one of them always kept the cash register in sight when he was there. This meant that, instead of trying to learn

184

something from his traineeship, he spent the time trying to get free from under their sullen, watchful gazes.

The proximity to the secondary school did not make matters better. His former classmates, who often passed by during free periods and lunch breaks, could not keep from looking into the shop and making cracks about him when the opportunity arose. The primary theme of their harassment was his presumed homo-sexuality, and as he thought about it, he suddenly recalled an episode from that time that he had not thought about since it happened, some thirty years before.

This incident had not affected him personally, but rather a brother in misfortune by the name of Sören, who was in a parallel class. He recognized the pattern. Sören, along with the rest of the football team, had been at a training camp in Finland. On the trip home, on the Finland ferry, they had apparently been drinking heavily and many of the boys got very drunk. One boy – a bully who for some reason went by the name Lasse Golare – got so drunk he let himself be lured into the toilet by the boy at the bottom of the peck-ing order, Sören. There, Sören subjected the poor, intoxicated Lasse Golare to a blow job, after which the deeply offended Lasse Golare marched out of the gent's and told all his teammates about the terrible thing he had experienced. The teammates reacted with great consternation, as did the coach who was along on the trip – to the extent that Sören was summarily kicked off the team 'for the boys' sake'. Lasse Golare – who, of course, was not the least bit homosexual – was praised as a hero and emerged with his honour intact.

Thomas smiled at this absurd story as he swallowed the last slab of black pudding and rinsed it down with half a glass of milk. He reached for the tabloid that lay unread on the kitchen table, and leafed through it to the spread with news from around Sweden.

Lise-Lott's gaze met his, and for a moment he thought that for the first time she was smiling at him in a friendly way. Then reality caught up with him and his heart began beating faster. He suddenly felt extremely thirsty, but could not force himself to stand up to get something to drink. He read through the article carefully, twice, and then jerked the pile of the past week's newspapers still lying on the table towards him. Further down in the pile he found the Sunday paper and leafed through it to the short item about the murder of the prostitute in Skärholmen. After reading this too a few times, he remained sitting, back straight, hands clasped around his knees, and stared vacantly ahead.

'What have I done?' he whispered to himself. 'What do I do now?'

Thursday Morning

On Thursday there was another meeting of the investigation team scheduled. Hadar Rosén had said that he did not plan to attend. Everyone else was present, except Westman. Sjöberg was somewhat indulgent about her poor time-keeping as she had so many otherwise positive qualities going for her. Despite her youth, she had no problem directing older colleagues. The male dominance at the workplace did not seem to affect her, and she was both enterprising and full of initiative. Besides, he knew that she usually stayed at work until late in the evening and never left behind a half-finished job. And this time Sjöberg knew, of course, that she had worked late the night before.

Five coffee cups stood ready around the conference table, as if waiting for the meeting's starting signal so they could be drained. Einar Eriksson kept looking at his watch, glaring at the door from time to time. Sandén balanced on his chair, while he distractedly drummed the table with his fingers and let his eyes rest on a framed poster depicting a girl on a swing. When the door flew open and Westman rushed in, cheeks red and out of breath with a teacup in her hand, he smiled sarcastically at her, but she grinned back, unconcerned, pulled out a chair and sat down. Eriksson sighed audibly.

'All right then,' said Sjöberg. 'Does anyone have anything new to report?'

He was met by nothing but head-shaking, except from Hamad, who began to speak.

'I have identified the "shifty toilet-paper salesman" who was not exactly shifty, unfortunately. I called around to some tennis clubs in the area and finally got a nibble. He is eighteen years old, his name is Joakim Levander and he plays for Enskede Tennis Club. It's true that he was going around those neighbourhoods for a while, trying to sell toilet paper with the club's emblem on. Without much success – it clearly worked better to sell by phone. The shifty thing about him was probably a goatee and an earring. And most probably a disillusioned demeanour.'

'When was this?' asked Sandén.

'It was the week before the murder. I took the boy over to Ingrid Olsson's house, but as far as he could recall no one answered when he rang and he hadn't noticed anything in particular either.'

'Had he run into any of the other characters during his wanderings through those streets?' wondered Sjöberg.

'He doesn't live in the area,' answered Hamad. 'I'm sure he ran into lots of people, but they were all unknown to him.'

'Sounds like we can remove him from the investigation

then,' said Sjöberg. 'Always something. I've been think-ing a little about Vannerberg's activities that evening, and I have concluded the following: Pia Vannerberg – this we can agree on – seemed both interested in and informed about what her husband was doing, both on and off the job. She says she is certain that Vannerberg was going to meet a seller. In our main hypothesis, we have assumed that she misunderstood or heard wrong. I don't think that feels quite right. This, in combination with the fact that Vannerberg actually left home in the dark that evening to meet someone we have assumed to be the buyer of number 13. Well, I talked to the buyer last night,' he continued, now turning to Westman. 'True, he did say to Jorma Molin that it was fine to drop by any time, but they had not agreed on any particular time. And he never said that Monday evening would be an especially good time either. According to him, there was no guarantee that his wife – or he for that matter – would be home, whether it was daytime or evening. He thought that the reasonable thing would have been for Vannerberg to call before he came over, if he didn't really happen to be passing by. I think that, as Pia Van-nerberg suggests, he really had scheduled a meeting with someone at Åkerbärsvägen 31 at six o'clock on Monday evening. This someone I believe is the murderer.'

'So you think this business at Åkerbärsvägen 13 is only a remarkable coincidence?' said Einar Eriksson sullenly. 'I find that hard to believe. Strange coinci-dences do not exist in this business.'

189

'In any event, that is what I believe happened,' Sjöberg persisted.

Hamad and Sandén nodded in agreement.

'And Lennart Josefsson's testimony?' asked Westman.

'Josefsson's testimony is interesting in any event,' Sjöberg replied. 'We have the footprints in the garden. Bella?'

'Yes, the strange man's footprints indicate that he climbed over the gate and jumped down on to the lawn by the side of the gravel path,' answered Hansson. 'Whether this occurred before or after Vannerberg entered the garden is impossible to say. One might suspect that the reason for climbing over the gate instead of going through it would be that the person did not want to make a sound. The gate makes noise, as does the gravel path. So that might indicate that the murderer followed Vannerberg there.'

'Which was observed by Josefsson,' added Westman.

'Why should the murderer – if he had arranged a meeting with Vannerberg at that address – also follow him there?' asked Sandén.

'That does puzzle me a bit,' Sjöberg admitted. 'Maybe he wanted to make sure that Vannerberg really went there. He didn't want to leave traces behind in the house for no reason.'

'He didn't leave any traces behind in the house anyway, damn it,' Einar Eriksson grumbled.

Sandén ignored Eriksson's lament and continued speculating.

'Perhaps Josefsson's testimony is not relevant. Perhaps the murderer climbed over the fence a good while before Vannerberg showed up.'

'Why climb when he could just go through the gate?' Westman interjected. 'Wouldn't he attract more attention if he climbed than if he went through the gate like a normal person, even if the gate made some noise?'

'That's exactly why I still think the murderer followed him there,' Sjöberg stated.

'So where do we stand?' asked Hamad.

'We're looking for a person who has a connection not only to Hans Vannerberg but also to Ingrid Olsson,' Sjöberg summarized. 'Perhaps to the extent that he actually wanted to create problems for Ingrid Olsson too, but maybe that's a little far-fetched. In any case, a person who knew that Ingrid Olsson's house stood empty.'

'The postman,' said Sandén. 'The bin men, hospital staff.'

'The neighbours,' Hamad added. 'A female Polish picture-seller, a drunk cyclist, the paramedics.'

'A woman with a Swedish appearance out for a walk,' said Eriksson sullenly. 'Any old pedestrian.'

'So, we're in agreement,' said Sjöberg, resuming command by means of a surprise attack. 'Our new main hypothesis is that the murderer arranged a meeting with Vannerberg at Åkerbärsvägen 31 on Monday evening. The murderer shadowed him there – why or from where we don't know, but probably from

Vannerberg's residence. Judging from the footprints, Vannerberg then walked around to the back of the house, and during that time the murderer presumably entered the house, where he waited for Vannerberg and finally killed him.'

'So we're going with the connection?' Sandén suggested. 'The Vannerberg–Olsson connection.'

'Yes, I think so,' Sjöberg answered. 'We will devote the next few days to trying to find a person who in some way has a connection to both Hans Vannerberg and Ingrid Olsson.'

'You might say that the buyer at number 13 has,' said Westman. 'He's a neighbour of Ingrid Olsson and bought his house through Vannerberg's estate agency.'

'Sure, why not?' Sjöberg replied. 'Even if he never met or spoke with Vannerberg, there is actually a weak connection there. I suggest that you, Petra, do the rounds of the neighbours. The neighbours who live close enough to have noticed that Olsson was away. Sound them out properly. Show them pictures of Vannerberg – alive and dead – and pay attention to how they react. And this applies to the rest of you too. Einar, you check on the postman, newspaper delivery person and bin men. And then run a background check on Ingrid Olsson. Sandén, you talk to the hospital staff and paramedics. By the way, do you know where Ingrid Olsson is staying right now?'

'She's staying with Margit Olofsson for the time being.'

'Poor woman,' Sjöberg sighed. 'She already has her hands full, being a nurse and all. When can Ingrid Olsson move back home again?' he asked, turning to Hamad.

'We were thinking about keeping the house until Sunday, to be on the safe side. In principle we're finished, but you never know.'

'That's good. I was thinking about going there today and going over it one more time. This time with a focus on any connection between Ingrid Olsson and Vannerberg. Jamal, you've done that once before, so you come with me. Anything else?'

'Yes, I was just thinking,' said Westman hesitantly, as she fingered the teacup in front of her. 'If Vannerberg scheduled a meeting with the murderer at Åkerbärsvägen 31, as it said in his diary, isn't it likely that the so-called seller called him at work to sort that out? Shouldn't we go through all the incoming calls, let's say, during the weeks when Ingrid Olsson was in the hospital? And to cover our bases, maybe even check his home phone and mobile?'

'Of course,' said Sjöberg. 'Do you want to do that, Petra, or do you feel like you have enough already?'

'I don't mind doing it,' said Westman without hesitation.

'Excellent,' said Sjöberg, downing the last drops of his coffee. 'Now we're cooking with gas.'

'Hey,' said Sandén. 'What's going on with the Christmas dinner on Saturday?'

'Of course,' said Sjöberg, turning to Hamad, 'I'd completely forgotten about that. Have you made a reservation?'

'Yes, by general request it will be an alternative Christmas dinner, seven p.m., at the Beirut Café on Engelbrektsgatan.'

'Beirut Café,' said Sandén. 'What do they serve there? Iced bombe and pomegranates? Sounds great.'

Westman glanced furtively in Hamad's direction. As usual, everyone laughed at Sandén, including Hamad.

'It is great,' said Westman. 'I love Lebanese food.'

'Yes, those Arabs,' Sandén sighed. 'They'll do anything to avoid eating ham, including eating testicles instead.'

* * *

The assault Petra Westman was subjected to over the weekend had been reduced to a story. True, she had only told it to a single person, but in her mind she had gone through the whole sequence of events an incalculable number of times. What she felt about the whole thing was shame. Shame at waking up in a bed in a strange house, not knowing who she had spent the night with. Oddly enough, she did not feel violated. She assumed that was because she had no recollection of what happened, but she wanted to get rid of the shame. At any price.

As long as she kept busy it was not a problem, but when she was trying to fall asleep she tossed and turned for hours while the embarrassing memories went through her mind, one after another. Naked and groggy between the Egyptian-cotton sheets, or in front of the bathroom mirror in the luxury home in Mälarhöjden. Or else stumbling in her new boots on the way out of Clarion's bar.

Besides, she could not shake off the doubt. Had she really been raped? Not in the traditional sense. If she had been attacked and raped, there would have been no doubt. Perhaps that would have left deeper marks. Perhaps she would have had injuries and diseases and God knows what. But there would have been no doubt. She would have avoided the doubt. And the awful shame.

For that reason she would follow through on this project. She was firmly resolved to put the polished senior physician under lock and key. With his charming smile and his damn laughter lines. And something told her that Mona Friberg would have nothing against that either.

With the information about Peder Fryhk's interest in war in the back of her mind, on Wednesday Petra Westman had made contact with the military. After numerous phone calls, she finally got hold of the now sixty-one-year-old major who had been Peder Fryhk's commander during his final months at KA1. He remembered Fryhk as a lone wolf, but gave her a tip about a former French foreign legionnaire of Hungarian origin who had been hired by the troop to train the coast commandos in hand-to-hand combat. Fryhk, according to the major, had shown a greater interest in this Andras Takacs than his fellow draftees, and he had the impression that they hit it off during the training.

Petra had an immediate feeling that she was on the trail of something interesting and thought it might be worth trying to contact Takacs. He was not hard to find. A Google search directed her to a karate club on Norrmalm where he was still training. She was told, however, that he was away and could not be reached until Thursday.

When Petra finally made contact with the Swedish karate champion with the Hungarian name, she was surprised to hear that he spoke with a French accent. She wondered how long he had actually been a legionnaire, but did not ask.

'I'm looking for information about a person by the name of Peder Fryhk, who did his military service with KA1 on Rindö. You reportedly met him during the spring of 1973, when you were training coast commandos in hand-to-hand combat.'

'Yes, I remember him very well,' said Andras Takacs. 'Capable guy.'

'Are you still in touch with him?' Petra asked.

'No, I haven't seen him since.'

'How would you describe him?'

'He was strong, and had a good head on his shoulders. He was extremely interested in the training. Asked a lot of questions.'

His French accent was almost a parody.

'About anything in particular?'

'About everything we covered. He always wanted to go a step further than the others, and as a teacher you feel flattered when a student shows such a great interest in what you're teaching.'

'But?'

'There was no "but" there. He was excellent soldier material.'

'Do you know if he had plans for a military career?' asked Petra.

'Not in Sweden anyway. I recall that he was very critical of Sweden's neutrality policy. On the other hand, he was extremely curious about the French Foreign Legion.'

Petra straightened up.

'I'm an old legionnaire myself,' Takacs explained. 'He wanted to know all about what it was like, what was required, what they did, and how you got accepted. I gave him all the information I had. I don't recommend becoming a foreign legionnaire to just anyone, because it's really no walk in the park, and I told him that. But I gave him a number of useful tips.'

'Did you get the impression that he was serious?' Petra asked.

'I don't consider that unlikely,' Takacs answered. 'He would have passed the admission test easily with the qualities he had.'

'Mentally too?'

'Are you joking? That kid was strong as an ox, both physically and mentally.'

Petra smiled to herself and noted that she and the

old foreign legionnaire presumably did not share the same concept of mental health.

Petra summarized the information she had. Peder Fryhk was an intelligent, educated man. Smart, polished, well-to-do. But he was also a liar. To show himself in a better light, he had lied about working for Doctors Without Borders. In reality he was a warmonger who had left behind a wife and child in order to murder people with whom he had no quarrel in foreign lands, with a uniform as a cover. Perhaps in Lebanon. Perhaps somewhere else. Perhaps he was just as well informed about all wars as the one playing out in Lebanon. Perhaps it had been extremely easy to rape women in that uniform. Perhaps, thought Petra, it was also the case that his daughter was the result of a rape. A rape that he camouflaged by going to the minister with his victim, shrewd as he was. Best for everyone involved. That could be the reason that contact between him and his wife, between him and the child, was for ever broken. A deeply hidden secret that was in everyone's interest to conceal. That must have been where it started, thought Petra. But a leopard never changes its spots. He was the person he had always been, only now he was considerably more cunning and had refined his methods.

Thursday Evening

It was almost three o'clock on Thursday afternoon when Sjöberg and Hamad got out of the car outside Åkerbärsvägen 31. The snow here, unlike in the city, had started to settle like a white blanket over the residential neighbourhood, and muffled all the usual sounds from the metro and a few busy roads in the vicinity. The quiet twilight snowfall evoked a feeling of Christmas spirit on the idyllic street, with its mature gardens and old wooden houses. It was hard to say what his colleague's sense of winter and Christmas was, but Sjöberg knew that he had moved to Sweden as a small child with his family, fleeing from Lebanon's civil war. Jamal Hamad was as Swedish as you could be in Sjöberg's eyes, except that he still refused to eat pork. Possibly, despite his Swedish wife, he was more Lebanese at home than he let on to his co-workers.

The two men looked like they were exhaling clouds of smoke as they inched their way with tiny, tiny steps up the slippery path to Ingrid Olsson's house.

'How the hell did they think the old lady would manage this hill in her condition?' Sjöberg exclaimed, without really being clear who 'they' were.

'Spikes,' Hamad answered pragmatically.

'Hmm,' Sjöberg murmured, taking the house key from his jacket pocket.

They climbed up on to the porch and stamped as much of the wet, packed snow from their shoes as they could, while Sjöberg unlocked the door.

It was dark in the house and Sjöberg fumbled for the switch on the wall inside. The house, for some reason, felt smaller now than it had the last time, when it had been literally swarming with people. It smelled old but not unpleasant, more cosy. But it didn't feel particularly cosy. The furniture gave an even shabbier impression today than it had before. Sjöberg got a sense that the furnishings had been chosen and placed without care. Ingrid Olsson appeared to be a very lonely person and it struck him just how many lonely people there seemed to be in this country.

His own mother, for example. His father had died from the complications of a mysterious illness when Sjöberg was only three years old. While he was growing up, they lived in a couple of different apartments in Bollmora, where his mother worked in the cafeteria at his school. As far as he could recall, she never socialized much and had no close friends. Her personality didn't invite that. She was basically a negative person, reserved and not easily amused.

Everything was in order and the house seemed clean. Hansson had done a good job as usual, Sjöberg observed. Not just as a police officer but also in purely human terms.

'What is it we're hoping to find?' asked Hamad as they stood in the living room, aimlessly looking around.

'Papers, books, photographs, souvenirs – how do I know? Anything that might suggest a connection between Olsson and Vannerberg. A connection that perhaps they didn't even know about themselves. Are there any storage spaces?'

'There's a basement and a garage.'

'No attic?'

'No attic.'

'We'll take the top floor then, to start with,' said Sjöberg. 'I haven't been up there.'

They went up the narrow stairway that led from the end of the hall and Sjöberg now understood why there was no attic. The upper floor was the attic, renovated into a living area; two rather large rooms in terms of floor space, but with steeply sloping ceilings, making large sections unusable for anything other than storage. One was Ingrid Olsson's bedroom and the other served as a kind of office. There was a desk and a wobbly little bookcase, plus a small table, on which there was a sewing machine.

They made a joint attack on the bedroom. While Sjöberg went through the drawers in the bedside table, Hamad turned on a transistor radio sitting on a stripped wooden dresser by a small window facing on to the garden in front of the house. Sjöberg was startled by the sudden sound, but then smiled in appreciation. The sixties music that was playing felt happy and alive, while

Ingrid Olsson's furnishings from the same period left an impression of sadness and hopelessness. The house also suffered from an almost total lack of books. Nor did Ingrid Olsson have any houseplants, which Sjöberg imagined must be unusual among women of her generation.

The bedroom concealed no secrets, nor did they find anything in the office that might be of interest to the investigation. The drawers in the desk mostly held sewing patterns, but also standard office supplies such as a stapler, hole punch, scissors, pens, paper, tape and glue. The bookshelves were full of old magazines from forty years ago, meticulously organized chronologically in various types of magazine holders. The two policemen observed that this was probably a gold mine for collectors and that Ingrid Olsson could surely make a fortune if she decided to sell them – the most interesting thing the house had revealed so far. On the other hand, they found no connection between Ingrid Olsson and Hans Vannerberg.

For a long time they worked in silence, each occupied by his own thoughts. Occasionally one might suddenly start a conversation or pick up the thread of an earlier one, which for one reason or another had languished.

'Maybe Ingrid Olsson is the murderer after all,' Hamad threw out, tired of the monotonous searching.

'She has an airtight alibi, as you know,' said Sjöberg.

'Yes, sure, but she could have hired someone.'

'Perhaps through an ad in the local paper: "Seventy-year-old woman seeks hit man for possible partnership."'

'Did you ask her whether she has a boyfriend?' Hamad wondered.

'No, you're right about that, damn it! Maybe the old lady has a man somewhere. She needn't be alone just because she's a widow.'

'We would have heard about him. Then she probably wouldn't have to stay with Margit Olofsson,' said Hamad.

'Presumably not. I think we'll have to abandon that theory.'

The top floor took a couple of hours for the two men to look through, the garage and basement another two, but they found nothing of any interest until they came to the main floor. Hamad was perched on a kitchen chair, rooting in one of the cupboards above the refrigerator, while Sjöberg sat at the kitchen table examining the contents of a drawer in which Ingrid Olsson apparently stored various objects with no particular home. Besides batteries, flashlights, rubber bands, a roll of cotton twine, drawing pins, a bicycle lamp, a few keys and a number of loose stamps of various denominations, the drawer also contained a bundle of papers. He leafed slowly through the pile, carefully studying all the receipts, discount coupons, bills, instruction manuals, account statements and warranties that passed before his eyes. A receipt from a grocery store in Sandsborg gave him the idea that perhaps Vannerberg and Olsson did their shopping at the same place, and he made a mental note of that for further investigation.

'Jamal, do you remember where Pia Vannerberg works?' Sjöberg suddenly asked.

He was holding a receipt from a visit to the dentist Ingrid Olsson had made a few months earlier at Dalen's Dental Health Service. Jamal Hamad was widely known at the police station for his extraordinary memory. If he had heard or read something, you could be almost certain that he would remember it, months, maybe even years later. In this particular case, Sjöberg was fairly convinced that his own memory did not betray him, but to be on the safe side he wanted to double-check.

'She works as a dental hygienist at the National Dental Health Service,' Hamad replied.

'Which office?' Sjöberg asked.

'At Sandsborg, over there,' said Hamad, with a gesture in a direction that Sjöberg was not capable of geographically assimilating. 'I think it's called Dalen.'

'Ingrid Olsson has a receipt from there,' said Sjöberg. 'Maybe this is the connection we're looking for.'

'Look,' said Hamad, glancing at his watch, 'we'll have to check that out tomorrow. It's already twenty past eight.'

'Oh boy,' said Sjöberg. 'Time really flies when you're having fun. And we haven't even got to the living room yet.'

'And the big job is waiting there,' said Hamad, a hint

of resignation in his voice. 'That's where she keeps her photos.'

Sjöberg suddenly realized that he had forgotten to phone Åsa. As he called her, Hamad concluded his work above the refrigerator and climbed down from the kitchen chair. Then the two men silently continued their hunt for the breakthrough lead.

It was already nine-thirty when they took on the last room in the house, the living room.

'I'm very curious about those photographs,' said Sjöberg, 'but I don't think I can keep going without anything to eat. I'll go and get us some food. What would you like?'

'Whatever. No pork.'

'Okay, we'll have to see what I can find. I'll be back as soon as I can.'

Sjöberg left the room and shortly after Hamad heard the outside door slam shut.

Ingrid Olsson had no particular order to her photos. Some were neatly placed in albums, but most were in the envelopes they came in after processing. Some were in large manila envelopes and others were piled in heaps right on the shelves in the cabinet. He chose an envelope at random and started leafing through the pictures. There was an eclectic mix of old black-and-white and colour photos. A few had notes on the back. One old black-and-white photograph, dated June 1938, depicted a man and a woman standing behind two small girls who each sat dangling their legs on a chair. All of them were oddly bundled up for the time of year. He guessed that this was Ingrid Olsson and her sister posing for the photographer along with their parents. Now Ingrid Olsson was the only one left of the people in the picture, and the man she later shared her life with was dead too.

The man who was presumably her husband appeared in a number of fading colour photos, which he assumed were taken during the seventies, on a trip to what might be a Spanish seaside resort. The two of them looked happy and tanned, and the pictures were nice, if not particularly good in the technical sense. There were also about a dozen pictures of a little wire-haired dachshund in various poses: by the food bowl, on the brown couch Hamad was sitting on, on a bed, on a lawn, in the arms of his master and mistress. Ingrid Olsson did not look much like her pictures from the seventies, but because he knew it was her, he could see the similarities that were there. She was thinner now, he thought. Her hair had been long and blonde before; now it was grey and cut short. She already had glasses at that time, but then they were large with heavy, brown plastic frames, as was the fashion then.

He stopped at a black-and-white photograph of a group of children, presumably a school class, lined up in two rows in front of a wall, where several old seasonal posters were hanging that he recognized from the windows of antique shops. The teacher stood behind them in the middle, looking serious, as did the majority of the children. He turned the picture over and read the handwritten text: 'Forest Hill '65/'66.' Then he bundled up the photographs, put them back in the envelope and turned to a beautiful album bound in light-brown leather.

Two albums and a dozen envelopes later, Sjöberg finally showed up with food.

'I couldn't find anything close by, so I thought it was just as well to go to McDonald's by Globen. McChicken – is that all right with you?'

'Super.'

Sjöberg unpacked the bag of food on the coffee table and divided the french fries and drinks between them. He was having a Big Mac himself, well aware that this type of food was detrimental at his age. True, he was not too overweight, and he also worked out several times a week. Two hours of exercise was part of his job, and he used them for strength training in the police station's own gym. He and Sandén also had a regular tennis slot in the Hellas tent at Eriksdal every Friday morning at seven o'clock, which they tried to make the best use of. He was already forty-eight, and it was crucial to keep your body in shape to prevent a heart attack.

'Did you find anything?' he asked Hamad, taking a bite of his hamburger.

'No, nothing special. Holiday pictures from the seventies and eighties, lots of pictures of some pooch – a dachshund. Maybe they couldn't have children. Old black-and-white pictures from ancient times. Nothing with a connection to Vannerberg. Provided they weren't on the same holiday in Spain in 1975.'

'We'll keep going until we've looked through everything anyway. If nothing else, to create a picture of Ingrid Olsson as a person. Have you seen her smiling in any of the photos?'

'Yes, actually. She was probably happier before, when she wasn't so lonely.'

'That's not so strange when you think about it. Even if the chance of making new friends increases with the number of smiles you spread around you.'

'By the way, I don't think there was a camera in the house during the fifties and sixties,' said Hamad.

'No?'

'No, there are almost no photos from that time, which is too bad. Just studio pictures of the bride and groom, as far as I could see, and those are from 1957.'

'So they got married in 1957,' Sjöberg said meditatively. 'Well, then they had thirty-three years together anyway, if the old man died sixteen years ago.'

'So, you think fifty-five is old?' Hamad said mischievously, watching Sjöberg stuff a handful of french fries into his mouth.

Sjöberg glanced at him, but chose not to reply.

'Are there any more recent pictures?' Sjöberg asked.

'Not many since the old man died. But she and her sister seem to have done a few things together. I found pictures from Prague and London and a few more everyday photos. She doesn't seem to have had any friends.'

They finished their meal. Sjöberg picked up the rubbish and wiped off the table with a damp paper towel. Then they continued ploughing through the piles of photographs. Sjöberg browsed through a stack of photos from a little cottage where Ingrid Olsson and her sister apparently spent a summer in the early nineties. He was struck by the absence of children in all of Ingrid Olsson's pictures. There were simply no children in her surroundings. Neither she nor her sister had kids, and clearly no one else did either, in the limited circle of acquaintances who appeared in her photos over the years. Of course it's like that, thought Sjöberg, if you or those closest to you don't have kids, then you just don't meet any kids. He had never thought about it before, but Swedish society was extremely age-segregated. Children went to school and nursery; adults worked and went to restaurants. Two separate worlds, and, as an adult, if you neither work with children nor have any of your own, you simply have no contact with them. How sad it must be never to hug a child, never experience the unmistakable aroma of a filthy child fresh from nursery, never take a pinch of smooth, soft baby fat.

His thoughts were interrupted by Hamad.

'Conny, look at this,' he said, placing an approximately thirty-year-old photo on the table in front of him.

The picture depicted a number of mostly toothless

children aged five or six who were lined up in front of the photographer. Farthest back to the left stood a woman in her forties, with long blonde hair and large glasses with brown plastic frames.

'What the hell –?'

Sjöberg felt a stab in his belly from tension. He turned the picture over and read the sprawling pencil notation on the back: 'Forest Hill 1974/'75', then he turned the photo face up and set it down on the table again.

'That's Ingrid Olsson!' he said excitedly, pointing at the only adult in the picture.

'Of course it is,' said Hamad eagerly. 'And what's more – I've seen a similar photo from the mid sixties. I have no idea where that picture is now, and I didn't realize then that Ingrid Olsson was in the picture. She didn't look the same.'

'Look for it then,' said Sjöberg. 'I'll go through the piles we haven't checked and see if I can find more pictures like this.'

'Maybe she was a schoolteacher in her past life?' Hamad asked himself, but Sjöberg had already figured it out.

'These children are younger than that. They're no more than five or six. She must have worked as a preschool teacher or nursery assistant. At that time, most Swedish women were housewives and took care of their own children, but some kids went to preschool for a few hours a day.'

'Maybe Ingrid Olsson was Hans Vannerberg's pre-school teacher. There we have our connection,' Hamad said.

'A very old connection, but it's the link we're looking for, I'm sure of it,' said Sjöberg.

Hamad tore open envelope after envelope of the pictures he had already looked through, while Sjöberg quickly browsed through the remaining piles. At ten minutes past midnight order was restored, in the room as well as in the cupboard with photographs under Ingrid Olsson's bookshelf. They left the house and went out into the now sparklingly cold winter night. In an envelope in his jacket pocket Sjöberg had three photographs, taken at Forest Hill Preschool and depicting groups of children from the years 1967/'68, 1968/'69 and 1969/'70. Maybe somewhere, on one of those pictures, was the little boy who now, as a grown man, was at the morgue at Huddinge Hospital waiting for his funeral. Brutally murdered with a chair in Miss Ingrid's kitchen.

Friday Morning

Even though he had not got to bed until shortly before one o'clock, he showed up at Eriksdal, changed and ready, at seven o'clock sharp on Friday morning. Sandén was already there, volleying against a backstop as Sjöberg came into the tennis hall.

'Good afternoon, Chief Inspector,' Sandén could not resist saying, even though he had probably not been there more than five minutes himself.

'Listen, I was actually working until midnight, while you sat at home munching pizza in front of the TV.'

Sandén, who was roughly the same age as Sjöberg, had considerably more difficulty maintaining his weight. This didn't concern him much. He was a bon vivant who ate what he liked and never worried about anything. He was always ready with a joke and was probably considered a bit loud by some, but you were seldom bored around Jens Sandén. They had met at the police academy and, though they weren't much alike, they had always stuck together and enjoyed each other's company. There had never been any rivalry between them either, which was a prerequisite for such a long and close friendship.

'How'd it go?' asked Sandén, hitting the first ball over the net.

Sjöberg returned it with a soft forehand stroke that placed the ball right in front of Sandén's feet.

'We'll discuss that later,' answered Sjöberg. 'After the match.'

They volleyed for a little while to warm up and served a few times before the always competitive match began. As the time approached eight o'clock, the four older women who usually followed them gathered on a bench to one side of the tennis court. The score was 6–3, 4–1 in Sjöberg's favour and they called off the match. They went over to the women and exchanged a few pleasantries. Then they sank down on the bench and wiped the sweat off their faces with their towels, while they watched the women skilfully volleying in pairs over the net. The two policemen always studied them as they got their breath back. It was easy to see that neither would have a chance against any of these ladies if they met in a singles match, but they sometimes toyed with the idea of challenging them in doubles. Just for the fun of it.

After teasing Sandén about his worthless backhand, which Sandén countered by reminding Sjöberg of how many of their matches he'd lost, Sjöberg changed the topic of conversation.

'How are the kids doing?' he asked.

'Fine. Everything's cruising along as usual for Jessica.

She nailed an oral exam the other day. "Fourier Analysis and Transform Theory" – what do you think of that?'

'You can pronounce it at least,' said Sjöberg with a sarcastic smile.

Jessica was twenty years old and studying to be an electrical engineer at KTH. Her older sister, Jenny, who was twenty-three, had a mild learning disability. Sandén was carefree by nature, but if he had one worry in life, it was Jenny. He always said that it would have been simpler if she'd had a serious disorder. Because her disability wasn't immediately obvious, society placed greater demands on her than were reasonable.

'And Jenny?'

'I can hardly bear to talk about it, but that damn snot-nosed kid who's running after her – he's got her thinking she should move in with him.'

'Oh boy. Not a good kid?'

'Right, what do you think? What do you think he wants with her?'

'But she's in love with him?'

'She's in love with him because he's interested in her. That's not so strange. But he's only after one thing, I'm sure of that. There's only going to be trouble.'

'Does he have a disability too?' asked Sjöberg.

'He is so-called normal intelligence. Otherwise I wouldn't be so worried. Then they would be in the same boat. But this fellow – he's going to use her like a doormat and she's going to go along with anything he asks. She's just too damn kind, Jenny.'

Sjöberg nodded thoughtfully.

'So what's he like?'

'He's a loathsome little jerk, that's what he is. When we spend time with them, he plays a damn charade and acts all loving and protective.'

He was spitting out the words.

'But have you talked to her?'

'Of course we've talked to her. But she's a big girl now and has to make her own decisions.'

'I guess she'll have to learn from her mistakes,' Sjöberg observed.

'Just hope the fall won't be too hard,' Sandén muttered, his face in the towel.

They allowed themselves some time in the sauna, where Sjöberg took the opportunity to report on Hamad's findings in Ingrid Olsson's house the night before.

'I think we've found the connection between Vannerberg and Olsson,' he said. 'We haven't confirmed it yet, but my intuition tells me we're on the right track.'

'Shoot,' said Sandén.

Sjöberg briefly related how they found the old photographs from the preschool.

'And?' Sandén asked.

'The old lady worked as a preschool teacher. As far as we could tell, she ran the Forest Hill Preschool for at least fifteen years.'

'And now you think that's where she met Hans Vannerberg?' Sandén asked hesitantly.

'Exactly. I just feel it. This is completely new information about Ingrid Olsson, and I'm willing to bet that Gun Vannerberg and little Hans have lived in Österåker. I sincerely hope this is the breakthrough we need.'

'You *feel* it?' Sandén didn't seem too impressed.

'Do you think I'm going out on a limb?'

'Well,' Sandén answered doubtfully, 'the only thing you've found out is that Olsson was a preschool teacher. That's not exactly sensational, is it?'

'Maybe not, but it's new information.'

'Sure, but for one thing, we don't know whether Vannerberg really did attend that preschool –'

'No, but *if* he did – then we have a connection between them!'

Sandén got up and poured a ladle of water over the sauna element. The room filled at once with steam and the hot air burned in their nostrils.

'Then we have a connection,' he said. 'But we have no one who knew that Ingrid Olsson was in the hospital.'

Sjöberg felt the wind going out of his sails. Maybe he had worked himself up unnecessarily. Counted on something in advance that wasn't there. His intuition seldom failed him, but this time maybe he had grasped at a straw which would turn out to be just that, a simple piece of straw.

'But maybe that person knew both of them at that

time. Maybe that person is also in the picture. Maybe we have a photo of the murderer!'

'I think we should start by checking up on whether Vannerberg actually did go to that preschool,' said Sandén matter-of-factly. 'And *then* we can move ahead on that track. Okay?'

'You're awfully critical today,' said Sjöberg, half joking, half serious. 'I'll have to think twice about beating you at tennis in future.'

They returned to squabbling about tennis, but Sjöberg felt a growing worry inside him. They finished their sauna, got dressed and left the sports facility on foot.

By nine o'clock Sjöberg was back behind his desk at the police station. He sipped a cup of hot coffee, and had a couple of Marie biscuits too, which he told himself you could indulge in when you've been playing tennis. He browsed through the quickly growing folder concerning the Vannerberg case until he found his note of Gun Vannerberg's phone numbers. He dialled her home number and let it ring ten times before he hung up. Then he tried her mobile, but got no response on that either. After leaving a message on her voicemail, asking her to contact him as soon as possible, he hung up and decided to visit Hamad, whose office was a little further down the corridor. But before he could stand up there was a knock on the door. It opened. Hamad had anticipated him and sat down in the visitor's chair.

'Good morning,' he said cheerfully. 'Did you get any sleep?'

'A few hours. I was up at the crack of dawn and played tennis with Sandén.'

'How'd that go? Did you win?'

'The tennis went fine. I won. But Sandén didn't seem to think that thing about the preschool was much of a lead.'

'No?'

'No. I've been trying to get hold of Gun Vannerberg, without success. But even if it does turn out that Hans Vannerberg had Ingrid Olsson as a preschool teacher, Jens doesn't think that will lead us anywhere. That was almost forty years ago.'

'If they knew each other at that time, then they lived in the same town,' said Hamad hopefully. 'In that case we should look for the murderer somewhere in the circle around them and their families. But first we have to establish the connection.'

'I'll contact Ingrid Olsson too, as soon as we're done here,' said Sjöberg.

'I'll talk to Pia Vannerberg about that receipt from the dentist in the meantime.'

'I think it's best if Petra does that. She's spoken to her before. It seems unnecessary to involve more people than necessary. But you could help Petra with Ingrid Olsson's neighbours. Let's go and see her.'

Sjöberg got up, taking his coffee cup with him but leaving the biscuits behind. Together they went across to Westman's office. The door was open and she was sitting at her desk, jotting down a few lines on a notepad, as they stepped into the room. She looked up and greeted them with a smile. Sjöberg sank down in her visitor's chair and Hamad perched on a corner of the desk.

'I'd like your help with something,' Sjöberg began.

'Let's hear it,' Westman replied, enthusiastic as always.

'As you know, we were in Ingrid Olsson's house yesterday and went through her belongings.'

Westman nodded attentively.

'There, among other things, we found a receipt from the dental office in Dalen, at Sandsborg. Here it is,' Sjöberg continued, placing the receipt in front of her. 'This just happens to be where Pia Vannerberg works. Could you phone her and check whether *she* maybe knew Ingrid Olsson? Stop by the dental clinic too, and see whether you can come up with any interesting information from her colleagues. Look in Olsson's patient records and so on. We also need her to send us a picture of Hans as a child. Can you arrange that?'

'No problem,' said Westman. 'But then I'll have to put the business with the neighbours and the phone numbers on hold for the time being.'

'Jamal will help you with the neighbours. You'll have to update him on the process. Have you talked to any of them yet?'

'The ones I got hold of yesterday afternoon. Everyone I talked to reacted normally to the pictures, and none of them had anything new to offer. Ingrid Olsson seems to be a very anonymous person in the neighbourhood, and so far I haven't met anyone who so much as exchanged a word with her.'

'How'd it go with the phone company?' Sjöberg asked.

'They're supposed to fax a list of the incoming calls on Vannerberg's home phone, mobile and the company line. They'll call me when they send the fax, but I can ask Lotten to forward the call to you.'

'Do that, please.'

Sjöberg left the office and his two younger colleagues. Since he was already on the move, he decided to find out how things were going for Einar Eriksson as well. Eriksson was not in his office, which Sjöberg took to be a good sign. The phlegmatic, moody Eriksson was out and about and, at best, that indicated he was doing what he was supposed to rather than moping in his office. It struck him that while playing tennis earlier in the morning he had been so full of his own business that he had forgotten to ask about Sandén's progress with the investigation, so he knocked on Sandén's door. When he got no answer he tried the door handle, but the door was locked, and he could only return to his own office and start on his own tasks.

He quickly washed down the two biscuits with the last of the coffee and pushed the cup aside. Then he picked up the phone and dialled Gun Vannerberg's number again, but there was still no answer. He pulled out the note of Margit Olofsson's home number, but no one answered there either. After talking to four different people at her workplace without getting any concrete answer regarding her whereabouts, he decided to go there. He asked Lotten in reception to take his and Westman's calls, and also take care of the fax from Telia when it came and put it on his desk. Then he took the lift down to the garage and got into the car.

The first person he encountered as he stepped into the hospital lobby was Sandén, who was having a cup of coffee and a Danish over an open newspaper in the cafeteria. Sjöberg cursed himself for not having thought that his colleague might already be there, so that he could have spared himself the drive. Sandén looked up in surprise from the Swedish handball results.

'Hey! What are you doing here? Are you sick?'

'I completely forgot that you were here,' Sjöberg replied, sitting down at the table. 'I'm trying to get hold of Margit Olofsson – or, more precisely, Ingrid Olsson – but it was impossible to reach her by phone. No one answers at her home number, so I thought it was best to come over. Do you know where she's hiding herself?'

'Who?'

'Margit Olofsson. Or Ingrid Olsson.'

'Okay, which one will it be?'

'Stop playing games. Either of them.'

'No, I don't know.'

'Then say so, you joker. So you haven't seen Olofsson today?'

'No, I haven't.'

'Then I guess I'll have to try to figure out where she's gone. How's it going for you?'

'Nothing new under the sun. No one I've talked to recognizes Vannerberg. Many people recognize Olsson, but no one knows her.'

'Have you had a chance to talk to the paramedics?' Sjöberg asked.

'Sure. The ones who picked up the old lady remember her, but no one showed any noticeable reaction to Vannerberg's massacred face. I imagine they've seen worse.'

'How long will you be here, do you think?'

'Rest of the day, I'd say. The personnel come and go here all the time so I thought I'd try to talk to as many as possible before I leave. And then I'll call it a day.'

'Are you doing anything in particular over the weekend?' asked Sjöberg.

'The in-laws are coming for a visit, so it can't get much worse than that,' Sandén answered with a forced look of distress.

Sjöberg knew that Sandén got along very well with his in-laws. He had met them several times himself and knew that they were nice people.

'I was thinking maybe you could all come over for a bite to eat tomorrow evening, but we'll have to do it another time,' said Sjöberg. 'We're going to Åsa's brother and sister-in-law's tonight, so we're sure to be hungover tomorrow.'

'Hello there. Have you forgotten the works do?'

'The works do? Damn it, it's the Christmas dinner tomorrow!'

'Raw liver and lamb testicles.'

Sjöberg got up looking amused and raised his hand in farewell.

'Good luck.'

'Get well soon,' Sandén answered, returning to the sports pages and his half-eaten pastry.

The first three people he talked to in Margit Olofsson's department had no idea where she was. The fourth was a short man who appeared to have passed retirement age long ago. Sjöberg wondered what in the name of God he was doing there. He had never previously encountered a male nurse that age. But the man was well informed. Margit Olofsson had taken her family – and Ingrid Olsson – on a Finland cruise and was not expected back at work until Monday morning. Olofsson and the nurse appeared to be very familiar, and the old man reported that the trip had been planned long ago – for the grandchildren's sake – and that Olofsson had let Ingrid Olsson go along, rather than leave her alone in a strange house. Sjöberg was not happy about this news, but thanked the man for his help. Then he took the lift down to the cafeteria and bought a bottle of mineral water and a ciabatta with Brie and salami, which he consumed in the car on his way back to the police station.

Friday Afternoon

As Sjöberg passed Lotten on the way to his office, he asked her to redirect his and Westman's calls to his extension. Neither Telia nor Gun Vannerberg had been in touch that morning, and he wondered whether Gun Vannerberg might have gone on a Finland cruise too. It occurred to him that from Malmö you were more likely to go to Germany or Poland, or even England. He had never thought of that before – that Finland cruises were not a Swedish phenomenon but more of a local thing for those living near Stockholm.

He sat down at his desk, picked up the phone and dialled Westman's mobile number. She answered almost at once, and Sjöberg asked her who she had talked to at Telia about the requested call logs. She gave him the details he needed, and he explained that, in his many years of experience in similar matters, it was best to be persistent if you wanted to get anything done. Petra Westman laughed irreverently at her impatient superior and wished him good luck. He wished her the same and called the relevant person at Telia. This turned out to be a young woman with a Gothenburg accent, who swore that she had the information right in front of her and was at that very moment in the process of faxing it over to the police. He traded his authoritative detective inspector voice for a gentler, more humane version, apologized for the inconvenience he had no doubt caused and thanked her. Then he went out to the copy room and waited until the fax machine started humming and the longed-for papers were spat out of the machine one by one.

The lists of phone numbers and accounts were long, and Sjöberg was astonished at how many calls were made to a normal family during a three-week period. Not to mention the mobile and the business line. They seemed to be in constant use day after day, and these were only the incoming calls on the pile of papers before him. He started to scan through the lists to see if any of the names came up frequently, but soon gave up. Instead, he called the woman at Telia back and asked whether they could possibly help him by sorting the accounts on the lists, so that he could get a better overview of how many times each subscriber called each number during that time period. She had no way of doing that, so Sjöberg phoned a computer-savvy acquaintance at the National Bureau and asked the same question. He couldn't help either, so Sjöberg had to tackle the monumental task on his own.

After staring at the meaningless numbers and names for a while longer, he decided to devote the rest of the day to going through the incoming calls on the business line with Jorma Molin. He called him and Molin dutifully promised to help, as best he could. Sjöberg felt a little guilty for further burdening Vannerberg's poor business partner, who had been left alone with the company on his hands, as well as his sorrow at his friend's death. He got on the metro anyway and went over there.

The office on Kungsholmen was the same, but Molin looked considerably more worn out than the last time they had met. They dispensed with the pleasantries and got straight down to the Herculean task of systematically going through the subscribers who had called the office during the weeks of interest, one by one. They could discount many calls immediately, while the great majority seemed irrelevant, but to be on the safe side these were put in parentheses. Four hours later, when they had gone through all the numbers on the detailed printouts, almost a hundred calls still remained that were unknown to Molin.

It was now six o'clock, time for Molin to shut up shop for the day and for Sjöberg to hurry home to change before the evening's dinner with his brother- and sister-in-law. Sjöberg left Jorma Molin at the little office with a shudder. Partly because yesterday's wintry weather had reverted to howling autumn winds and ice-cold rain, and partly out of sympathy for Molin, who was a pitiful creature with his mussed hair, big, sorrowful, brown eyes and quiet, toneless voice.

*

Just as he was about to step on to the escalator that would lead him down into the metro system his mobile rang. To avoid losing the connection if he went down into the underworld, he stopped and stood next to some staggering winos who were begging under the roof outside the Västermalm shopping arcade. It was Gun Vannerberg finally calling back.

'Yes, I happened to think about your frequent moves during Hans's childhood,' said Sjöberg. 'I just wanted to ask, did you ever live in Österåker?'

'No, we only lived in cities,' Gun Vannerberg answered. 'You know, in my business . . .'

'I thought you said you lived in Hallsberg.'

'Yes, we did for a while.'

'But that's no city.'

'Oh, yes, you bet it is.'

'No, not really. Believe me. But that's of no significance . . .'

The female voice in the receiver interrupted him.

'It's a lot bigger than Österåker.'

Sjöberg had no desire to bicker about that too, so he asked instead, 'So, did you live anywhere else in the Stockholm area?'

'Did we live anywhere in the Stockholm area? No, actually, we didn't,' Gun Vannerberg replied. 'We never got that far north. As long as Hans was living with me, we kept to Östergötland, Närke and then Södermanland, of course, but never the Stockholm area.'

One of the intoxicated men nudged him and yelled

in his face, and Gun Vannerberg sounded so sure of herself that Sjöberg could think of no other questions to ask. Instead, he quickly ended the call and fled the street in disappointment, down into the metro.

* * *

Hamad and Westman were on Åkerbärsvägen in Enskede, dividing up the remaining addresses in the door-knocking operation between them. They stood close together under Hamad's umbrella. Westman's was back at the office. The rain pattered against the taut nylon and the sound made it seem heavier than it really was. There was a call on Westman's mobile and with frozen fingers she pulled the vibrating apparatus out of her jeans pocket.

'Westman,' she answered curtly.

'Where are you?' asked an angry voice on the other end.

'At work,' Westman answered uncertainly.

In the racket under the umbrella she could not tell who it was.

'Who is asking?'

'Rosén. Where are you?'

'In Enskede. We're knocking on doors . . .'

'I want to speak to you. When will you be back?'

The prosecutor sounded really annoyed and she felt

herself shrinking as she stood under the umbrella with the phone against her ear.

'I won't be able to come in later today, but –'

'Then we'll have to do it over the phone.'

Hamad was studying her curiously and she turned her back to him, but remained under the umbrella.

'What are you up to?' Hadar Rosén almost roared into her ear. 'I'm getting information that you are improperly putting the economic crime unit to work and running amok in the registers. ISPs and ASPs and conducting unauthorized searches in the crime register.'

She was prepared for this sort of problem, but she had imagined it would come from Sjöberg, not Rosén. She knew how to handle Sjöberg, but a hopping mad, nearly-six-foot-six prosecutor was much worse.

'I can explain,' Westman ventured, feeling Hamad's eyes on her neck.

'Yes, you'd better come up with a really good explanation. I don't want to hear about any personal vendettas in my district.'

'This is no vendetta,' she stammered, but realized at the same moment that was exactly what it was.

'I can issue you a warning about this.'

'Don't do that,' said Westman, pulling herself together. 'He figures on the fringes of the investigation and I've got certain indications that not everything is as it should be. My searches confirm that.'

'I see,' the prosecutor retorted, ice in his voice. 'No convictions, no overdue payments, no conspicuous business deals, no hits in the ASP. The guy has a spotless past, damn it. And since when is Mälarhöjden on the outskirts of Enskede?'

'You know very well what I –'

'Perhaps you think I have no insight into what you're doing, but you think wrong.'

Rosén spat the words out into her ear and she knew that what he was saying was right.

'I've read everything that's been written in this investigation. I own this investigation, Westman. And I have not read a word about Mälarhöjden or any suspicions that some doctor at KS is supposed to be running around killing people with kitchen chairs.'

'On Monday –' Westman began.

'On Monday at nine you will be in my office. And then I want a written account.'

'Written account . . .' Westman echoed as the prosecutor ended the call.

She sighed heavily and put the phone away before she turned towards her associate with a guilty smile.

'What was that all about?' Hamad asked. 'Did Sjöberg go off his rocker?'

'I wish. No, it was Rosén.'

'What?' Hamad exclaimed with sincere surprise. 'Have you fallen into disfavour with the prosecutor's office? What are you up to? A vendetta?'

'We'll discuss it some other time.'

'Hey, come on!'

Westman simply shook her head, a look of resignation in her eyes, and they resumed the work they were there to carry out.

* * *

'Speech is silver, silence is . . . what?'

She sat whispering the words, barely audible even to herself.

'Two letters . . . must be a chemical notation . . .'

Chemistry had never been her strong suit. No school subject, besides gymnastics, had really been her strong suit, but she had done well in life anyway. She sipped her wine, cut off a large piece of cucumber and set it on the cutting board. Possibly inspired by the crossword, she cut some horizontal slits across the light-green surface and then a couple of vertical ones, after which the cucumber separated into a dozen thin rods that fell on to the cutting board. Using the knife, she gathered them together and placed them in the salad bowl, then she took another sip of red wine and attacked a different corner of the crossword.

Cooking, and housework in general, were not occupations she greatly enjoyed. Ironically, that was just how she spent most of her time these days. After two years of community college and with mediocre grades she had moved to Stockholm in search of adventure. Even without good qualifications or any work experience, she soon got a job at a trendy bar near Stureplan. She had her appearance and her open, somewhat provocative manner to thank for that, and she made no secret of it.

On the nights when she was not working she made the rounds of Stockholm's nightlife and had no problem finding plenty of friends and admirers. It was not long, as she stood behind the bar mixing exotic drinks and pouring beer, before she was headhunted, as she liked to call it. An intoxicated, good-looking and very prosperous lawyer offered her a job as a secretary at his office. She didn't hesitate. He paid well and she devoted her days to uncomplicated paperwork, making coffee and other small services he wanted done. On weekday evenings they went to expensive restaurants and slept together, and on weekends – which he mostly spent with his wife and children – she moonlighted at the popular bar and continued to entertain her male acquaintances from other branches of society. It was the booming eighties and Stockholm was swinging.

By and by, however, even Stockholm started to seem boring and she decided to test her wings (so to speak) in the even more glamorous occupation of airline stewardess. Her lack of education was no obstacle here either, and now she had some work experience besides. She got a job at SAS and travelled the world. Troublesome passengers and many hours of hard toil in cramped aeroplane aisles were compensated for by amazing parties, beautiful people and one stormy relationship after another in a never-ending flood of champagne and piña coladas.

Finally she met her Prince Charming, the SAS pilot Jonas, who, with his dark, almost raven-black hair and his clear blue eyes, was the handsomest man she had ever met. From a constant swarm of female admirers he chose her, and she was just as quick to dismiss her own pining cavaliers and wannabe lovers for his sake.

After a grand wedding, with almost two hundred guests, she found out that there was an estate outside Sigtuna which had been in the family for generations, where he thought they should live. Jonas was going to realize his dream: to fly on weekdays, and ride and hunt small game in his free time. He expected her to quit her job as a flight attendant and stay at home on the estate, taking care of the household, the horses, the dogs and the children. In the honeymoon phase of their relationship she had not objected to this, which she now deeply regretted. There had been no children and her time in the country was lonely and boring. She who was used to the good things in life – magnificent parties and a large circle of friends – now found herself almost fifteen years later sitting childless and alone on their estate, which still felt foreign to her. Jonas was seldom at home, which naturally did not improve the odds of having children.

Despite her disappointment at this abrupt, unexpected change in her life, she kept up her usual good spirits. Her body was still like a twenty-year-old's – perhaps she could thank her childlessness for that. Her blonde, naturally curly hair had retained its shine, and her face showed a conspicuous absence of wrinkles. She also knew that her husband still adored her, even if her own feelings had cooled considerably. She could leave when she wanted, and maybe she would one day.

Katrina and the Waves were booming from the CD player in the living room, which made Carina suddenly feel joyful. The song recalled many pleasant memories and she could not sit still when she heard it. She emptied the wineglass in one gulp and refilled it while she sang along with the refrain.

She got up and danced over to the stove, put on a pair of oven mitts and opened the oven to remove the moose steak. Hot steam welled up from the open door and she squinted and turned her face away until it dissipated. Gripping the pan firmly with both hands, she lifted the aromatic piece of meat on to the counter, filled a small stainless steel measuring cup with gravy and poured it over the meat a few times before she placed it back in the oven.

The wine was going to her head and her cheeks felt warm and rosy. She went over to the kitchen window and looked through the steady rain into the darkness, out over the horse meadow and towards the illuminated road to spot for the bus that would hopefully be bringing Jonas. Admittedly he hadn't called, so the plane was probably delayed, but sometimes he surprised her. After peering out for several minutes she saw the bus arrive and stop for a moment, then drive on and disappear beyond the curve. In the weak light at the bus stop she could see a solitary figure come hurrying across the road, enter their little lane and get swallowed up by the shadows among the trees. Happy that the past week's solitude was now finally over, she went back to the stove and turned on the ring under the potatoes, after which she sat down at the table again, took another sip of wine and continued her fruitless attempt to solve the impossible crossword.

Diary of a Murderer,
November 2006, Friday

The bus stopped and let me off in the rain on a deserted country road on the Uppland plain. I've never liked Uppland, and yet as a child I always dreamed of it. I imagined that the big Uppland towns, despite the inhospitable landscape around them, would welcome an odd sort like me, in contrast to rolling, attractive Södermanland, with its small, cookie-cutter, working-class towns and narrow-minded inhabitants.

I made my way across the road and on to the small gravel lane leading up to the farm. The November darkness enclosed me in its wet, ice-cold embrace, and I knew that I was invisible from the illuminated windows in the main building. The wind howled in the treetops, but nothing can frighten me now. Now I am the one you should be afraid of, and I continued with undisturbed calm past a few hedges and a small patch of forest.

There was soft light coming from the stable, but no sign of anyone inside. Some dogs were barking somewhere in the vicinity, but that did not bother me. I sneaked around the house, and through the beautiful sash windows I could see large, furnished rooms, with warm colours and wall panels and wooden furniture. The upper floor was dark, and on the ground floor a solitary woman was sitting in a large, modern kitchen with a rustic touch, doing a crossword puzzle. Something was boiling on the stove and a bottle of wine was already opened. The aroma of meat and spices forced its way into the autumn chill outside the kitchen window, and suddenly I felt hungry.

I took careful hold of the door handle and discovered it was locked. Even though the element of surprise would be lost, I had to ring the doorbell. After a few moments the door opened and Carina Ahonen looked out at me with surprised blue eyes. I cannot maintain that I was struck with amazement, because she was very pretty even as a child, but she looked much younger than the forty-four I knew her to be. What surprised me more was that as soon as she opened her mouth, she lost all the dignity that the pretty face, wavy blonde hair, well-proportioned figure and proud posture gave her at first glance. Despite (or perhaps because of) the fact that the broad Sörmland accent had been exchanged for a more standard Swedish, marked by a vowel inflection normally associated with upper-middle-class suburbs like Danderyd or Lidingö, she immediately gave the impression of being stupid. Her gaze looked unsure, while her way of talking betrayed self-righteousness and condescension. In brief, her very appearance played into my hands, and after a few minutes with her I had all the tools I needed to carry out my fourth murder: impassioned hatred and a big carving knife.

'Who are you?' asked Carina Ahonen, after studying my no doubt out-of-date and definitely drenched appearance for a few moments.

'Have I come at a bad time? Are you in the middle of dinner?' I asked cunningly.

'No, I'm waiting for my husband to come home. Did you come on the bus?'

'Yes, I did,' I answered truthfully. 'But no one else got off here. In case you were wondering.'

'I see,' she sighed, unable to conceal a certain resignation, and I could tell that so far the circumstances had not thrown any spanners in the works for me. 'So, what do you want?'

'May I come in?' I asked politely. After a moment's hesitation she answered, 'Sure, be my guest.'

The door locked behind her and I wriggled out of my jacket and handed it to her imperiously. She looked surprised, and observed me with some scepticism before she took the soaking weatherproof jacket and hung it up.

'We knew each other a long time ago,' I said.

'Yes?'

'Preschool.'

She made no effort to escort me from the hall into the house, so I had to take the first step myself. She followed me into the kitchen and looked at me suspiciously as I pulled out a chair and made myself at home at the long, farmhouse oak table. On it, besides the crossword and a ballpoint pen, was a rough cutting board and a big knife.

'What do you mean, preschool?' she asked antagonistically.

I had a feeling she would have treated me with the same antipathy if I had told her she'd won a million in the lottery. It wasn't what I said that provoked irritation, but the fact that I was the one saying it. Me – a disgusting person, with an ugly face, so-so body, ridiculous haircut and out-of-date clothes. I radiate 'loser', exhale 'loser', look like a loser. And Carina Ahonen saw that the moment she opened the door. She could sense it before I even opened my mouth. This made me furious.

'We went to the same preschool. In Katrineholm – Forest Hill.'

'I don't remember you.'

'Do you remember anything at all from preschool?'

'Sure, but not you.'

The way she looked at my clothes and not at my face when she talked further underscored the contempt she felt for me. I could have killed her right then, but that would have been too merciful. I debated with myself about how to continue, but could not come up with anything other than that a little wine would be really nice.

'Are you offering a glass?' I asked.

She was surprised, presumably by my pushiness. In

any case, she stared at me incredulously for a few moments, then she shook her head and took down a wineglass from a cupboard, filled it halfway and placed it in front of me on the table. Then she sat down across from me and took a sip of her own wine.

'Cheers,' I said, raising the glass before I brought it to my mouth.

She glared morosely out of the window.

'Why so hostile?' I asked.

'What the hell do you really want?'

'I'm just saying that we went to the same preschool. And so I dragged myself out here to the wilderness in the rain, and you can't so much as spare a smile. Not particularly hospitable, if I may say so.'

There was light coming from the oven door and I realized that was where the nice aroma was coming from. A plan began to sprout in my mind.

'You weren't exactly invited. Now tell me who you are.'

From the back pocket of my jeans I pulled out the worn black-and-white photo from 1968, unfolded it and set it in front of her.

'This is me,' I said, pointing at where I sat cross-legged on the floor in the front row of children.

Her face unexpectedly broke into a smile, and it did not take her long to find herself, in the top right-hand corner, right next to the teacher.

'And there's me,' she said, happy now. 'I'm not sure I have this picture.'

'Do you recognize anyone else?'

'I recognize her,' she answered, her finger on the stomach of Ann-Kristin.

'Dead,' I said, taking a sip of wine.

'Dead?' asked Carina, with some alarm.

'Ann-Kristin is dead,' I repeated.

'Her name was Ann-Kristin, yes. How did she die?'

'She was strangled in her apartment last week. After being tortured. But she was a prostitute, so probably no one really cared that much about it.'

'Good Lord!' Carina exclaimed, with an uncertain smile on her lips, but her eyes revealed the prurient interest this news aroused in her.

She looked at me curiously and I smiled courteously back. I had brought out the worst in her.

'This one then,' I continued. 'Do you recognize him?'

I was showing her Hans. In the very front, in the middle. He was on one knee, grinning toothlessly into the camera. I emptied my wineglass in two quick gulps and Carina, who had thawed out considerably, did not take long to refill it while she tried to think of his name.

'Valdenström, Vallenberg, Vannerberg . . . His name was Hans Vannerberg, wasn't it?'

'Bravo,' I said. 'He's dead too.'

'Him too? It feels awful when people your own age are starting to die, don't you think?'

'Not particularly, to be honest. It was worse when they were alive,' I answered dryly.

'What do you mean by that?' she asked, without waiting for an answer. 'So how did he die?'

'Beaten to death with a kitchen chair. Nose broken and then "poof", the bridge of his nose pushed right into the brain.'

I demonstrated the procedure with my hands wrapped around the legs of a pretend chair.

'You're joking . . . Is it something contagious?'

'In Miss Ingrid's kitchen,' I clarified, pointing to our old teacher.

'No, stop fooling around! What happened? Is she dead too?'

Schadenfreude glistened in her eyes and, giggling, she poured herself another glass of wine too.

'No, she's still alive.'

'More, more!' Carina Ahonen cried enthusiastically. 'Tell me more! I want to know all the details.'

Her earlier frostiness was now gone, and it occurred to me forty years too late the simplest way to people's hearts.

'Lise-Lott,' I said. 'Do you recognize her?'

'No, I don't think so,' Carina answered, shaking her head. 'But wait . . . Don't tell me she's the mother of two in Katrineholm who was drowned in a footbath a few days ago!'

'Bingo,' I said.

She suddenly turned her eyes to me with an inquisitive, slightly guarded look.

'How do you know all this?' she asked carefully. 'Are

you a police officer or something? Is that why you're here?'

'No, I'm not a police officer,' I answered. 'I know all this because I'm the one who killed them.'

She stared sceptically at me for a few moments and then suddenly she started to laugh. Imagine that – someone who's taken so long to give me the slightest smile suddenly just laughs at everything I say!

'You joker,' she chuckled, giving me a friendly thump on the back.

Quick as a lizard I grabbed hold of her wrist, stood up and pulled her arm up behind her back in what is known as a shoulder lock (thanks again, Hans, for the good tip). She let out a scream and I reached quickly for the kitchen knife on the cutting board. With the knife against her throat, I was able to shove her over to the refrigerator. Its mirrored door was exactly what I needed.

'You still don't remember me?' I asked threateningly.

'No, I . . . Well, maybe . . .'

'That's what's so funny. Imagine if you'd recognized me. Imagine if, at some point, you'd thought about how things had turned out for that poor child you constantly tormented. Then maybe this evening would have ended differently.'

She was breathing heavily now and her body suddenly started to shake, as if she had a chill. Her voice had become shrill, on the verge of screeching.

'I did not torment you! I never hit you!'

'There are many ways to torment a small child. You chose the simplest. You led the audience, the cheering section. Without your encouraging shouts and your scornful smiles, the terror would not have had a breeding ground. You weren't the one holding the axe, but you were the one who decided who would be beheaded. You were the one who set the pace and provided the tone, what was right and what was wrong. You were the one who decided that I was the ugliest and most disgusting little kid who ever set foot on this earth, and that mark could never be washed away, Carina. That's how it works in a little town like Katrineholm. You've barely taken your first steps before a sugary-sweet, little power-abuser like you shows up and puts you at the bottom of the social status ladder. If you ever dare try to climb up a rung, you're immediately kicked down by the lackeys on the next rung up. And at the very top there you sit, directing us all, out of everyone's reach. You could have let me be. If you didn't like me, you could have been content with that. But you just had to spread your venom and let everyone know what a miserable specimen I was. You had to enhance your own excellence by showing the other children my – just my – imperfection. And why I was the chosen one I still don't understand, to this day. I don't really know who I am either – or who I could have been, if you and your ilk hadn't crushed the little me that once was sprouting in a small, soft, innocent child's body. And you destroyed it, you beat it black and blue and you punched holes in

244

it and made it hard and rough. You bent its straight back. You not only destroyed my childhood, you took my whole life from me. What you did then – what you did, Carina – was to destroy a person's life. You sentenced me to a life without friends, a life without pleasure, a life in complete isolation. That is a serious act, don't you get it? Neither one of us has a life to look forward to now. But what separates us is that you have a life to look back on, while I have nothing. All because of you.'

She was staring at me in the mirror with big, wide-open, blue eyes, and I felt her pulse pounding in her wrist. I was struck by the sudden desire to disfigure this beautiful woman before I killed her.

'I . . . I realize now how wrong I was,' she tried ingratiatingly.

'Unfortunately, it's a little too late to wake up now,' I said, as I let go of her arm and instead took a firm grip on the blonde hair falling over her shoulders.

I sawed through the hair on the back of her head with the carving knife, and when I was finished, and her head was hanging forward as the last strand of hair was removed from her scalp, I quickly moved the knife back against her throat. The sharp blade paralysed her and she did not dare move. Panting rapidly, she looked at the image of herself in the refrigerator with tear-filled eyes.

'What can I do?' she sobbed in desperation.

'It's too late to do anything now. I do and you feel.

How ugly you've become,' I smiled, but she did not reply. 'What's in the oven?'

'A moose steak,' she answered, and the tears running down her face left black marks of mascara on her cheeks.

'A moose steak? Oh, thanks! And to think how hungry I am. Shall we take a look at the steak?'

I shoved her ahead of me over to the oven.

'Open the oven now.'

She carefully cracked open the oven door and let the steam issue out from the narrow opening before she opened it all the way. In the oven was a long pan on a grill at chest height, and I forced her head into the oven with brute force. The edge of the long pan struck her nose and cheeks, and the oven grill ended up on her chin. It sizzled as the hot metal burned the thin, sensitive skin on her face, but the unpleasant sound was quickly smothered by a frightful howl that made the windowpanes in the kitchen rattle. She managed to get her head out of the oven from pure reflex, but in her shaken condition, and with the increasing pain from the burns, she could do nothing but hysterically stamp her feet, holding her hands in front of her mangled face, screaming out her torment.

I took a step back and witnessed the drama in fascination for a few moments. Then, as I approached her with the knife in my hand, she simply struck out wildly around her, without seeming to care about the consequences. She forced me to cut her on the forearm.

When she noticed that she was bleeding she calmed down a little. I put my arm around her throat and once again dragged the wriggling creature to the refrigerator's mirrored door. I forced her to look at her disfigured face, and she wept in desperation at the sight of the two broad, parallel burn marks.

'That wasn't pretty,' I said in a smooth voice. 'Not pretty at all. You do realize you are an ugly person, don't you?'

For a few moments of indecision, I seriously considered leaving her like that, just for the joy of knowing she would be a very unhappy, and presumably also terrified person for the rest of her life. Finally, however, I listened to reason and decided to go on with my work.

'Imagine having to live with such a handicap,' I said philosophically. 'Having to put up with people's curious, maybe even disgusted looks every time you set foot outside your door. Hear their giggling, see in the corner of your eye how they can't help but turn around to stare at you. Feel how they point and whisper behind your back. And the children, not to mention the innocent children, how they openly discuss and question your appearance. No, listen, Carina, that's not something you would wish on your worst enemy. Or what do you say?'

Carina Ahonen said nothing, simply stood shaking and gasping for air, with her hands before her eyes. The burns were too painful to be touched.

'It's better that we end this now, so I can eat. You can be grateful, Carina, that the torment was so brief.'

Without hesitating, I quickly made a deep cut with the carving knife across her throat. A fountain of blood sprayed in an arching, deep-red pattern of drops over our mirror image on the refrigerator, and she sank, lifeless, down on to the oak parquet floor. Finally, it was quiet and peaceful.

I presume that I wasn't fully responsible for my actions, but I went over to the stove and checked with a fork whether the potatoes were done. They were, so I put some potatoes on a plate, took the marvellously sweet-smelling moose steak out of the oven and carved a big, juicy, pink slice. In the refrigerator I found a fresh salad to go with it, and then I sat down at the kitchen table, drank what was left of the wine and enjoyed Carina Ahonen's Friday dinner. Without so much as casting a glance at the recently so lively person on the kitchen floor.

I now feel, to an even greater degree than before, that basically I am not a physical person. In reality, I'm not at all suited for physical activity, which I've always known, and I'm not a particularly suitable executioner either. The murder of Hans was in many ways a disappointment, but still the beginning of something big. The murder of Ann-Kristin might well be considered the high point of my career, and that's the murder I prefer to think back on. But afterwards, I felt very strongly that I couldn't bear to carry on with that sort of thing any more. Killing is one thing, torture another.

It's too physical somehow. Chinese water torture might be something, but I'm impatient too. I want results, and besides, there's always the risk that someone will show up.

The murder of Lise-Lott was a real flop. The stupid cow didn't understand a thing and you couldn't really expect her to either. She did get to suffer for quite a while, but I doubt whether she even knew who I was. And now – now here I sit with blood on my hands again. This time in both the figurative and literal sense.

I was nervous about this, I have to admit. Before, I acted according to my heart, but this time my heart was not really in it. Putting Carina Ahonen to death was a purely logical decision, based on certain philosophical assumptions I made. Namely, that fawning, passivity and Schadenfreude are associated with evil. She always fawned on those who were the driving force in the physical abuse, and praised them for their actions; with her passive presence she took an active part in the terror, and her Schadenfreude reflected her drive to injure and wound others. Besides, she was the one who established the norm for all that was important: appearance, behaviour, vocabulary, interests. Power radiated silently from her, and a wrinkle of dissatisfaction on her sweet little doll's face sent the soldiers out to attack anyone who defied the unspoken rules formed behind her glistening corkscrew curls. Such a person is evil without a doubt, isn't she? And thus does not deserve to live. Yet I wasn't able to mobilize any real hatred before I began the task I had set myself. No, no feelings at all really, except possibly a small measure of old contempt.

Only a few weeks ago the very thought of killing a person on such flimsy grounds – nay, on any grounds at all – would have been completely foreign to me, but today it's an everyday event. It's time to stop now, before I become so blasé that boredom gets the upper hand.

Friday Evening

It was almost seven when Sjöberg got home on Friday, wet, miserable and late. Since Thursday morning he had only seen his wife in a sleeping state, and he had not seen the children at all. He did not even have time to take off his wet trousers before he was ordered to put the little boys to bed. The girls rampaged around his legs in their eagerness to tell him about things that had happened during the day, and Jonathan screamed while Sjöberg changed Christoffer's nappy. The disappointment at the day's failures disappeared temporarily somewhere in his mind under a compact layer of stress and irritation at the children's loud voices. Twenty minutes later, when the girls were sitting in front of the DVD player eating popcorn, the twins, full of wholegrain porridge, were babbling in their cots, Simon was sitting in front of his computer and Åsa was in the shower, he finally had time to remove his soaked trousers. Then the doorbell rang and, half-undressed, he had to run over to the entry phone to let the babysitter into the building. The door to the bathroom was locked, so he couldn't get at his bathrobe and instead had to wriggle unwillingly back into his wet trousers.

The babysitter was the sixteen-year-old half-sister of

Simon's friend Johan, from one building down, who was there every other weekend. Her name was Anna, and she was a reliable girl with a mind of her own. The kids liked her a lot. There was also the added security of knowing there was help available in the neighbouring building if anything were to happen.

This was the first time they were leaving the twins at home with Anna as babysitter, but problems were unlikely, since the boys usually slept through the night. The girls rushed out into the hall when they heard the doorbell, and threw themselves into Anna's arms when Sjöberg let her in. Then he went back to the bedroom to freshen up and change quickly, before it was time to go down to the street to the pre-arranged taxi. Not until they were buckled in on the backseat and had pointed the taxi driver in the right direction was there time for Sjöberg and his wife to have a moment for each other.

When you saw them next to each other, there was no doubt that Lasse was Åsa's brother. Both were tall and slender, even if Lasse, who was a few years older than Åsa, had the beginning of a beer belly, which he tried to conceal by means of tunic shirts and loose-fitting sweaters. Both of them were also true blondes and had similar greenish, almost cat-like eyes. Sjöberg's sister-in-law, Mia, on the other hand, was dark, short and a little plump, with a marvellously contagious laugh. They had no children, and though they loved kids and were the best babysitters you could imagine, Åsa was convinced that they were childless by choice, even if she had never dared to bring up the question with either of them. Sjöberg was more doubtful, but yielded to his wife's presumed knowledge of her own brother. Lasse was an interior designer, which was definitely not reflected in their own, rather carelessly arranged home, and Mia worked as a manager at an IT company. They travelled a lot and this was Åsa's main argument that their childlessness was by choice.

Not until Sjöberg sank down in the somewhat worn but comfortable corner couch and took the first gulp of Lasse's specialty, vodka and Red Bull, did he feel how tired he was. The tension of the past couple of weeks started to release little by little, and the strong drink had an immediate effect. His disappointment at Gun Vannerberg's negative response about the family's possible residence in Österåker bubbled up to the surface again and he let out a deep sigh. He could hear the siblings' voices from the kitchen as Mia sank down next to him on the couch, holding out a small ceramic bowl of mammoth green olives towards him.

'Why the dejected sigh?' she asked curiously.

He took an olive and tossed it in his mouth.

'I'm just exhaling after a long, strenuous week with the dregs of society,' he answered jokingly, depositing the olive pit in an ashtray that had clearly been swiped from a restaurant in the neighbourhood.

'Oh boy,' said Mia. 'What are you working on now?'

'A murder in Enskede. A forty-four-year-old estate agent who was beaten to death in an old lady's kitchen.'

As he spoke, he happened to think of another forty-four-year-old, and remembered that Mia had actually grown up in Katrineholm.

'By the way, did you hear about that mother of two in Katrineholm?' he asked. 'The one who apparently drowned in a tub of water a few days ago?'

'Yes, I read about that,' Mia replied. 'A gruesome story.'

'Did you know her?'

'No, I didn't. She was three or four years younger than me, so we weren't in high school at the same time. I didn't even recognize the name. What was it again?'

'No idea,' Sjöberg answered, taking another olive.

'I think my mum said her name was Lise-Lott or something like that. No, I don't remember anyone by that name. This case you're working on now, has there been anything in the papers about it?'

'Yes, quite a bit actually, but that was a couple of weeks ago.'

'Do you think you'll catch him?' Mia asked hopefully.

'Maybe we will sooner or later, but right now it doesn't look good.'

'Then we'll stop talking about that and entertain ourselves instead. It will ripen over the weekend and then you'll solve it on Monday!'

'Let's drink to that,' said Sjöberg, taking a substantial

gulp from his glass and almost getting an olive pit caught in his throat.

Lasse called from the kitchen that the food was served and they got up from the couch, taking their glasses with them. On the large, round kitchen table a pasta buffet of unusual proportions was set out. There was a bowl of spaghetti alla carbonara, a pan of home-made gnocchi swimming in cream sauce with cheese and diced pork, a saucepan of tagliatelle with pesto smelling of garlic, a pan of homemade lasagne, and another bowl of spaghetti in a sauce made of cream, onion and chicken liver. Alongside this, a large dish with a colourful salad of tomatoes, avocado and moz-zarella, and a tub of freshly grated Parmesan cheese. Lasse stood behind the groaning table opening several bottles of Italian red wine of varying origins. Sjöberg's jaw dropped, and all he could manage was a question about whether both of them had lost their jobs, con-sidering the time it must have taken to prepare this, as promised, 'simple' Friday dinner.

They sat down around the table and dug into the amazing dishes. Sjöberg ate until he was about to burst; the sound level in the kitchen rose as the levels in the wine bottles sank, and topics of discussion flew thick and fast around the table. After the main courses were finished, a sweet, smooth panna cotta was served, decorated with raspberries and blueberries on a mirror of raspberry coulis. With this they drank a white port wine – and their intoxication grew.

After they had cleared the worst of the dinner debris, they retired to the soft sofas of the living room. While coffee was brewing, Mia took out her favourite game, 'National Encyclopedia', and they debated whether they should play individually or in teams. Sjöberg, who was an individualist and hated losing, proposed the former.

'It's already eleven,' said Mia, 'and we know that you'll win if we play individually. But if we don't play in teams, we'll be sitting here all weekend.'

Something clicked in Sjöberg's head, and he suddenly sobered up. There it was again, that accent that had haunted him since the story about the murdered woman in Katrineholm on the TV news the other day.

'Wake-end,' said Sjöberg quietly, but the others heard it and looked at him in surprise.

It was the policeman from Katrineholm who had talked that way, but who else? It was very close now, it was right there in the back of his mind and wanted to come out. In what context had he heard that, very, very recently?

'Wake-end,' he said again, louder this time.

The other three people at the table exchanged glances among themselves, and once again looked curiously at Sjöberg, giggling expectantly. He did not notice them, though; it was so close, so close . . . He knew it was important. Something in his subconscious told him this was decisively important, he just knew it.

And then suddenly it came to him. He remembered

his first conversation with Gun Vannerberg. The grieving, strangely dressed Gun Vannerberg sitting on a
chair across from him in his office at the police station
and asking to look at the remains of her murdered son.

'I know that they would prefer that we not come
until after four, but I'll ask.'

'Is that so?' Gun Vannerberg had answered. There it
was, what the policeman had said in the TV interview.

'When did you last see your son?'

'Last *wake-end*. He was with his youngest daughter,
Moa, and came to see me in Malmö, where I live.'

And where was this sudden insight leading him?

'What are you up to, darling?' Åsa interrupted his
musings.

'I've got to go to the loo,' Sjöberg answered, getting
up from the couch and quickly leaving the room.

The others shook their heads and laughed, wondering, but returned to the game preparations.

Sjöberg went into the bathroom and sat down on the
edge of the tub. So the policeman on the TV news comes
from Katrineholm, like his sister-in-law, but Gun Vannerberg comes from there too, he thought. Mia nowadays
spoke a smoothed-out variation of the Katrineholm
dialect, but Gun Vannerberg's accent was the same as the
policeman's, he was sure of that. So had Hans Vannerberg lived in Katrineholm? In that case, why had his
mother withheld this information from Sjöberg? Sandén
would have laughed if he could see him now, but Sjöberg
was sure that he was on the trail of something decisive; he

felt it intuitively, and this time he relied on his intuition. But where did Ingrid Olsson come into the picture?

He got up and rushed back into the living room. Three pairs of curious eyes were turned on him.

'I need an atlas,' he said excitedly.

'An atlas?'

Lasse looked at him in bewilderment.

'A map of Sweden, whatever.'

'I don't know where our atlas is,' said Mia. 'I don't think –'

'I've got to have one. Now.'

'Maybe the neighbour has one,' Lasse suggested.

Mia saw the seriousness in Sjöberg's eyes and got up purposefully.

'I'll go and ask the neighbour,' she said, walking resolutely out into the hall, putting on a pair of shoes and going out of the door.

'What is this all about, Conny?' Lasse asked. 'You look completely wild.'

'He's thought of something,' Åsa answered in his place. 'He's thought of something important that has to do with the murder.'

'The murder?'

Lasse looked at him with fascination.

'Are you sitting here drinking and solving murders at the same time?'

'Yes, I hope so,' Sjöberg answered with an absent-minded smile.

At that moment the door opened again, and Mia

trudged in holding *The Motorist's Road Atlas of Sweden*. She handed the book to Sjöberg, who immediately started searching in the alphabetical index in the back.

'What are you looking for?' Mia asked.

'Katrineholm,' answered Sjöberg. 'I want to see where Katrineholm is . . .'

'I could tell you that,' Mia suggested, but Sjöberg took no notice of the others right now.

He led his index finger along one of the columns and mumbled, 'Katorp, Katrineberg, Katrineberg, Katrinedal, Katrineholm – there it is, page sixty-two . . .'

He flipped back to the page in question and studied the map for a minute or two. His eyes ran over the names of lakes, cities, towns and villages. He continued to search purposefully until he found what he was looking for. There it stood, clear and obvious in bold, black letters, right between Katrineholm and Hallsberg: *Österåker*.

Sjöberg closed the atlas with a thud and looked at his beloved wife with a rather apologetic expression.

'I'm afraid there's going to be some work for me this weekend,' he said ruefully.

But inside he felt a growing exhilaration.

Saturday Morning

When he woke up on Saturday morning he had a pounding headache. Although he had switched to drinking water by eleven, when he made his startling discovery, and taken two aspirin besides, and had at least ten glasses of water right before he crept into bed, he was unable to outwit the hangover. It only got harder as the years passed, and now he decided, as he had so many times before, to quit drinking alcohol altogether. A resolution he would abandon by Saturday evening, if he knew himself.

He let Åsa sleep for a few more hours. After all, he would be leaving her to take care of the kids alone for the better part of the day. Even though he knew that the tasks he had before him were urgent, a few hours here or there would not make any difference. Hans Vannerberg was dead, after all, and his self-imposed Saturday assignment could not change that fact.

At ten o'clock he finally woke his still soundly sleeping wife. He had been up with the five kids for almost four hours, so his conscience was mostly clear. He snuggled down next to her between the sheets, enjoying for a few minutes her warm, soft body against his own. Then he apologized and promised to be back as soon as possible, probably before the twins woke up from their afternoon nap.

He hugged the children and sent them in to their sleepy mother, then he slipped quietly out of the door so the little boys would not try to follow him barefoot out into the dirty stairwell.

When Sjöberg came out on the street he noticed to his surprise that the heavy clouds had scattered and the sun was peeping out for the first time in weeks. There was a strong wind and the temperature was about freezing, but he decided to walk to the police station anyway. The playground at Nytorget was already full of children, and on the benches along the side sat their parents, keeping the children in sight while they played. He did not envy them. Sitting and watching in a playground was not one of Sjöberg's favourite pastimes.

Instead of walking down Östgötagatan to the police station, he took the pedestrian path past Eriksdal. The wind was blowing right at him and he regretted not bringing his scarf. Under the bridge, two winos sat yelling, wearing far too little clothing for the season. Sjöberg pushed his hands deeper into his pockets when he saw them. The walk was just what he needed, however, and when he sat down at his desk he already felt more energetic.

He started by phoning Margit Olofsson's house again to try to have a few words with Ingrid Olsson, but as he had feared, no one answered. Then he tried both of Gun Vannerberg's numbers, but got no answer there either. Finally, he called Pia Vannerberg. She was at home. He asked if she had any objection to him coming over for a short visit and she answered in a flat voice that she did not.

He took the envelope with the old photos from Ingrid Olsson's preschool, left the police station and took the path back up to Skanstull to get a southbound metro. At Enskede Gård he got off the train and walked the last stretch. Pia Vannerberg's mother opened the door for him, and it was with some relief that he noted the recent widow was not alone in her grief.

Pia Vannerberg had no make-up on and she looked tired and worn out. She was moving in slow motion and spoke slowly too, which made Sjöberg think she was on tranquillizers. It was quiet in the house. The children were nowhere to be seen, nor was their grandfather. Sjöberg assumed he had taken the grandchildren out in the relatively nice autumn weather. Mother and daughter sat down on the couch and Sjöberg in the armchair, like the last time he was there. He took out the photos and set them on the coffee table in front of the two women.

'I really have just one question,' he said, directing himself to Hans Vannerberg's widow. 'I understand that this is difficult for you, but I would like to know whether you recognize Hans in any of these pictures.'

She looked for a long time at two of the pictures without recognizing any of the children. On the third photograph, which according to the writing on the back depicted the group of children from 1968/'69, she found him immediately. She pointed to a little boy with dishevelled light-blond hair and a big smile that showed he was losing his baby teeth. He was on one knee in the middle of the front row, and somehow gave the impression that he was on his way. He wore a checked flannel shirt whose sleeves ended halfway up to his elbows and which let a little of his stomach peep out. He was certainly the first person an observer's eyes were drawn to.

'There he is,' said Pia Vannerberg in a cracking voice. 'That's Hans, there's no doubt.'

'Did Hans ever live in Katrineholm?' asked Sjöberg.

'He was born there. I know he lived there for a while, but not how long. He moved so much as a child. You'll have to ask Gun.'

'I thought I did,' Sjöberg said cryptically, 'but there must have been a misunderstanding.'

He got up and extended his hand.

'Thanks, Pia. You've been a great help. I apologize for disturbing you like this.'

'Don't mention it,' said Pia Vannerberg, giving him a limp handshake without getting up from the couch.

He picked up the pictures, put them back in the envelope and stuffed it in his jacket pocket, and left the Vannerberg family.

*

On the platform at the metro station the wind was so strong that he had to take shelter behind a wall. The trains did not run very often on Saturdays, and it would be more than ten minutes before the next one came. Sjöberg stood with his hands in his pockets, stamping his feet to keep warm. He wondered about all the misunderstandings about the little village in Södermanland, Österåker, and cursed his own narrow-mindedness. Ingrid Olsson had said when they met, right after she found the body of Hans Vannerberg on her kitchen floor, that she had lived in Österåker before she moved to Enskede. He had assumed it was the Österåker outside Stockholm she was referring to and given it no further thought. Sloppy. Then he remembered how the dialogue with Gun Vannerberg the previous afternoon had developed.

'Did you ever live in Österåker?' he asked.

'No, we only lived in cities,' Gun Vannerberg answered.

'You said you had lived in Hallsberg. That's no city.'

'It's a lot bigger than Österåker,' she answered, and from her perspective she was quite right.

He had assumed she didn't know what she was talking about, but of course she did.

'So, did you live *anywhere else* in the Stockholm area?' Sjöberg had continued.

'Did we live *anywhere* in the Stockholm area?' she answered, and Sjöberg had thought it was a pure 'who's on first?' conversation.

It had been too, but he was the one responsible for the blunders.

He took out his mobile and called Gun Vannerberg again. This time she answered.

'Excuse me for calling and disturbing you like this on a Saturday morning,' Sjöberg said politely. 'Did I wake you?'

'Yes, you did, actually,' Gun Vannerberg replied sleepily. 'I worked last night.'

'I only want to know whether you and Hans lived in Katrineholm at any time. Did you?'

'You're really doing your research, aren't you? Yes, we lived in Katrineholm. Actually, for a pretty long time. I grew up in Katrineholm and lived there until Hans was about to start school. Then we moved to Kumla.'

'Why didn't you tell me that before?'

'I thought I listed a whole bunch of places where we lived.'

'You never mentioned Katrineholm.'

'Does it matter?'

'Yes, it does.'

There was silence for a moment, before Gun Vannerberg started speaking again.

'I think we talked about how we had moved here and there. We never moved to Katrineholm, only away from there. I guess it was obvious to me somehow that we had lived there, because I'd always lived there.'

'I understand. So Hans went to preschool in Katrineholm?'

'I guess so. Yes, now I remember, he did. Green Hill, Sunny Hill . . . it was some "hill" name.'

'Forest Hill?'

'That sounds right.'

'Do you remember his teacher?'

'No, I don't know if I ever met her.'

'Ingrid Olsson?'

'That sounds familiar. No, I don't know, I . . .'

'Do you remember anyone else from that preschool, any other children?'

'No, not a chance. That was so long ago. It was Hans who went to preschool, not me.'

'Just one last question. Do you recall that I asked whether you had lived in Österåker?'

'Sure, it was just yesterday you asked that.'

'Then you were thinking of the Österåker outside Katrineholm, I assume?'

'Yes, of course. Are there others?'

'There must be places called Österåker scattered all over this country. Now I won't bother you any more. Thanks.'

Sjöberg was seized by an almost irresistible urge to call one of his colleagues to talk about his discovery, but he calmed down and decided that it could just as well wait until Monday. It was Saturday. Everyone had worked hard the past couple of weeks and needed their weekend rest. He still felt somewhat bitter towards Sandén, who would normally be the first one he would call, because of the cool reception given to his now confirmed theory regarding the connection between Hans Vannerberg and Ingrid Olsson. And he was in no particular rush to call the prosecutor, Rosén, who was really the one to whom he should first report progress in the investigation.

On Sunday he would have a conversation with Ingrid Olsson no matter what, once she was back from her cruise. He decided to let the whole thing rest for the time being. Now he would take the weekend off, or at least one day, and devote the rest of Saturday to his family.

* * *

Petra Westman had had a hard time falling asleep on Friday night. The conversation with the prosecutor in the afternoon made her anxious. At two o'clock in the morning she lay in the dark, still going over and over her awkward situation, tossing and turning without falling asleep. At last she felt hungry, which also kept her from sleeping. She went out to the kitchen, and had two sandwiches and a glass of milk. She felt full, but not sleepy. Then she lay down and read until four-thirty, when she finally dropped off.

She did not wake up until lunchtime, and then only because the phone rang.

'Did I wake you?'

'No,' said Petra, still half asleep.

She looked at the clock on the bedside table: quarter past twelve. She tried to shake life into her body. Perk up now, Petra. This was the call she had been waiting for all week: Håkan Carlberg was calling from Linköping.

'Am I calling at a bad time?'

'Yes, you did actually. No, it's not a bad time, but you did wake me up.'

He laughed.

'I didn't fall asleep until four-thirty,' Petra excused herself. 'The prosecutor plans to give me a warning because I've been doing unauthorized searches in the police computer registers. I have to spend the weekend on a written report of what I've done and why.'

'Then perhaps I have something that can relieve the pain,' said Håkan Carlberg.

Petra sat up in bed, suddenly wide awake.

'You had alcohol in your blood, but so little you could have driven a car when the sample was taken.'

'I don't think that would have gone too well,' said Petra.

'No, I don't think so either. You also had so much flunitrazepam in your system it would have knocked out a two-hundred-pound man.'

'Are you serious? What is that?'

'Rohypnol – the date-rape drug. How much do you weigh?'

'About 59 kilograms.'

'As I thought. You must have had approximately six half-milligram tablets in you, and the normal dose for insomnia would be *one* such tablet to start with. I must say I'm impressed that you woke up after four hours. And that you were so lucid.'

'Lucid,' Petra scoffed. 'I could hardly stand up.'

'Iron will and good physique,' said Håkan with admiration. 'You must still have been seriously affected when we saw each other.'

'And the fingerprints?'

'There were two different sets of prints, one on each bottle. But there was no match for either of them. One set would certainly be yours, so that's not so strange. But as I said – no hits.'

'I know he hasn't been convicted. So he must not have left any traces behind at a crime scene before,' Petra sighed.

Relieve the pain, she thought. I'm not going to Rosén on Monday and tell him that I'm on the trail of a rapist; a senior physician who presumably has raped many women but who never leaves any traces behind and who has never been indicted.

'Not in the form of fingerprints,' said Håkan Carlberg.

'What do you mean?'

'I did a DNA test on one of those condoms.'

'And?'

'And found your DNA on the outside and his DNA on the inside.'

As expected. But she heard in his voice that he had something in his back pocket.

'His DNA has been found at two crime scenes before. A woman who was raped in Malmö in 1997, and one in Gothenburg in 2002.'

'Bingo,' said Petra. 'You have no idea how grateful I am.'

'Just make sure you put this character away. I am in Your Majesty's Secret Service until you ask me to appear.'

Saturday Afternoon

This time Sjöberg remembered to put his scarf on before he left home. Which he was grateful for now, as he sat in the grandstand in the biting wind, watching a gang of eight-year-old boys try to kick a ball into the goal on the artificial turf at the Hammarby football pitch. His scarf was the wrong colour, however, he realized when he saw the other parents and spectators.

Simon Sjöberg had been playing football with Hammarby at Kanalplan all autumn, until the practice sessions moved into the Eriksdal school gym a few weeks ago. This friendly match, against a five-man team from Marieberg, was being played outside, however, due to the nice weather. Sjöberg drew the conclusion that 'nice weather' in a football context had no connection to temperature and wind strength, but took into account only the colour of the sky.

Beside him he had his two daughters, Sara and Maja, who, completely uninterested in the match, each sat tapping on a Nintendo DS. Åsa was at the Eriksdal pool with the twins, which Sjöberg would have preferred to sitting here freezing.

His interest in football was limited to Sweden's matches in the major championships, but as far as he could tell none of the boys on the field were future stars. On the other hand, they were rather cute as they ran and chased the ball with deadly serious expressions, shouting, 'Offside!', 'Man on!' and 'Yellow card!' Sjöberg applauded when anyone did anything surprising with the ball, whether it was a home player or someone from the opposing team.

Play flowed back and forth across the shortened field, and it was a long time before one of the Marieberg players, with a little luck, finally managed to push the ball past Hammarby's goalie. Sjöberg had to admit that he did not feel any great disappointment, but instead sat and clapped politely. Below him, a man in a suit suddenly leaped up and rushed down to the goal line.

'It's time to take off that little bastard!' he screamed at the astonished home-team coach, who Sjöberg knew was the father of one of the boys on the team. 'Take off that little red-haired piece of shit, he can't cut it!'

The 'little red-haired piece of shit' was one of Simon's classmates whom Sjöberg didn't know particularly well. But from what he had seen, the boy, who was playing right back, was doing no better or worse than the other boys on the pitch. The coach, an unathletic type in street clothes who was volunteering his time, stood speechless and terrified, staring at the furious dad. Sjöberg noted that the woman accompanying the man had also stood up, but she stayed in the stands, gesticulating wildly. It took a few seconds for him to react, but when he met Simon's perplexed gaze from down on the field, a calm came over him that he had not felt in a very long time.

He stood up and resolutely took the few steps down to the field, with an air of authority that he did not recognize in himself. The stands were completely quiet and the match being played on the neighbouring field had also stopped. With all the weight he could muster he placed his hand on the man's shoulder and got him to turn towards him. They were the same height, but Sjöberg felt considerably taller at this moment, as he spat out the words into the man's face in a controlled voice.

'What kind of example is this? You're disgracing yourself and the sport in front of these kids and their parents! A grown man, picking on a little boy. You're nothing but a coward.'

Then he led the speechless man back to the stands and pushed him down on the spot where he had just been sitting.

'And you sit down too,' he said in a disdainful tone to the woman, who now looked as though she would like the ground to swallow her up.

When he looked back to the football field he saw that the red-haired boy had started crying. It was one of the proudest moments of his life, as he watched his eight-year-old son go over to the subject of the altercation and put his arm around his shoulders. The other boys in the team followed his example, and, after the coach on the opposite team whispered something into the ear of one of his players, the Marieberg boys also went up and consoled him.

Sjöberg returned to his place in the stands to supportive applause from the spectators, but avoided meeting their eyes. Instead, he continued to appreciatively observe the ring of children on the field. But it was as if an ice-cold hand took hold of his heart when his eyes suddenly fell on the little boy standing alone in the home team's goal.

Conny Sjöberg was pondering this incident later that afternoon while, clad in an apron, he stood in the kitchen peeling potatoes. He was preparing dinner with the children when Sandén phoned and asked if they could go out for a beer.

'Go to the pub?' said Sjöberg with surprise. 'I thought your in-laws were coming to visit.'

Just as he said that he remembered the conversation in the hospital cafeteria the previous day, and an uncomfortable feeling washed over him.

'Damn it!' he exclaimed, looking sheepishly over at Åsa, who was doing a puzzle with the little boys at the kitchen table.

She glanced up at him, with a look that could kill.

'The answer to your question is no, not under any circumstances,' said Sjöberg grimly.

'Oh boy,' said Sandén maliciously. 'Are you in the doghouse again? See you. I hope.'

Sjöberg hung up. He had completely forgotten about

the damn Christmas dinner. For a moment he considered calling to cancel, but that was inconceivable. He was the one who had instigated the whole thing; he was the biggest advocate of team-building, as it was called these days. True, he had opposed having this Christmas dinner on a Saturday for one thing, and in November for another, but that's what happens when you get too late a start. And he had delegated responsibility for organizing it to Hamad, so the only thing to do was bite the bullet.

'We have our Christmas dinner tonight,' Sjöberg said dejectedly to his wife. 'I completely forgot about it.'

'With significant others, I presume?' said Åsa in a sarcastic tone.

'You know the budget doesn't allow for that.'

'Well, my work is having their Christmas dinner tonight too. So I guess you'll have to try to get a babysitter.'

'Don't be silly, Åsa. I understand that this is really stupid and ruins Saturday evening and all that, but what am I supposed to do? I'm the boss, damn it.'

'You've been working today, you'll be working tomorrow. You can't be gone the whole week and then work all weekend and go to a work party on Saturday night. And just count on the fact that I'll take care of everything! I have a job to do too. And a life to live.'

'I know that full well,' said Sjöberg. 'I do my part. It just gets this way sometimes, you know that. Sometimes it's the other way around. When you have a lot to do at work and it's not as stressful for me, then I do the ground service.'

'I see, and how often does that happen? My job is always stressful. I'm a teacher, damn it.'

The children looked at their parents in dismay. Now Mum was swearing, too – that was a bad sign.

'Run out and stare at the TV or something,' said Sjöberg, with an irritated wave of his hand, to the three older children. 'Mum and I have to talk.'

The children slunk away and Sjöberg closed the door after them. They continued the quarrel in hisses.

'What if I was the one who decided at five o'clock on Saturday afternoon that I was going out with my friends? Huh? What would you say then?'

Åsa's eyes were flashing lightning bolts now and Sjöberg felt that he was also starting to get really angry.

'Then I would say, "How nice! You need to socialize with your friends in peace and quiet, without obligations. Have a nice evening!" I guess that's the natural thing to say,' he answered in a patronizing tone that made Åsa boil over.

'You can say that, because it never happens!'

'In that case, it's your own fault.'

'No, it's your fault! I have no opportunities to go out with friends because you're never home and I have to be here to take care of the children. And the cleaning and the cooking and everything else too.'

'I think I'm the one who has an apron on right now.

And you're sitting at the kitchen table with a drink in your hand.'

Sjöberg took a big gulp of his beer while Åsa went on.

'Should I be grateful because I get let off the cooking for one night a week? I don't get the impression that you're especially grateful for the other six nights.'

'How hard is it to boil macaroni and heat up frozen hash in the microwave?'

He knew he was being unfair now, and that his condescending attitude drove Åsa up the wall, but what was he supposed to do? She was cursing and swearing and he had to go to the damn Christmas dinner.

Åsa got up and pointedly left the kitchen to sit in the TV room with the older children. Christoffer and Jonathan heedlessly knocked all the puzzle pieces on to the floor before they toddled off after her. Sjöberg hoped that the older children would come back and help him with dinner, but they didn't. He picked up the puzzle from the floor and set the kitchen table for six. Then he went to the bedroom and changed into a pair of nice-looking jeans, a clean shirt and a new sports coat he had not worn before. He told himself it would annoy Åsa even more that he was wearing it when she was not coming along.

When Sjöberg was finished cooking he made sure the kitchen was spotless. Even the stove was clean, although there had been three saucepans of food on it.

He went into the TV room, gave all the children a kiss and declared that dinner was ready. Finally, he kissed Åsa on her head and said that he had to go. To the degree that ice-cold anger can be felt through the roots of someone's hair, he felt it now. Half an hour later he was sitting with Sandén at St Andrew's Inn on Nybrogatan with a pint of Erdinger Hefeweizen in front of him.

Saturday Evening

Everyone was already seated when Sjöberg and Sandén came sauntering in fifteen minutes late.

'Oh, Conny, I've been saving a place for you,' Lotten chirped.

That settled the seating arrangement, and Sandén ended up in the remaining place, across from Sjöberg on Petra Westman's right.

'You have to be nice to the inspector now, he's had a falling out with his wife,' said Sandén to Lotten.

Sjöberg glowered at Sandén, who, heedless, shouted something about balls to Hamad, who was sitting at the other end of the table.

'Is it anything serious?' Lotten asked in a voice that you might use when speaking to a very small child.

Petra, too, was curious to hear Sjöberg's response.

'I forgot about the Christmas dinner, but that gasbag called and reminded me,' said Sjöberg, with a nod in Sandén's direction. 'I'm not very popular at home right now, but it will blow over by tomorrow. Cheers.'

They sipped the red wine, which was Lebanese and tasted very good.

Hamad tapped his glass with a fork and welcomed everyone.

'I'm sorry to have to disappoint some of you, but the kitchen is currently out of lamb's testicles. On the other hand, at this very moment, they are preparing some raw lamb's liver for Jens.'

Everyone applauded and Sandén was happy to be at the centre of things.

'For those who don't care for that, various other dishes will be brought out in turn. To start with, there's bread, vegetables and various Lebanese sauces for dipping. Then there will be salads and cold meats, fried cheese, raw beef, ox tongue and so on. That's something for you, Sandén. Then there will be grilled meat, and when everyone is satisfied, there will be dessert. There's something to suit every taste, I promise. Merry Christmas!'

Everyone toasted each other and the sound level rose as the evening proceeded. The table was loaded with good food and Sandén ate his raw liver, to everyone's great amusement. Lotten soon tired of flirting with Sjöberg and instead started discussing dogs with the caretaker, Micke, who was sitting diagonally across from her. Petra, who was sitting across from Lotten and next to Micke, tried at first to get involved in their conversation but quickly lost interest. Instead, she tried to join in Sandén's and Sjöberg's conversation, but without much success since she hadn't been part of it from the beginning.

Hadar Rosén was sitting in solitary majesty at one end of the table, to give him room for his long legs. Einar Eriksson was on one side of him and Hamad on the other. Eriksson did not say much in the early part of the evening, but Hamad exchanged a few words with him and thought that even he seemed to be having a nice time. He was eating with enthusiasm and actually had some wine, without making a fuss about it. Hamad noticed that Petra cast the occasional furtive glance in their direction during the evening, but could not decide whether it was him or Rosén she was looking at. After a few glasses of wine, he tried throwing out a little feeler to Rosén.

'I heard you gave Westman a proper spanking,' he said quietly.

'You might say that,' Rosén answered coolly.

'What was that all about?' Hamad attempted, but the prosecutor was unrelenting.

'I'm sure she'll tell you if she finds it appropriate.'

The prosecutor then began a conversation with Eriksson, with whom he suddenly seemed to have a great deal in common. Hamad was unconcerned, and turned instead towards Bella Hansson, seated on his other side. As soon as he had turned his back she had been an unwilling audience to Lotten's and Micke's endless dog conversation, trying to look interested. She brightened up and they resumed their own conversation, which, as far as Petra could see, lasted for most of the evening.

At a quarter to eleven Sjöberg got a text message from Åsa: 'Forgive me for losing my temper. Hope you're having fun at the party. The food was excellent. Love you most in the whole world.' Sjöberg replied with: 'It was my fault. I'm a clumsy oaf. Coming home to you soon. xoxo.' Eriksson announced that it was time for him to go home and Rosén also took the opportunity to excuse himself. Petra got up from the table and mumbled something about going to the toilet, which no one heard. Hamad noted, however, that she left the table just as the prosecutor left for the evening.

She followed Rosén down the stairs, plucked up her courage and went up to him as he stood in the cloak-room, putting on his overcoat.

'I'd like to talk to you, Hadar,' she said, trying not to look nervous.

Einar Eriksson glanced at her quickly, then resumed tying his scarf.

'Now?' said Rosén, glancing at his watch.

Whether that was ironic or not, Petra did not know, but she nodded hopefully.

'Goodnight,' said Eriksson, starting to leave.

They answered his goodbye and Petra proposed that they sit for a while in the bar, and Rosén agreed.

'This conversation has to stay between us,' said Petra. 'You can do what you want with me, but I don't want you to tell this to anyone.'

Rosén looked at her suspiciously, and declared that he did not intend to make a decision about that until he had heard what she had to say. Petra was prepared to take that risk, and told the story of what she had been subjected to a week earlier for the second time. Rosén listened attentively without interrupting. After

282

ten minutes, he took off his coat and placed it on his lap. After another five minutes, she was done.

When Hamad and Bella Hansson came down the steps Petra looked up. Hamad had his hand on Hansson's shoulder, but nonchalantly removed it when his eyes met Petra's. He winked at her as they passed, and they left the restaurant without coats.

'This is what I *know*,' said Petra to Rosén. 'This man is not just any old rapist, but a well-functioning member of society who conceals a cunning sex offender behind a prim and proper façade. He rapes women in his own home and when they wake up they believe they've had a one-night stand while drunk. This is what I *think*: he has been raping his whole adult life. I think that his daughter was the result of a rape, but he was so shrewd even then that he concealed it through marriage and, just like that, there's no evidence. Love does not interest him – violence is his thing. A woman who gives herself to him is uninteresting. It's the element of violence that gets him going. And what could be a better environment for rape than war? So he becomes a foreign legionnaire. Then he can ravage freely for years without anyone raising an eyebrow. After he tires of military life, he comes home and has to continue some other way. So he refines his methods. He's a doctor besides, so he has easy access to drugs. Do you understand? He prefers unconscious women to willing ones.'

'And what do you want me to do?' asked the prosecutor, who up to that point had not said a word.

'For one thing, I want you to overlook my unauthorized computer access. Let that disappear in this murder investigation. Only you and I know about it, and it won't do any harm.'

Rosén studied her thoughtfully over his glasses.

'For another, I want you to see to it that Peder Fryhk is arrested.'

'For what? We have no police report and no evidence, because you intend to keep out of it.'

'For a rape in Malmö in 1997, and another in Gothenburg in 2002,' said Petra.

'How do you know that?'

'Because I had the semen from my rape DNA tested. His DNA matches that of the perpetrator of those rapes.'

Rosén sat silent, thinking. Through a window, Petra could see Hamad leaning forward in a way that suggested he had his palms against the wall. She concluded that Hansson was standing in between, with her back against the wall.

'But if you don't file a report, we can't use the semen from your rape as evidence,' the prosecutor said. 'Besides, it's doubtful we can build a case even if you were to file a report, since you haven't exactly gone by the book.'

'I don't intend to file a report, and I'm aware that this DNA test won't do as evidence. But now we know that he committed these rapes. Arrest him as a person of interest, swab him and *then* do a DNA comparison, according to the rules.'

'On what grounds could we arrest him?'

'A tip from the general public or whatever you want. Show a picture of him to the victims and let them point him out. You can solve that problem yourself.'

'Why are you so afraid to file a report?' Rosén asked.

Petra was forced to think for a moment before she answered.

'I'm a cop. I don't want to be the subject of an investigation conducted by my colleagues. I don't want them to know anything about this. Can you understand that?'

Hadar Rosén nodded meditatively.

'If, for some reason, he was not convicted of these crimes, I might feel threatened,' Petra continued.

'Why is that?'

'Because I'm a police officer, and because he gets arrested right after I've been to his home.'

'Does he know you're a police officer?'

'I don't think so. I keep my police ID behind the driver's licence in my wallet. But I'm not sure. He may have found it, if he went through my things thoroughly.'

'You are aware that he will get out again in a few years? Even if he goes to jail.'

Petra nodded.

'How many years do you think he'll get?' she asked.

'The maximum sentence is six years. He'll be out after –'

'It's all the same,' said Petra. 'We'll cross that bridge when we come to it. In the meantime, at least we can keep an eye on him.'

The prosecutor studied her for a while without speaking. Petra was calmer now that she'd revealed the truth, but she always felt uncomfortable when she found herself under a magnifying glass.

'So, what do you say?' she asked, unable to conceal her uncertainty.

'I'll see what I can do,' Rosén answered. 'God have mercy on you if you're wrong.'

'And the meeting on Monday –' Petra began.

'. . . we'll have anyway,' the prosecutor grunted. 'But you don't have to turn in a written report, for the time being.'

A hint of a smile passed over his face.

Just as the prosecutor was leaving the restaurant Hamad and Hansson came back in again. Petra joined them on the stairs and Hamad placed his hand on her shoulder and asked her to sit with him. While she was away, Sandén and Sjöberg had taken their wineglasses and moved over to the seats left empty by Eriksson and Rosén, so Petra fetched a chair and sat at the corner of the table, between Hamad and Sjöberg. Micke and Lotten were still talking tirelessly about their dogs.

'What did he say?' Hamad whispered in Petra's ear.

'Who?' Petra whispered back.

'Hadar.'

'About what?' Petra teased.

'About the vendetta.'

'Vendetta?'

'You know what I mean.'

His eyes gleamed with curiosity in the soft light.

'He said I could keep my job.'

'But tell me now! Don't be so damn secretive!'

He tousled her hair a little and made her feel like a kid.

'You seem to have your hands full anyway,' Petra replied curtly.

'How many wives can you have over there?' said Sandén in an audible tone.

Hamad met his eyes across the table and shook his head. Petra felt a sting of irritation and looked at Sjöberg, who tried to look neutral. Bella Hansson pretended to be interested in how often you have to groom standard poodles.

'Yes, one at home and then two new ones on the hook here tonight,' Sandén went on.

'Leave it alone!' Petra exclaimed. 'Drop that racist talk. Pretty soon there'll be something about camels too.'

Sandén put his hand over his mouth and pretended to be embarrassed, and Sjöberg knew that in fact he was. He gave him a light tap on the arm with a clenched fist.

'If it interests you, I'm getting a divorce,' Hamad answered, looking seriously at Sandén.

'Oh, hell,' said Sandén. 'I didn't know that. I'm sorry.'

Petra and Sjöberg looked at Hamad in surprise.

'But Jamal, why didn't you say anything?' Petra asked, placing her hand on his arm.

'I guess it's not the first thing you blurt out when you get to work in the morning.'

'But –'

'It was finalized last weekend. It's sad, but that's how it is. Cheers.'

Petra's glass was still at her old place, but Sjöberg handed her Hadar Rosén's half-finished glass so that she too could join in the toast.

A few minutes later Sandén had managed to get everyone at the table to laugh out loud several times, even Lotten and Micke, who could no longer make themselves heard. With Sandén as conductor, one topic of conversation followed another, and everyone at the table was drawn into the group. The mood was suddenly better than it had been the whole evening, and they did not leave the restaurant until they were politely but firmly asked to. By then, all the other guests had long since departed and it was already half past one.

Sunday Morning

Sjöberg discovered, to his disappointment, that the paperboy had failed to show up that morning. He had to be content with yesterday's *Aftonbladet*, which he had not had time to read. He sat at the kitchen table trying to read the paper while he ate his own breakfast and helped his twin sons to swallow their little sandwiches and yogurt without too much catastrophe. The other children were sitting in front of the TV watching a rerun of last night's children's programme, while Åsa was in the shower. During half a minute of peace, while both boys were chewing their liverwurst sandwiches at the same time and in silence, he was able to skim an article inside the paper, which on the placards had been marketed with the headline 'Party-Going Friend Brutally Murdered':

'A forty-four-year-old woman, Carina Ahonen Gustavsson, was found on Friday evening murdered in her home, a remote estate in the Sigtuna area. The woman was discovered at ten o'clock by her husband when he returned from a trip abroad. She had been brutally assaulted and killed with a knife. The time of the crime has not yet been established, and the police have made no statement concerning a possible perpetrator.'

The majority of the story was taken up, however, by an interview with an old acquaintance and B-list celebrity, who told about her friendship with the murdered woman twenty years earlier.

Christoffer put an elbow in his bowl and yogurt splashed in all directions. Jonathan laughed encouragingly at his brother, and Sjöberg gave up his attempt to read the newspaper and devoted his attention to the children instead. He felt a nagging worry taking hold in his gut, but had neither time nor energy to figure out what it was that disturbed his otherwise good Sunday mood. He finished breakfast as quickly as he could and went to shave.

As he was standing in front of the mirror with the razor against his cheek, he noticed that his hand was still not completely steady. Once again he had woken up in the small hours, damp with sweat, heart pounding, and made his way to the bathroom to shake off the horrid dream. Or was it so horrid . . . ? The dream itself was not terrible per se, but that was how he experienced it. And as it went on, it had become horrid in more ways than one. Since the woman in the window had assumed Margit Olofsson's form, he had started to doubt his reason. Good Lord, he was living with the world's most marvellous woman, and nothing could get him to leave Åsa. No woman in the world could compete with her and he loved her with all his heart.

But yet . . . the dream now felt almost erotic, and he caught himself again and again feeling a kind of longing for that dream figure. Margit. Olofsson. It was sick. She was quite nice-looking though. She had amazingly beautiful hair, that was undeniable, but she was rather heavy and much older than Åsa. She had grown-up children, even grandchildren. A charming and open manner, of course, but he had barely spoken to her. In terms of appearance, Åsa beat her by several lengths. Yet this woman aroused something inside him that he could not put his finger on. Something enticing and warm, but which still made him shudder with discomfort.

Hamad was almost euphoric when Sjöberg called and told him about his discovery.

'That's just what we said!' he exclaimed. 'We knew it the whole time! How'd you figure it out?'

'The dialect,' said Sjöberg. 'I noticed that Gun Vannerberg had the same accent as a policeman I heard being interviewed on TV the other day. About that murder in Katrineholm, you know. There was a woman who was drowned in a tub of water.'

'And?'

'It struck me that Katrineholm was not a city that had been mentioned in the investigation in any way. On the other hand, the name Österåker had come up. I found Katrineholm on a map and there it was – Österåker! A small village, or township or whatever, about twenty miles outside Katrineholm. Ingrid Olsson lived in the small community of Österåker outside Katrineholm, not the Österåker outside Stockholm. Hans Vannerberg had her as a preschool teacher in Katrineholm, and Gun Vannerberg has now confirmed that. The reason she didn't mention the city before was that she grew up there, so it was not a place she had moved *to*, but simply *from*. It fell between the cracks, so to speak. I went to see Pia Vannerberg too. She pointed out Hans on one of the pictures.'

'Oh, hell. Have you talked with Ingrid Olsson about it?'

'No, she's been on a Finland cruise with Margit Olofsson and her family, so I haven't been able to reach her. She's moving back home today, so I thought we could have a chat with her now. If you feel like dragging yourself in, even though it's Sunday?'

'Of course. It will be a pleasure.'

His colleague's youthful enthusiasm was a relief, but Sjöberg could still not quite get rid of an irritating sense of discomfort.

Yesterday's fresh breeze had died down, but in return the temporary sunshine had once again disappeared behind a thick mantle of threatening clouds. Sjöberg took a detour to pick up Hamad, outside his apartment in one of the buildings on Ymsenvägen in Årsta, before they made their way to the familiar old wooden house in Gamla Enskede.

*

It was Margit Olofsson who opened the door. Sjöberg was quite unprepared for this and reacted with an embarrassed smile that he felt was unbecoming. She greeted them happily and beckoned them in. Sjöberg felt that she could read him like an open book, but convinced himself that he most likely had the mental advantage. He adopted a preoccupied expression and tossed out, as though in passing, some words of praise about her concern for her former patient. Margit Olofsson sparkled back and informed them that Ingrid Olsson herself was upstairs unpacking her bag. The two policemen made their way up the narrow stairway and, to their surprise, found the elderly woman perched on a chair in the bedroom. They saw no sign of a crutch and Sjöberg drew the reassuring conclusion that Ingrid Olsson had been in good hands during her rehabilitation. They did not expect a smile, but she greeted them courteously and got down from the chair when they entered the room. They sat down on her bed and Sjöberg explained that there were a few questions they needed answers to.

'For one thing,' he said, 'I wonder whether the Österåker where you told us you lived before you moved here is the Österåker in Södermanland, outside Katrineholm?'

'Of course,' she said, sounding surprised. 'Was there anything unclear about that?'

'No,' said Sjöberg, a little embarrassed, 'I guess it was

more that, as a Stockholmer, I assumed you came from the Österåker just outside the city. That was careless of me, I admit, but it's good to get that cleared up at last.'

'Does that have any significance –?'

Sjöberg interrupted her with yet another question.

'If I've understood things correctly, you worked as a teacher at a preschool in Katrineholm?'

'That's right. Forest Hill was its name.'

Sjöberg removed the envelope with photos from his jacket pocket and searched for the picture from 1968/'69.

'Do you recognize anyone in this picture?' asked Sjöberg.

Ingrid Olsson took the photo and held it so far from her that her arms were almost straight.

'No. Good Lord, this must be forty years old. Well, I recognize myself naturally, but there is no way I would recognize any of the children.'

'No?' Sjöberg asked doubtfully.

'No, never.'

She turned over the picture and confirmed her assumption about the age of the photograph.

'1968. That wasn't exactly yesterday.'

Her eyes swept over the black-and-white picture and stopped on one of the children.

'But this girl I actually do remember,' she corrected herself, pointing at the smiling little girl with light-blonde braids and a neat dress in the upper right-hand corner. 'I'm quite sure her name was Carina Ahonen.'

Something clicked for Sjöberg and he tried feverishly to recall where he recognized that name from, but without success.

'A real little jewel,' Ingrid Olsson continued, and Sjöberg noticed that, for the first time, the old woman was almost showing emotion. 'She had a very lovely singing voice, I recall, and she was so sweet and nice.'

'No one else?' Sjöberg coaxed, feeling a vague sense of unease.

'No, no one else.'

'This is Hans Vannerberg,' said Sjöberg, pointing at the little boy in the middle of the picture. 'He was the man you found murdered in your kitchen.'

He watched her face, trying to read her reaction. Hamad too looked at her with tense expectation.

'No, I don't recognize him,' she answered, shaking her head. 'He looks like a real little scamp, and I didn't have much patience for them, I can tell you that,' she said, pursing her lips.

After trying unsuccessfully to get Ingrid Olsson to recognize any of the other children in the picture, or even to remember anything concerning this particular class, they felt compelled to leave her. Their theory had been completely confirmed, even though Ingrid Olsson's surprising lack of any memory of these children made their work more difficult.

When they came back downstairs, Hamad stuck his head into the kitchen and called out a cheerful 'Thanks' to Margit Olofsson. Sjöberg, half-hidden by his colleague, shuddered all over and mumbled something inaudible in farewell, without looking in her direction.

'What do we do now?' Hamad asked in the car, as they were leaving Åkerbärsvägen and turning on to one of the equally idyllic small cross streets.

'We have to find out the names of these children. Look them up and see whether there's anyone who remembers anything. What do you think about Ingrid Olsson?'

'Strange woman,' said Hamad. 'It doesn't seem to bother her particularly that a person was murdered in her home. One of her old pupils, at that. The only thing she had to say about him was that he looked like a scamp and she clearly didn't like that. More or less as if it served him right to be murdered, because he looked mischievous in a picture from 1968. Remembers nothing. Well, besides Carina Ahonen, of course. She was apparently teacher's pet. What do you think?'

'One got that impression,' Sjöberg muttered, trying once again to remember in what context he had heard that name before.

Then his mobile rang. It was twelve o'clock and just as Sjöberg answered, the heavens opened and it started to snow heavily, but neither of them noticed that. It was Mia on the phone, Sjöberg's sister-in-law.

'Thanks for the other night!' said Sjöberg. 'It was a heavy but pleasant evening. And then winning that game to top it off.'

'It's called hospitality,' Mia said jokingly, but her voice had a tinge of seriousness and she quickly changed the subject. 'Listen, Conny, I don't know if this has any significance, but I thought I should call you right away, to be on the safe side.'

'Yes?'

Sjöberg listened intently to his sister-in-law's somewhat incoherent description of her realization.

'You asked me last Friday if I knew anything about that woman in Katrineholm. You know, the one who was murdered earlier in the week, Lise-Lott Nilsson.'

'Yes, what about her?'

'Well, I didn't recognize her at all, as you no doubt recall. Did she have anything to do with your investigation?'

'No,' said Sjöberg impatiently. 'I was just curious in general. What about it?'

'Well, you see now . . . I don't want you to think I'm silly or sensationalist.'

'Out with it. What is this all about?'

Sjöberg could feel, without knowing why, the tension churning inside him, and his heart started beating faster.

'There was a woman murdered on Friday too.'

'Yes?'

'And I recognized her. A forty-four-year-old woman

from . . . it wasn't in the paper. There it said she was from Sigtuna, but I know that originally she was from Katrineholm. Her name was Carina Ahonen.'

Sjöberg braked abruptly, without bothering to check in the rearview mirror first. Fortunately, there was no one behind him. He felt as if his heart had stopped, and he just sat gaping with the phone in his hand for several moments. Hamad stared at him excitedly, not understanding a word of what was being said on the phone.

'Hello?' said Mia. 'Are you still there?'

'Thanks, Mia,' said Sjöberg when he had caught his breath. 'That was incredibly important information. I'll call you later.'

He ended the call and put the phone back in his inside pocket. Hamad was still looking at him, wide-eyed.

'What's this all about?' he said at last.

'I don't know,' said Sjöberg. 'I have to think.'

'You're in the middle of the road,' Hamad informed him.

'I know. Wait a little.'

'Come on now! Who was that?'

'It was my sister-in-law, Mia. She said that Carina Ahonen was murdered . . .'

'Carina Ahonen? But that was her, damn it – the teacher's pet!' Hamad exclaimed. 'How did she know that?'

'I knew it too. I just didn't make the connection. It's been gnawing at me all morning.'

Sjöberg seemed clearer now and his voice was controlled, but eager.

'Hans Vannerberg, aged forty-four, from Katrineholm is murdered two weeks ago in the house of his preschool teacher, Ingrid Olsson. Yesterday, another of her old preschool students from the same group was murdered, Carina Ahonen. The other day, another forty-four-year-old woman from Katrineholm, Lise-Lott Nilsson, was murdered – the one drowned in the tub of water, as I mentioned. I'd lay odds she's somewhere in that picture, too. And perhaps there are even more. Three murdered forty-four-year-olds in two weeks, all from Katrineholm. Jamal,' said Sjöberg, emphasizing each syllable, 'I think we're on the trail of a serial killer.'

'You're joking,' said Hamad, without thinking for a moment that he was. 'A serial murderer? You're out of your mind! How many of those have there been in Sweden?'

'Not many, but we have one here, I'm convinced of it.'

Were there other victims? He remembered something he'd read, but he could not think what it was. Would there be more? Now it was crucial to act quickly. He retrieved his phone from his inside pocket again and entered Sandén's number; at the same time he ordered a perplexed Hamad to call Petra Westman and Einar Eriksson. Hamad did as he was told while Sandén answered Sjöberg's call.

'Hi, Jens, it's Conny. Be at the office in half an hour; something has turned up.'

He ended the call immediately, then phoned Hadar Rosén and left the same brief message. Then he started the car again and drove quickly back to the police station, while Hamad informed Eriksson and Westman about the hastily summoned meeting.

Sunday Afternoon

At exactly twelve-thirty, all six of them were assembled in the conference room at the police station on Öst-götagatan. No one seemed irritated, not even the usually gloomy Einar Eriksson. Instead, everyone was sitting in tense anticipation, observing their resolute boss as he started to speak.

'Our focus on a possible connection between Hans Vannerberg and Ingrid Olsson has borne fruit,' Sjöberg began, and then he related how recent discoveries led to today's breakthrough in the investigation.

The meeting participants followed his account attentively, without interrupting.

'Earlier in the week a forty-four-year-old woman by the name of Lise-Lott Nilsson was murdered in Katrineholm. The papers said she was drowned in a tub of water. We have not yet been able to prove any connection to Vannerberg, but I would be surprised if we don't find one. I haven't had a chance to speak with our colleagues in either Katrineholm or Sigtuna to confirm this, but that will be the first thing we start working on after this meeting. There may be more victims we don't know about, and worse yet, there may be more victims to come if we don't figure this out right now. In short, I believe we're dealing with a serial killer here.'

Sjöberg fell silent and looked around for reactions and questions. The first one to open his mouth was the prosecutor.

'Well done, Sjöberg. Just as you say, this puts the case in a different light. We need to act quickly. We have to focus on identifying and locating the other children in this preschool class, not only to warn them but obviously also to look for a motive and a perpetrator. And we have to coordinate our respective investigations in the various districts.'

'The press,' said Sandén. 'What information should we give to the media?'

'None at all, at the moment,' Sjöberg replied. 'It could interfere with the investigation. If we have problems locating the others involved, we may ask the press for help as a last resort, but not unless we have to.'

'Okay, what do we do now?' asked Hamad.

'I suggest that, to save time, Jens immediately makes contact with someone at the municipality in Katrine-holm who can give us the information we need concerning that preschool class. We want all the children's names and addresses. Petra, you get hold of someone at the census bureau who can help us find information about where these people are today. And we want that information as it arises. We can't afford to wait until the whole list is compiled. Instead, we want each name as soon as it becomes available so we can begin our search as quickly as possible. I'll contact the people responsible for the investigations within the police departments in Katrineholm and Sigtuna to see what they've learned so far. Einar and Jamal are on standby, and will dive into the search process as soon as we have the slightest thing to go on. Einar, you contact the districts and get information about all murders that have been committed in Sweden during the past month. Jamal, to start with, you may as well go and get sandwiches for everyone.'

'I want frequent updates,' said Rosén to Sjöberg.

'Will do,' Sjöberg promised, getting up from his chair. 'Work hard now, do you hear me? You'll get time off in lieu when this is over.'

Five chairs scraped against the parquet floor and three police officers and one prosecutor left the meeting room with determined expressions. Sandén lingered behind for a moment and gave Sjöberg an encouraging pat on the shoulder.

'You and your damn intuition. But you're a lousy tennis player,' he added, laughing, and then he too left the room.

Sjöberg went to his office and closed the door behind him. Before he was even in the chair, he had picked up the phone and was dialling his sister-in-law's number. It was Lasse who answered but, after a few quick pleasantries, he asked him to put Mia on the line.

'What now?' said Lasse, but immediately handed the phone to his wife.

Sjöberg presumed that his brother-in-law was well informed about their conversation earlier in the day.

'Tell me,' said Mia. 'I'm dying of curiosity.'

'What I'm telling you now is highly confidential,' said Sjöberg. 'You must not utter a word of this to anyone, do you understand that?'

'Absolutely,' answered Mia.

'It turns out that the murder I'm working on is closely connected to what you told me this morning. And, presumably, with what we talked about on Friday. We seem to be dealing with a serial killer. A serial killer with very strong connections to Katrineholm.'

'Wow,' said Mia.

'And you can help me a little, if you don't mind. Extremely informally, if you know what I mean.'

'Of course.'

'The police don't normally work this way, you understand. But if you can, I would like you to do a little social research for me. You have contacts in Katrineholm, after all.'

'What do you want me to do?'

'Are you familiar with Forest Hill?'

'Sure, that was a preschool when I lived there.'

'Exactly. During the 1968 to '69 school year, there was a group of children there, led by a certain Ingrid Olsson. That group included Carina Ahonen and Hans Vannerberg, the murder victim in the investigation I'm working on. Now, I haven't yet got the names of any more children in the group, but that's only a matter of time. I'll be in touch with more details when I have any. I would like you to discreetly ask around and find out whether anything special was going on in that group of children – what the social structure was like, if there were any children who stood out in one way or another, et cetera. Do you understand?'

'I'll see what I can do.'

'But not a word about this to anyone.'

'I'll be silent as the grave.'

'Good. I'll be in touch.'

Sjöberg hung up and then picked up the phone again. This time he called information, who connected him to the Katrineholm police department. The on-duty constable who took the call referred him to an Inspector Torstensson, who was off for the weekend. He promised to locate him as soon as possible and have the inspector call Sjöberg back right away. Sjöberg hung up and repeated the procedure with the Sigtuna police. Then he went out into the corridor and got a cup of coffee and returned to his seat just in time to receive Hamad's delivery of a sandwich for lunch.

Halfway through his meatball sandwich the phone rang. It was a Chief Inspector Holst from the Sigtuna police. He was very shaken by what Sjöberg had to say, and reported in turn that they had secured fingerprints at the scene of the crime that almost certainly belonged to the murderer. He also reported that the murder of Carina Ahonen could be considered relatively brutal; judging by appearances, it involved torture. Her hair had been cut off and she had had severe burn wounds that were incurred shortly before death. Finally, her throat was cut. The whole thing was a very bloody affair. Sjöberg promised to be in touch again after he had spoken to the Katrineholm police. He felt sickened by the information his colleague in Sigtuna had interrupted his lunch with. He sat for a long time thinking about what he had heard.

Everything indicated that the murderer was someone out for revenge. The question was simply why. The first murder, of Hans Vannerberg, seemed more like a crime of passion, even if the planning of the whole thing had been fairly refined. Then the murderer appeared to have warmed up. Lise-Lott Nilsson, it seemed, had been drowned without mercy, and Carina Ahonen had been outright tortured before her execution. What could these individuals have done to deserve such punishment? The perpetrator must be a disturbed person, likely to have been seriously abused during childhood. Hans Vannerberg had been a scamp, that much he understood. But were his boyish pranks so serious that someone would have hated him for almost forty years to the extent that he – or she, for that matter – finally snapped and then murdered him? The thought was dizzying. That hatred must have been hard to live with. He had heard somewhere that trauma tends to return in memory after ten years. Could the same be true after forty years? Was this possibly the result of some out-of-control mid-life crisis?

His musings were interrupted again by the shrill ring of the phone. This time it was Torstensson in Katrineholm. Sjöberg recounted his theories, but Torstensson evidently had a hard time believing what he was hearing. He asked the same questions over and over, and seemed to need extra reassurance of the credibility of his Stockholm colleague before he gave in. Torstensson then described in detail the murder of Lise-Lott Nilsson. Here too there were clear fingerprints to go on. The murderer was evidently either inexperienced or unafraid, but presumably both. Lise-Lott Nilsson, just as the media had reported, had been drowned in a tub of water, more precisely, her own footbath. According to Torstensson, there were no visible signs of physical torture, but Sjöberg had the definite feeling that the mental torture that preceded the murder had been just as painful. The medical examiner's report did not contain anything to indicate repeated periods underwater, but Sjöberg assumed, based on what he had heard about the murderer's methods so far, that the drowning itself was only the end of prolonged torment. Perhaps the murderer had been subjected to similar treatment as a child?

He left his office and went over to Sandén, who was on hold to the municipality of Katrineholm. He had managed to bring in a number of municipal employees who had been off for the weekend, who were now in the process of going through old binders. For now, he could do nothing but wait.

Then Sjöberg went to see Westman, who had just made contact with someone at the National Registration Office. As he entered the room she put the phone on speaker. The woman on the other end readily promised to help when the time came with searches in the central reference register, and to locate information herself about the individuals who were currently registered in the Stockholm area. However, she could not do searches in the local registers, but offered to supply a telephone number to personnel at the local tax offices involved. She also suggested that she contact the relevant personnel in Katrineholm and Norrköping, where one might expect to find some of the persons being sought.

Sjöberg moved on impatiently and knocked on Eriksson's door, further down the corridor. Eriksson was scrolling through old domestic news on the computer screen and Sjöberg got dizzy trying to follow it.

'Have you found anything, Einar?' he asked, looking from the flickering letters to his colleague.

'A little,' Eriksson answered. 'I'm waiting for word from police districts all over the country, and in the meantime I'm searching the Internet. I'm printing out everything I find, but I haven't decided whether any of this is of interest. You can go out and have a look on the printer if you're curious.'

Sjöberg went out to the copy room, somewhat surprised by Einar Eriksson's sudden frenzy. On the printer were extracts from a dozen newspaper pages, and he stood next to the copy machine and began to study them. His eyes ran over the black-and-white pages, which brought a series of tragic events to light: a murder with racist undertones at a sausage stand in Nacka; an apartment disturbance that escalated into a knife fight in Skellefteå; a member of the Hell's Angels beaten to death at a party in Malmö; a woman in Burträsk strangled by a jealous ex-boyfriend; the discovery of the body of a Polish berry-picker who had disappeared in June 2004 in Ångermanland; a presumed settling of scores in the underworld which resulted in a Serbian father of three being shot to death at a restaurant in central Stockholm; an unidentified body with stab wounds that floated up in a plastic bag in Edsviken; and a nineteen-year-old boy knifed to death by a gang of skinheads in a metro carriage.

The printer started humming again and Sjöberg picked up the fresh printout. Here it was, the week-old news that had been nagging at the back of his mind: a prostitute and mother of three killed in her apartment in Skärholmen. That a prostitute should die at a young age was perhaps not that sensational; but it was not her youth he reacted to, but her age. She was forty-four, and now, when he read the article again, he found to his dismay that she had also been tortured before she was murdered.

He was just about to leave the copy room to go and

inform Sandén and Westman about his discovery when it started humming again, this time a fax. He stopped and waited for the machine to finish. Slowly, a full page was printed out – finally he was standing with a complete list of Hans Vannerberg's preschool classmates in his hand. He rushed into Sandén's office. As he crossed the threshold, Sandén was just finishing his call with the municipal official in Katrineholm. They called in Westman, and the three police officers crowded around the coveted list and quickly ascertained that Sjöberg's fears had been verified. Besides Hans Vannerberg, here too were Carina Ahonen and Lise-Lott Johansson, whom Sjöberg guessed had later married Nilsson. Another twenty children were on the list, but they recognized none of the other names.

'A serial killer,' Sandén sighed. 'I've never seen the like.'

Sjöberg held up Eriksson's printout in front of his colleagues.

'So what do you think of this? Einar has been productive.'

'Wonders never cease,' Sandén mumbled, but Sjöberg pretended not to hear him.

'A prostitute with three children who was found strangled in her apartment in Skärholmen a little over a week ago. She was forty-four years old and was tortured before she was murdered.'

'Call Skärholmen right away,' said Sandén.

'I'll do that. We'll let Einar continue with the press

for a while longer, but the two of you and Jamal will get started on this. I'll make the call, then I'll be back.'

He left the office confident that the important work they had before them would continue at a rapid pace. The question was whether that would be enough. Three, perhaps four forty-four-year-olds murdered in less than two weeks. Now it was crucial to get out into the field quickly to prevent further bloodshed.

The police in Skärholmen were also caught napping by the news. They gave him the name of the murdered woman, Ann-Kristin Widell, confirmed, as expected, that she was born in Katrineholm and gave her name as Andersson before she was married. Then he got a detailed account of the brutal murder. If possible, it was even more sadistic than the other three. The woman had been tied to the bed, perhaps raped – that was hard to determine, given the woman's occupation – and then had her hair and even her eyebrows cut off, was burned with cigarettes, assaulted vaginally with scissors, and then finally strangled. Sjöberg knew that it was urgent, very urgent, to find and bring in this maniac.

Four hours later, with the help of the woman at the registration office in Stockholm, and the personnel at local tax offices around the country with whom she put them in contact, they managed to locate all the children in Ingrid Olsson's preschool class from 1968/'69:

Eva Andersson, Sibeliusgatan 9, Katrineholm

Peter Broman, Rönngatan 7B, Katrincholm

Carina Clifton, Husabyvägen 9, Hägersten

Urban Edling, Hagelyckegatan 18, Gothenburg

Susanne Sjöö Edvinsson, Sibyllegatan 46,
Stockholm

Staffan Eklund, Lokevägen 57, Täby

Anette Grip, Vinsarp, Sparreholm

Carina Ahonen Gustavsson, Stora Vreta, Sigtuna

Kent Hagberg, Idrottsgatan 9, Katrineholm

Katarina Hallenius, Lötsjövägen 1A, Sundbyberg

Lena Hammarstig, Sköna Gertruds Väg 27,
Katrineholm

Stefan Hellqvist, Almstagatan 6, Norrköping

Gunilla Karlsson, Paal Bergs Vei 23, Oslo

Thomas Karlsson, Fleminggatan 26, Stockholm

Jan Larsson, Krönvägen 3, Saltsjö-Boo

Jukka Mänttäri, Sågmogatan 25, Katrineholm

Lisc-Lott Nilsson, Vallavägen 8, Katrineholm

Marita Saarelainen, Jägargatan 21A, Katrineholm

Eva-Lena Savic, Djupsundsgatan 24,
Norrköping

Annika Söderlund, Hagaberg Norrsätter,
Katrineholm

Christer Springfeldt, Sunnanvägen 10K, Lund

Hans Vannerberg, Trädskolevägen 46, Enskede
Gård

Ann-Kristin Widell, Ekholmsvägen 349,
Skärholmen

Four of the children were now dead, eight were still in or near their home town of Katrineholm, six were in the Stockholm area, two in Norrköping, and the remaining three were registered in Gothenburg, Lund and Oslo.

Sjöberg made an agreement with the other districts involved to immediately start working on the Stockholmers with Skärholmen; the Katrineholm police would take care of their eight, plus the individuals residing in Norrköping; while the Sigtuna police could wait for the time being. For the present, Oslo, Lund and Gothenburg were given the lowest priority in the investigation. Sjöberg had a strong feeling that they would find the person they were seeking in Stockholm. It was there that the first two murders had taken place, and that was where Ingrid Olsson lived. This suggested that the murderer was also in Stockholm, even if Sjöberg could not be sure of that. Given the circumstances, Oslo, Lund and Gothenburg seemed too far away to be acted upon right now.

Because the suspect was considered very dangerous, it was decided that the police would work in pairs when they visited the people on the list. They were to be armed as well. Sjöberg took a colleague from Skärholmen with him on a home visit in Täby. Sandén and Eriksson headed for Saltsjö-Boo, while Hamad and Westman made their way to Kungsholmen.

* * *

It was already Sunday, and tomorrow it would be that time again. Time to face reality, time to face his solitude. The true solitude that he found when he was with other people. He happened to think about Sofie, a young woman who had started in the post room a while ago. She was very overweight, but that did not seem to have any great significance nowadays. When he was growing up, a girl like that would have had a life not worth living, so Thomas instinctively felt sorry for her.

At noon on her first day at work, she had ended up right behind him in line in the cafeteria. After paying for his cabbage pudding, he took his tray and went to sit at his usual spot, at the far end of a table that could seat sixteen. To his surprise, she showed up immediately, and with a friendly smile asked if she could sit across from him. Naturally, he had no objections to that, but she had barely set her tray down before Britt-Marie – another co-worker – came up and placed a friendly hand on her shoulder and asked if she wouldn't like to sit with them instead. They, Thomas knew, were a clique of eight or ten people from the post room who usually had lunch together at a table further away. He had never been asked and Britt-Marie did not dignify him with even a glance this time either, but he had no difficulty understanding what was going on in Sofie's mind. Flattered to be asked and curious about her new co-workers, she thanked Britt-Marie for the invitation, took the tray and followed her over to their table. Before she left, she touchingly tilted her head and asked Thomas if he wouldn't like to join the others too. He was halfway out of his chair when he changed his mind. 'No, I always sit here,' he answered stupidly, whereupon Sofie left him with a slight shrug. Since then they had not so much as exchanged a word. However, he often saw her in lively conversation with their co-workers, conversation that usually changed from a normal tone of voice to whispers when he showed up.

At least at home he had TV, books and newspapers to keep him company. Above all, the happy voices and laughter on TV that got him out of bed and took him on adventures into the world, and into other people's living rooms. He loved the family shows, with songs and games and a cheering audience, hosts cracking jokes, and beautiful performers in glittering costumes. They made him forget his loneliness. They looked him in the eye and spoke right to him. Not many real people did that. They barely seemed to notice what little sense of self he felt he had.

In a little while a rerun of *Class Reunion* would start. A well-known person would get to see his old class-mates again for the first time in years and then compete with those classmates against another celebrity and his or her old class. Thomas thought it was fascinating the way the class sat there together, happy and enthusiastic, remembering all the fun they'd had in their schooldays. Wasn't it true that in every class there was someone like him? Maybe not. Maybe he was unique in that respect.

He would never appear in a programme like *Class Reunion*, and no one would miss him either. No one would even remember that he was in their class. He remembered all his classmates, all the kids from preschool. He could sit and look at old class photos and, without hesitation, rattle off the first and last names of every one of them. Yet he was sure that no one would recognize him. Strange, really, considering that he was the one who stood out, he was the one everyone noticed, who walked the funniest, wore the worst-looking clothes, said the stupidest things, was the worst at football, and was the weakest of the boys.

The programme had not started yet, so he watched the three-minute news broadcast. Suddenly, there was someone smiling at him again. A lovely smile in a tanned face, framed by curly, light-blonde hair.

'Carina Gustavsson,' said the news reporter, 'a forty-four-year-old flight attendant, was found on Friday evening murdered in her home outside Sigtuna.'

'Gustavsson?' Thomas murmured. 'Carina Ahonen . . .'

'The murder was preceded by a violent assault,' the reporter continued. 'According to the police, the victim was tortured. The suspect is still at large, but the investigation team has secured evidence and hopes to arrest the perpetrator within the coming days. The motive for the crime is still not known, but the police admit that the brutality suggests it may be a case of revenge.'

A segment followed with pictures from the crime

scene and an interview with the police department's spokesperson.

A wave of discomfort washed over him, and he suddenly felt completely powerless, almost paralysed. It felt as though the ground was starting to crack below him. He had to do something, not just sit here and wait. His eyes fluttered aimlessly between the TV and the cold, white textured wallpaper behind it. He looked down at his hands and noticed that they were shaking. His pulse was pounding in his ears and he was afraid for the first time in as long as he could remember. If you were already floundering at the bottom of society, there was nothing to fear. Any unhappiness was drowned in the great flood of misery that constituted life itself. But now, now he felt fear taking hold of him – fear and the compulsion to act. He decided it was time to seek out yet another person from among the shadows of his past.

Suddenly the doorbell rang. Startled, he jumped out of bed as if shot from a cannon. Without having time to think it through, he unlocked the door, regretting it before it had opened completely. Who could be looking for him at this time on a Sunday evening? Certainly not someone he had any desire to talk to. But now it was too late. They were standing there, a man and a woman in civilian clothes, waving police identification. How could he have been so stupid?

'Detective Assistant Petra Westman, Violent Crimes Unit, Hammarby Police,' the woman said authoritatively.

'Detective Assistant Jamal Hamad,' said the man.

Thomas said nothing. He just looked at them in shock, unable to make a sound.

'We're looking for Thomas Karlsson,' said the woman. 'Is that you?'

Thomas stood quietly for a moment, just staring at them.

'Yes,' he answered at last, but his voice did not hold. It sounded like a hiss.

He had not used his voice all weekend. Now he had to clear his throat, and as he did so, his face turned beetroot red.

'Yes,' he said again, with better control now. 'That's me.'

Most of all he wanted to disappear, but he stood there, with shaking hands and shifting gaze.

'May we come in for a moment?' the male police officer asked, looking serious.

Thomas did not answer, but took a few steps backwards, as if it was an order. To him, all words sounded like orders. The two police officers stepped into the little hallway and looked around suspiciously. The woman closed the door behind them.

'First of all, we would like to know what you were doing on the following days,' said the female police officer.

She listed a number of dates and times, but Thomas was not able to concentrate on what she was saying. He answered anyway, reflexively, which surprised him.

'I was at home,' he said, with his eyes directed down towards the brown hall mat. 'At home or at work.'

'Strange how you know that just like that,' said the female police officer. 'Wouldn't it be best to take a look at the calendar before you answer? Excuse me, but it doesn't give a particularly credible impression when you answer so quickly.'

'I don't have a calendar,' said Thomas, ashamed. 'On weekdays between six and four I'm either at work, or on my way there or back. Otherwise I'm at home. On weekends I'm always at home.'

'Is there anyone who can confirm this information?' the male police officer asked.

'Well, at work there must be someone who knows when I'm usually there . . .'

'And otherwise?'

'I guess it's hard to prove that I'm at home when I'm at home.'

'You don't see anyone?'

'No,' Thomas admitted. 'I'm mostly by myself.'

'Mostly?'

'Always, then. I'm always alone,' said Thomas suddenly, in a loud, clear voice – why, he didn't really know.

The two police officers exchanged a quick glance and the woman wrote something down on a small pad.

'Why are you asking me this?' Thomas asked.

'May we come all the way in?' the policeman asked.

Thomas nodded and went ahead of them into the

kitchen. The female police officer remained out in the hall, diligently making notes on her pad. They sat down at the kitchen table and Thomas looked hopelessly at his hands, which seemed to have a life of their own, on his lap.

'You have no family?' the policeman asked.

'No,' answered Thomas.

'Can you tell me a little about yourself?'

Thomas thought the policeman looked friendly, but his eyes were vigilant and wandered over the impersonal contents of the kitchen. From the hallway not a sound was heard. Was there so much to write about him?

'Please?' the policeman repeated.

Thomas did not dare look him in the eyes, but cleared his throat again and told, stammering, the little there was to tell about his empty life.

'Tell me about preschool,' the policeman encouraged him.

Thomas turned completely cold inside.

'Preschool?'

'Yes, exactly. I want to know what preschool was like.'

'I don't know. Preschool? That was a long time ago . . .'

'Were you happy? Who did you play with? Are you in touch with anyone from that time?'

'In touch? No, not in touch.'

Thomas wrung his hands, which were now completely sweaty. What should he say? It felt unpleasant to lie to the police, but you could not dress the truth in words, the truth was like a grey blanket over his entire existence.

'I must ask you to please answer my questions,' the policeman said commandingly, and his voice cut like a knife in Thomas's ears.

'Childhood . . . was a nice time. It was fun going to preschool. We drew . . . and played. I played with . . . no, I don't remember.'

'Why don't you look me in the eyes?' the policeman asked, not as friendly now. 'You're not lying to me, are you?'

'Lying? No. I played with . . . a girl whose name was Katarina,' Thomas lied.

They had never played, never even exchanged a word as far as he could remember. But what could he say?

'I would like to take your fingerprints,' said the policeman, setting something that looked like a stamp pad in front of him. 'All fingers, one print in each square here.'

He indicated a paper with ten printed squares. Thomas placed one hand on the table and the policeman touched it. His hand was so damp with sweat that the policeman immediately pulled his own hand back, and Thomas felt his face turning bright red again. His pulse was pounding in his ears and he wished they would leave him in peace now. But he obediently pressed his fingers against the inkpad and then against the rough surface of the paper, one at a time.

'There have been a number of brutal murders,' said the policeman, watching Thomas intently as he did what he was told.

Thomas felt like he was about to start crying and a hard, painful lump was growing in his throat. He said nothing, but tried as best he could to look the now almost-threatening man in the eyes.

'Four of your classmates from preschool have been murdered during the past two weeks,' the policeman continued, 'and we have reason to believe that you too may be in danger. For that reason we ask you to be on your guard and not to let any strange people into your apartment. We're finished now, but we'll be in touch again.'

He got up from the table and gave Thomas a little pat on the back. It was impossible to tell whether this was intended as a friendly, sympathetic or threatening gesture, but the feeling from the touch lingered on his skin under his shirt, as if he had been burned. He remained seated until he heard the outside door close behind the two police officers. Then he got up on wobbly legs, stumbled into his bedroom and lay down on the bed. He lay there for a long time, crying, and when the tension was finally released he fell asleep there, in the foetal position, with his clothes on.

Monday Morning

By eight o'clock on Monday morning everyone in the investigation team was already in the conference room for a review of Sunday evening's work. Hadar Rosén and Gabriella Hansson were also at the table, and their colleagues in Katrineholm, Skärholmen and Sigtuna were included by phone. The expectant silence was broken only by scattered yawns. Westman sought Rosén's gaze, but when she did catch it his eyes were completely neutral and revealed nothing about what he was thinking. Finally, Sjöberg began to speak.

'Welcome, everyone, this is Chief Inspector Conny Sjöberg, Hammarby. We'll have to speak loudly and clearly because we're on a conference call. Are you there in Katrineholm, Sigtuna and Skärholmen?'

Affirmative responses in raspy voices were heard from the speakers on the table.

'To start with, I hope that those of you who aren't in the Hammarby district have sent all the fingerprints to Stockholm by courier?'

This had been done, and the fingerprints would be in Hansson's hands at the lab later that morning.

'Then I propose that we go through the names on

the list in the order they appear and then have the party responsible for each person report on what they found out yesterday evening. Are you all with me?'

There were no objections, and the verbal reports were given in the proposed order. The names were dealt with one by one, and, as it turned out, almost all had been at home. Of the twenty-three individuals who had been in Ingrid Olsson's preschool class, four, of course, were dead. No attempt had been made to get hold of the three living in Gothenburg, Oslo and Lund, and two who were still registered in Katrineholm. One person living in Stockholm could not be reached. In summary, thirteen individuals had been questioned the evening before, and six had not yet been found.

Of those the police had been able to speak to, the majority were completely average people, who reacted as expected to the visit by the police and did not seem to have anything to hide. A few had scattered memories from their time in preschool, but most of those questioned recalled little or nothing. A few of those who were still living in their home town knew, or knew of, each other, but none recalled that they had also gone to the same preschool.

One of the men who lived in Katrineholm, Peter Broman on Rönngatan, turned out to be an alcoholic, and when the police barged into his apartment a party with some twenty people was going on. They had not welcomed the appearance of the police and a fight broke out, but fortunately no one was injured. The man had been convicted of a number of petty thefts, as well as other similar violations, but never of any violent crimes.

When they came to Thomas Karlsson, it was Hamad who initially spoke for himself and Westman.

'Thomas Karlsson reacted very strangely to our visit. One moment it was as though he was petrified, and the next moment he was shaking like a leaf. He was sweating profusely and incoherent. He had a hard time understanding and answering our questions. Would not look us in the eyes. As we were leaving I thought he was about to start crying. To start with, he claimed not to remember anything from preschool, but then it came out that he used to play with someone named Katarina. That must be this Katarina Hallenius in Hallonbergen.'

'We haven't got hold of her yet, but we'll try to confirm that with her when we do,' Sandén interjected.

'I got the feeling he was lying,' Hamad continued. 'But it wasn't just that. He was, like . . . really strange too, don't you think, Petra?'

'Yes, he was,' Westman agreed. 'I don't think he's really right in the head.'

'And he has no friends either,' said Hamad. 'No family. No one who could confirm his whereabouts at the time of the murders. "I'm always alone," he almost screamed at one point.'

'Does the guy have a job?' asked Sjöberg.

'He works in the post room at a company in Järfälla. We'll have to check what they have to say about him there. In summary, he was a very odd duck, this Thomas Karlsson.'

'We took prints of his shoes,' said Westman. 'He had one pair of shoes in the hall. He had almost no possessions. The apartment was nearly bare. No pictures, no flowers, no curtains, nothing. A few pieces of furniture, but just the bare necessities, a few books and magazines, that was it.'

'Did he appear threatening in any way?' Sjöberg asked. 'Is he capable of murder?'

'He was absolutely not threatening,' Hamad replied. 'On the contrary, he almost gave the impression of being scared to death. Is he capable of murder? What do I know about what goes on in his mind? Fear can be a reason to kill people. No idea.'

'Okay, he seems to be our likeliest candidate, so far anyway. Now we'll wait for Hansson's analysis of fingerprints and shoe prints. We'll continue the hunt for the remaining people and Sigtuna will make contact with Oslo, Lund and Gothenburg. Now let's break. Thanks, everyone.'

Sjöberg ended the conference call and Hansson gathered up the fingerprint samples that the officers who were present had collected the evening before. She also took Westman's competently acquired shoeprint with her to the laboratory. The remaining police officers, in the company of Prosecutor Rosén, lingered in the conference room for a while longer.

'Now we have a few hours' wait ahead of us before Bella gets back to us with the initial analysis from the lab,' Sjöberg began. 'I propose that Eriksson run all these individuals against the crime register and so on to see what we can find on any of them. Westman will make another visit to Ingrid Olsson. Now that we have all the students' names, perhaps we can bring some dormant memories to life. Go through each and every one and try to get her to remember anything from that year. Hamad and Sandén will continue to search for the remaining person, Katarina Hallenius in Hallonbergen.'

'This Thomas Karlsson,' said Rosén, 'shouldn't we assign a couple of men to keep an eye on him?'

'I think it's too early at this point,' Sjöberg replied. 'We'll wait for the lab results first, and make a decision on that later. We don't know anything about him. Maybe he's just shy and unsure of himself.'

Rosén agreed and the meeting was over. Petra once again tried to make silent contact with the prosecutor. He took his time gathering his papers, without raising his eyes. When he was finally ready, everyone had left the room except Petra, who had waited behind. He looked at her in silence for a few seconds and then said, revealing nothing by his facial expression or tone of voice, 'This is more important. Do what you have to do. At five we'll meet in my office.'

* * *

When he woke up the next morning he wasn't sure where he was at first. In his dream he had walked on a long pier. Below the pier there was presumably water, but you could not see it because a thick layer of fog covered it and billowed up around him like big clouds of smoke. It was twilight and cold, he had on a red quilted jacket, ski pants and a pair of clumsy black ski boots with blue laces. With every breath he took, steam came out of his nostrils. Behind him he heard the children's voices. They did not see him in the fog, but they knew he was out there because the voices were coming closer. The end of the pier could not be seen, but as he walked and walked it became clear that the pier was very long. Suddenly, there was no longer anything under his feet and he fell, arms flailing, into the cold, damp void. He opened his eyes and found, to his surprise, that it was completely light around him. He lay there quietly for a while, waiting for reality to return to him. The dream slowly released its grip and he discovered that he was on top of the covers with his clothes on. The lights in the room were on and the blind was not pulled down. He did not move, did not even look at the clock, just lay there for a long time, completely relaxed, looking into himself.

At last hunger got the upper hand. His stomach growled discontentedly for breakfast, and he stretched and sat up on the edge of the bed. He could see through the window that it was already light outside, which meant he would be late for work. That didn't matter, because he didn't intend to go there anyway. Today he was going to look up a woman he had not seen in a very, very long time. Just thinking about it caused a surge in his belly, as if he were riding a roller coaster.

* * *

She took hesitant steps on the wet pavement, as if she was waiting for something or as if every step hurt. Now and then she stopped and poked with her foot among some old, rotting leaves, or in one of the small, blackened snowdrifts that were scattered reminders of yesterday's winter weather. In one hand she carried a small suitcase; the other was plunged deep in the pocket of her coat. Her collar was folded up as protection against the cold wind. As she passed the familiar black iron gate she stopped and stood for a long time, gazing across the large garden with its fruit trees. Although it was midday, the outdoor lights were on and the old pink house looked welcoming, despite the high, dense hedge that surrounded it. Then she started walking again, with the same slow steps, but she did not go far. After fifty metres she turned and slowly walked back to the iron gate, where she remained standing, deep in thought.

Thomas followed her, with some excitement. He had not seen her in many years, but she was not all that different. Soon he would get up the courage to make himself known, but first he wanted to watch her for a while.

He was well hidden. He could not be seen at all from his position crouched behind a car parked across and further down the street, even if the woman were to look unexpectedly in that direction. She walked around a little more and finally she laboriously opened the heavy gate and stepped on to the gravel path that led to the house. Thomas got up from his hiding place and crossed the little street with aching knees. Resolutely, he followed the pavement towards the gate. Just as he was leaning down to avoid some low-hanging tree branches, he heard a car engine behind him. He turned reflexively to look at the car and found, to his amazement, that it was the policewoman from last night who was behind the wheel. She slowed down, came up alongside him and rolled down the window. Thomas felt the fear from yesterday come over him again and, without knowing why, he started running.

* * *

Petra Westman was in the car on her way to Ingrid Olsson's house in Gamla Enskede, worried about what would be said in Hadar Rosén's office at the end of the day. She felt extremely uncertain about him. He was not the type to show his feelings much. Unless he was furious. Either he would recommend that the disciplinary review board give her a warning, or he would accommodate her request and have Peder Fryhk arrested. Either alternative was a good enough reason for nail-biting, a habit she was not prone to. On the other hand, her stomach was in an uproar and she had already been to the toilet more times this morning than she normally would all day.

As she turned on to picturesque Åkerbärsvägen, she was able to put aside her anxieties temporarily and thought instead that this is how she would like to live one day. In a beautiful old house with a mature garden and abundant climbing roses, a small vegetable patch to potter in, and a lawn for the dog to run around. And maybe children too, if she ever had any. Nice neighbours you could sit with under the fruit trees and drink wine. And organize barbecues and play croquet. At this time in November it looked empty and deserted, but in the spring and summer the area would liven up, you could be sure of that. People in minimal clothing, and kids playing football and skipping on the little street.

Suddenly she saw a man crouching on the pavement. He looked familiar, but before she could think about how she knew him he turned towards her and looked her right in the eyes. It was that character from yesterday,

Thomas Karlsson! What business did he have in this neighbourhood? Instinctively, she drove up to him and rolled down the window. Before she could open her mouth, he took to his heels and started running. She jumped out of the car and took off after him. He had a lead of fifteen or twenty metres, and she thought that she probably should have driven after him instead, but it was too late for that now. He raced up the street, without turning around. He was a man and she was a woman, but she was in good shape and had always been a good runner. Despite her bulky winter clothes, she started gaining on him, but she had no idea what she would do with him if she caught up. She had left her service pistol in the cupboard at the police station – no orders had been issued on being armed for a visit to Ingrid Olsson. She had a pair of handcuffs in the glove compartment of the unmarked police car, but how would she get to them?

She caught him up before the crest of the hill. She threw herself at him with all her weight, and he fell flat on his face on the wet asphalt. She straddled him and wrenched his arms behind his back. Then she caught her breath for a few moments before she took her mobile out of the inside pocket of her jacket. She entered Sjöberg's number, and he answered before she even heard the ring.

'It's Petra,' she panted into the phone. 'I've caught Thomas Karlsson outside Ingrid Olsson's house. I need reinforcements, quickly.'

Then she ended the call and put the phone back in her pocket.

'You are arrested on suspicion of the murders of Hans Vannerberg, Ann-Kristin Widell, Lise-Lott Nilsson and Carina Ahonen Gustavsson. Now lie quietly and calm down, do you understand?'

* * *

Thomas said nothing and did not move but, with tears streaming down his face, he felt the icy cold of the asphalt spreading from the skin on his face and into his body, where it finally squeezed his heart until only a sharp little piece of ice remained.

Twelve minutes later he was sitting in handcuffs, shaking with cold, in the back seat of a police car.

Monday Afternoon

Once again Sjöberg was at his desk with a sandwich in front of him, and once again he had a hard time finishing his meagre lunch. Some constables were now in a car on their way to the city with a suspected serial killer in the back seat. A forty-four-year-old man who had never been convicted before, who had never been in trouble with the law, had never stood out in any way, but instead lived a quiet life in solitude in a little apartment on Kungsholmen. He had always paid his bills on time, never been in contact with the social services or mental health system, and yet he was being held as a suspect in no fewer than four sadistic murders.

This was astonishing. What could have happened to bring out such a dark side of him? The victims were people he most likely hadn't seen since he was a child, a very young child at that.

When news of the arrest reached Sjöberg, after first arranging reinforcements for Westman, he called Sandén and Hamad in from Hallonbergen. They were still searching for the only person on the list who had not yet been located. By now they were presumably in their car, on the way back to the police station, preparing for the initial interrogation of Thomas Karlsson, who would be charged as a suspect in the murders. Sjöberg felt tense as he waited for the confrontation with Karlsson, and wondered how he would manage to handle Karlsson's alleged fear and nervousness. Perhaps they ought to have a psychologist on hand? No, that sort of thing would have to wait. The main thing now was to prevent any further victims by ensuring that they had indeed arrested the guilty party.

The phone rang yet again – all morning he had been flooded with calls from colleagues involved in the investigation around the country, journalists wanting an update on the developments in the Vannerberg case, the prosecutor, the police chief and so on – but he answered dutifully anyway. It was Mia, his sister-in-law, who wanted to speak to him.

'I've done some research, as we agreed, and now I have a little information that I think will interest you.'

Sjöberg had forgotten, in the general confusion after Petra Westman's breathless voice had requested reinforcements, about having asked his sister-in-law for help. The idea of trying to form an impression of the atmosphere in Ingrid Olsson's preschool class almost forty years earlier felt superfluous now.

'Go on,' he said politely. 'We've arrested a suspect for the murders, but tell me anyway. I'll be seeing him in a little while, so it might be good to have something a bit more concrete to go on.'

'It's not Thomas Karlsson you've arrested, by any chance?'

Sjöberg remained silent for a moment, but then said, 'I can't answer that.'

'Of course you can, otherwise I can't tell you what I've found out. And it will interest you, because I knew his name, right?'

'Okay, okay,' Sjöberg sighed. 'Now tell me.'

'I talked with *that* friend in Katrineholm I love to talk about childhood memories with. Just because he has such a good memory. He's the same age as me and it turned out that his little brother, Staffan Eklund, was actually in that preschool class. My friend and his mother both remembered things from that time. On the other hand, his little brother didn't remember a thing. The police had already been in contact with him, but he was completely blank.'

'Get to the point, please,' Sjöberg encouraged her impatiently.

'Okay, here it is. At that time they lived in a pretty bad area. They were building a house and were going to move away from there as soon as the new house was finished, but for the time being little brother was in that preschool. There was evidently a crowd of really nasty kids and his mum was not at all happy about his playmates. They got into fights and misbehaved and two of the children, above all, distinguished themselves as real brats. Guess what their names were?'

'No, tell me.'

'Hans and Ann-Kristin.'

'You don't say . . .'

'Hans and Ann-Kristin dominated that group of children completely and stirred up the others against a couple of poor things they put at the bottom of the pecking order. One of them was Thomas Karlsson, the other was a girl, and they both got beaten up every single day. And the whole class was in on it, Staffan too, to his mother's great disappointment. Probably due to peer pressure, he couldn't really see what was right and wrong. They did horrible things to those children, each worse than the last. Besides beating them black and blue, once they almost drowned one of them, they cut off their hair, ripped their clothes; they laid one of them in front of a car on the street. There were teeth knocked out, and serious mental abuse along with it. Can you imagine? They were only six years old!'

'What kind of person do you become if you're subjected to such things?' Sjöberg asked.

'In a small town like Katrineholm it works this way,' Mia continued. 'Once you've been labelled, it's like it can't be washed off. I imagine that the bullying wouldn't have stopped; instead, it would have carried on into school and presumably after, in some form or other, until one day you move away. So it's hard to rehabilitate yourself. Maybe these children started it, but then others would have taken over and carried on the pattern.'

'Carina Ahonen then, where does she fit into the picture?'

'She seems to have been the one really pulling the strings. A sharp little doll who never used force herself, but who was the initiator of the mental terror. She was the one who decided who was good and who was bad, what was right and what was wrong. Everyone adored her, adults and children alike, but in reality she was the cheerleader and opinion-maker. In a negative sense.'

'It sounds like we're talking about a Mafia organization, not about six-year-old children,' Sjöberg sighed.

'People are always the same. The world runs on power and violence, at all levels.'

'And Lise-Lott?'

'A real ruffian. A stupid lackey with a great need for attention. I guess she behaved like most of the others, only more so.'

'And Ingrid Olsson did nothing, I'm guessing?'

'Exactly right,' Mia answered. 'Staffan's mother tried to talk to her a number of times about the unpleasant atmosphere among the children, but she got nowhere. Ingrid Olsson thought her job was to watch over and stimulate the children during the time they were at pre-school. There was no trouble on the preschool grounds and she could not control what the children said to each other. What happened outside the gates when they left was not her responsibility. The children and their parents had to manage on their own, she thought. Poor Thomas had no rights at all. At last, almost forty years later, I guess he decided to take matters into his own hands. What was he supposed to do?'

'Nothing,' said Sjöberg.

*

Thomas Karlsson was a man of normal build, some-what below average height, with what might be called an ordinary appearance. He had brown hair, several weeks past due for a haircut, and was dressed in blue jeans and a blue cotton shirt. Sjöberg introduced him-self and then sat down in the interrogation room to wait for Sandén, studying the suspect in silence. He did not seem to notice the scrutiny, but sat looking down at his hands. Nor did he appear particularly frightened or nervous, as Sjöberg had expected. Dejected, if any-thing. He had mournful blue eyes and his posture suggested resignation.

When Sandén stepped into the room he looked up, shifted a little in the uncomfortable chair and straight-ened up.

'So your name is Thomas Karlsson,' Sjöberg began. 'This is Inspector Jens Sandén and we are here to question you about the murders of Hans Vannerberg, Ann-Kristin Widell, Lise-Lott Nilsson and Carina Ahonen Gustavsson. Do you know the people I've named?'

Thomas raised his head and looked him in the eyes for the first time.

'Yes,' he answered. 'We went to the same preschool.'

'Why did you murder them?'

When Sjöberg got no answer, he continued.

'This is what's called an initial interrogation. This is the first questioning that we have with a suspect immediately after the arrest. Later there will be more questioning, and then you have the right to have a lawyer or legal representative with you. Do you understand what I'm saying?'

'Yes.'

'Do you admit that you are guilty of these crimes?'

Thomas hesitated for a moment, then answered.

'No.'

'Why do you think we've arrested you, then?'

'Don't know,' Thomas replied.

'What were you doing outside Ingrid Olsson's house?' Sjöberg asked.

'I was afraid something would happen to her.'

'Indeed?' said Sjöberg. 'But I'm not, because you're sitting here with us, safely in custody. There won't be any more murders. Are you sorry that your friends from preschool are dead?'

Thomas did not reply, but instead sat drumming his fingertips against each other. There was a knock on the door and Sandén went to open it. Westman waved him out into the corridor and their whispering voices could be heard, but not what they were saying.

'That was a difficult time for you, so I hear,' Sjöberg continued.

Thomas looked at him in bewilderment, without saying anything.

'Preschool,' said Sjöberg. 'I've heard you didn't have such a great time there. Can you tell me what they did to you?'

'They hit me,' said Thomas.

'All children fight. It doesn't sound all that bad.'

Thomas blushed. Sjöberg observed him in silence and Sandén came back into the room and whispered something in his ear.

'But now you've been able to hit back,' Sjöberg said quietly.

He saw the blood vessels on the man's neck become visible. Perhaps there was an underlying rage festering below the insecure surface.

'Tell us what you were doing at Ingrid Olsson's on Monday evening two weeks ago, when Hans Vannerberg was murdered there.'

No answer. Sjöberg put on a cunning smile and continued in a silky voice.

'We have positive evidence that you were there. We have found prints of your shoes in the garden, and soon we will have verified your fingerprints on the murder weapon. You've already lied to us once. You maintained that you were at home that evening, but we know you were on Åkerbärsvägen in Enskede. What were you doing there?'

Thomas's face was now beetroot red, but he collected himself and answered the question.

'I was following Hans Vannerberg.'

'Okay then. You were following Hans Vannerberg. And then?' Sjöberg smiled triumphantly.

'Nothing. He went into the house and I waited outside, but he never came out, so I went home.'

'Yes, that is a plausible explanation,' said Sjöberg

sarcastically. 'But soon we will have identified the fingerprints on the murder weapon and what will you say then?'

Sjöberg received no answer, but the eyes he met were close to terrified. Sjöberg did not give up, but pressed on with another question.

'Why did you follow him in the first place?'

'I ran into him on the street. I was curious.'

'And Ann-Kristin Widell, you just followed her too?'

This was taking a chance and Sjöberg knew it, but it hit the mark.

'I went to see her.'

'Just like that? On the evening of her murder?'

Thomas nodded in reply.

'Curious about her too?'

'Yes.'

Sjöberg could not believe his ears. Until now they had had no traces of Thomas Karlsson in Skärholmen and no witness reports, but he willingly admitted that he was there.

'And what did you see then? Perhaps a savage murder? That you yourself committed?'

Thomas twisted his fingers nervously in his lap.

'Visitors,' he answered. 'There were a lot of people who came to visit that evening.'

'What kind of visitors were they? Murderers?'

After a moment's hesitation, Thomas met Sjöberg's gaze.

'Customers,' he said curtly, lowering his gaze again.

Sjöberg inspected the quiet man for a while without saying anything. Sandén, who until now had not opened his mouth, took over the questioning.

'And then we have Lise-Lott Nilsson, what do you know about her?'

'She's dead.'

'You didn't by chance happen to be there too, when she was murdered?'

'No. I read about it in the newspaper.'

'You're lying through your teeth,' said Sandén, 'and before long we will have identified your fingerprints at all four murder scenes. Then you can say whatever you like, but you can expect life imprisonment. Don't you have anything reasonable to say to put an end to this meaningless interrogation?'

A shake of Thomas's head was the only reply, whereupon Sjöberg declared the interview over and requested that Thomas Karlsson be transferred to the jail.

* * *

Thomas did not know where his sense of calm had come from, but in the car en route to the jail an unexpected feeling of security suddenly appeared. Even though he had just been sitting in a sterile interrogation room, held for a number of very serious crimes, there were people who cared and worried about him. The police officers saw him and took responsibility for him. They talked to him and they would see to it that he got to eat and sleep, that he had clean clothes and did no harm to himself. True, they despised him, but he was a person and he had aroused their interest. He felt like a small child being rocked in a secure embrace – no one could do him more harm than he did to himself. The contemptuous condescension and insinuating questions of the police gave him value. He was a significant person now.

But during the walk to the jail cell, where he would spend the hours until the lawyer arrived, something happened that made him reconsider. Thomas, in handcuffs, and the two constables escorting him were guided through the corridors of the Kronoberg prison by a burly guard. They passed a social room, where some young men sat playing cards. One of the men called out to the guard, wanting to know who was with him.

'A new friend,' the guard answered curtly, without stopping.

For just a fraction of a second Thomas met the young man's gaze, but that was enough for things to go wrong. Before anyone realized what was happening, he threw himself forward and head-butted Thomas, making him fall to the floor. The guard, who was considerably larger than the assailant, overpowered him without difficulty, while both police officers brusquely hauled Thomas up from the floor, without taking into account that he was injured. Blood was gushing from his nose and down on to his clothes. When his head cleared, it occurred to him that, in their eyes, he was at least as dangerous as the man who had attacked him. He also realized that he would not cope well with being in prison. It would almost certainly be ten times worse than preschool.

* * *

Sjöberg left the interrogation room feeling dissatisfied. He could not get a handle on this peculiar man. He had made no effort to either defend or explain himself. Maybe he wanted to go to prison. Was he one of those criminals who wanted to show off and brag about his evil deeds? His story was very strange too. That he admitted following Hans Vannerberg to Ingrid Olsson's house was one thing, since they had evidence that he had been there, but why did he admit that he had also gone to see Ann-Kristin Widell? And why didn't he admit that he had done the same with Lise-Lott Nilsson and Carina Ahonen Gustavsson? The story didn't make sense. Everything seemed clear, but Thomas Karlsson's conduct in the interrogation room was puzzling.

'A sick bastard,' Sandén said, when they were sitting in Sjöberg's office a few minutes later, each with a cup of coffee.

'Do you think so?' said Sjöberg.

'Of course he's sick, he's killed four people.'

'What if he hasn't though? What if the fingerprints don't match?'

'Of course they'll match. You don't mean to say you're in doubt?'

'No,' answered Sjöberg, 'of course it's him. But he behaved really strangely during the interrogation, in my opinion.'

'In what way?'

'He admits that he's been at two of the murder scenes at the time of the murders, but not at the other two.'

'Maybe he's confused. Maybe he doesn't know what he's done.'

'You don't believe that,' said Sjöberg dismissively. 'On the one hand, he's afraid and nervous, on the other, he does nothing to deny the accusations. Or even tell lies about mitigating circumstances.'

'I guess he hasn't found his "true self",' Sandén suggested.

'No, apparently not,' Sjöberg answered thoughtfully. 'He had a difficult upbringing.'

'Where'd you get that from?' Sandén asked with surprise.

Sjöberg told him about his sister-in-law's private surveillance and Sandén gestured that his lips were sealed.

'Poor devil!' he exclaimed when Sjöberg was done. 'Makes you wonder how that poor girl has managed in life. If he turned out to be a serial killer, what might have become of her.'

'Probably just a normal, peaceful person,' thought Sjöberg. 'Many children have a hard time, but strangely most of them turn out human anyway.'

Their conversation was interrupted when the phone on Sjöberg's desk rang. It was Lennart Josefsson, the neighbour of Ingrid Olsson who had previously testified that two men passed by outside his window on Åkerbärsvägen the evening of the murder. This time he wanted to report that an unknown woman had passed by on the street outside several times that morning, finally entering Ingrid Olsson's gate. Josefsson had also seen the arrest of Thomas Karlsson, and for that reason he had hesitated to call in about the strange woman for quite a while, but ultimately decided to do so. Sjöberg thanked him for the tip, but dismissed the whole thing as irrelevant to the investigation. It was probably only Margit Olofsson visiting Ingrid Olsson to make sure she was coping properly back in her own home.

The phone immediately rang again. This time it was Hansson at the forensic lab with the information that Thomas Karlsson's fingerprints did not match any of those at the murder scenes. She had been able to determine that all the samples belonged to the same person, but this person was not Thomas Karlsson. This hit both policemen and the entire investigation like a cold shower. With the conversation with Lennart Josefsson fresh in his memory, Sjöberg immediately came to the conclusion that the two men who had been observed outside Ingrid Olsson's house on the evening of the murder must have been Thomas Karlsson and an additional person who was in league with him.

During the following hours, while they waited for

Thomas Karlsson's lawyer to arrive at the police station, further reports came in from the forensics lab. None of the fingerprints taken from the people questioned from Ingrid Olsson's old preschool class matched those at the four murder scenes.

* * *

Katarina had not yet taken off her coat. She was sitting on her suitcase in the hall, playing the scene over again in her mind. How many times she had done so she did not know, but one thing was certain: this was not what she had imagined. This was not the way it should end, alone again, misunderstood.

After wandering back and forth on the street for a while, she had finally gathered up her courage, and went through the gate and up to the house to ring the doorbell. Her heart was beating like a piston in her chest, but she was optimistic. All her hope rested on her old preschool teacher. Miss Ingrid was fond of children, so she must be fond of people. She would understand – console her and understand. Naturally everything would have been different if Ingrid had been at home when she had first sought her out, before everything that had happened in the past few weeks. Then, perhaps, Ingrid would have been able to stop her, put her on a better path. She could have helped her find the strength to forgive and go on. But she had not been home. Katarina kept the house under surveillance for days, but Ingrid had not shown up. So she had been forced to go to work, without Miss Ingrid's approval. And for that reason there was a little seed of doubt inside her when the door opened.

'Yes?'

How beautiful she was. She had cut her long hair and had a youthful short hairdo instead. Miss Ingrid looked enquiringly at her with clear eyes, behind a pair of glasses that suited her finely chiselled face. The wrinkles of age were well placed and gave her a distinguished expression.

'My name is Katarina. Katarina Hallenius. You were my preschool teacher many years ago. I would really like to talk to you.'

Ingrid inspected her without saying anything.

'May I come in for a moment?' asked Katarina.

'I don't know. I've been ill and –'

'I can help you. I've been looking forward to seeing you, Miss Ingrid.'

The gaze that met hers was a trifle sceptical, but that was not strange after so many years. She must get the chance to show who she was, so she took a step closer to the older woman. Ingrid took a step back and Katarina interpreted this as an invitation and entered the hall. Ingrid backed up a few more steps.

'What's happened to you?' asked Katarina.

'I broke my hip. Old people . . .'

'You're not old,' Katarina smiled. 'But I can take care of you.'

She carefully closed the door behind her and set her suitcase down on the floor. Then she took an old photograph out of a compartment on the outside of the suitcase.

'Look here!' she said happily, placing herself close by her old teacher. 'Here I am. Do you remember me now?'

She felt that Ingrid Olsson's gaze was still directed towards her instead of the picture and gave her yet another smile.

'Look!'

Ingrid did as she was told.

'No, I must confess that I don't recognize you. But I just can't –'

'Wait, I'll help you,' Katarina interrupted and fetched the stool, which she placed behind Ingrid. 'Sit down.'

Katarina sat down across from her on her suitcase and, with some hesitation, Ingrid sat down too. She said nothing and still did not return the smile, so Katarina decided to start her story.

She told about Hans and Ann-Kristin and all the other children. She told about terror, mistreatment and loneliness and what life had been like after the difficult time at the preschool. Not for a moment did she blame her old teacher for all the terrible things she had been subjected to. Yet Ingrid made only one brief comment during Katarina's hour-long monologue.

'What happened outside the preschool was not my responsibility. In my classroom there was no fighting.'

Katarina tried to get her old teacher to understand

that it was not just about hitting and kicking, but about the whole game. She had a hard time holding back the tears, and at one point placed her hand on Ingrid's, but the teacher resolutely lifted it away with a pained expression.

Gradually, Katarina started to worry that she wouldn't be able to get Miss Ingrid to take an interest in what she had to say. In a final, desperate attempt to get her to react, Katarina talked about what had driven her to kill Hans Vannerberg, and how after that she had also looked up Ann-Kristin, Lise-Lott and Carina Ahonen.

Ingrid sat stiff as a poker on the stool and observed her in silence, without changing her facial expression.

'May I sleep here?' asked Katarina, when the words came to an end. 'I'm so terribly tired.'

'No,' said Miss Ingrid. 'You may not.'

A long time had now passed since silence had fallen in the hall. The two women sat quietly, observing each other. The suitcase, whose only contents were a washbag, a couple of changes of clothes and a few diaries, started to be uncomfortable to sit on. Slowly, it occurred to Katarina that there was nothing for her here either. No warmth, no consolation. Her beloved preschool teacher did not remember her, and obviously had no interest in lightening her burden. Her indifference to Katarina's life story was apparent. And indifference was a deadly sin.

* * *

Ingrid was lying on the sofa in the living room. Her wrists ached from the tightly pulled cord that rubbed against her bare skin, and the blood was pounding in her bruised fingers. Her feet were also tied together, but the pain in them was not as noticeable. It was very wet underneath her and she shivered quietly, lying there in the cooling urine.

'I don't intend to harm you,' Katarina had said. 'Just like you, I don't intend to do anything. I do intend to let you lie here until you rot, in your own filth. You'll get no food, no water and no medicine. I'm not going to torment you; the torment will come from yourself. Your hunger, your thirst, your bad conscience, your needs of one kind or another. I'm not going to provide for your needs. You're your own responsibility, aren't you? That's how you see it, true?'

At first Ingrid was too dazed to take in what the woman was saying, but now hours had passed and she'd had plenty of time to think and listen. How long did it take to starve to death? That probably didn't matter; the hunger would gradually disappear until at last only a great, unbearable thirst would remain. How long could you live without liquids? A week, two weeks? She still felt no hunger, but her mouth was completely dry, so dry that she found it difficult to speak. But right now it was the pain in her wrists and the unpleasant pounding of the pulse in her fingers that she was most aware of. It felt as if her hands were going to burst and she wished they would simply go numb.

At first she had not understood who the unpleasant woman was and what she wanted, but Katarina talked uninterruptedly for an hour and at last the words sank in. She was one of the children in the murdered Hans Vannerberg's preschool class thirty-seven years earlier. She insisted that she had been badly treated by the other children and Ingrid's own guilt in the whole thing rested on the fact that she, in her capacity as teacher, had taken no steps to stop the so-called bullying.

The woman was obviously completely out of her mind, but even so, Ingrid could not help feeling rather unjustly treated. She had always done her best at her job, been friendly and nice to the children, and she felt that the children had liked her. She worked hard for many years at the preschool, taught the children to sew and make things, sang with them and played games. Of course, they could be a little annoying at times, and bickered with each other, but when Ingrid had been present there were never any fights or other mistreatment of the type that Katarina described.

Of course, she had no control over what happened after the children left the preschool. You have to draw the line somewhere, and in this case it was simple: the line was at the gate at noon, when the children's day at the preschool was at an end.

'You knew what was going on, you could have talked to the children,' Katarina said.

Ingrid had no memory of any mistreatment, but in any case she answered, 'I was a preschool teacher, not a therapist. Or a child psychologist, for that matter.' But this did not go over well. After an unexpected outburst of complete madness, Katarina put her on the couch, hands and feet bound.

She had roared that Ingrid was a human being after all, and as such, you don't just stand by and watch other people – children – destroy one another. Ingrid had not made any objection, but inside she knew that, in fact, this was the only way to survive. Even as a little girl, Ingrid had learned not to poke her nose in other people's business. When her father resorted to clenched fists against her mother, she realized that it was best for all concerned if she stayed out of the way. It was a wicked and nasty world they lived in, but if everyone minded their own business, existence would be more tolerable. I am the forge of my own happiness, she thought, and you are yours, Katarina. Of course, she did not say this out loud, but she knew this was the way life worked.

The ache in her hands only increased and it was now beginning to feel unbearable.

'Please, Katarina, can't you loosen the cord a little?' she begged pitifully. 'It hurts so terribly.'

'It hurts to live,' Katarina replied with a smile. 'You're the forge of your own happiness, so make the best of the situation.'

The insane woman had read her thoughts and obviously had no intention of doing anything to relieve her torment. Ingrid felt the stealthy onset of hunger. Her interest in food had ceased long ago. Food simply had no taste any more, but even so, she felt hunger pangs like anyone else and would need to eat a little something so as not to become confused and nauseated. Now she was lying here completely helpless, hungry, thirsty and in severe pain, and it would only get worse. Katarina said she intended to live in her house until her time was up, until Ingrid's time in the hourglass had run out.

There was no hope that anyone would come to visit, or even miss her. She was completely alone in the world, and she felt the tears streaming as she thought about that. She did not know when she had last cried – it must have been many years ago, perhaps when her sister passed away. Now she was alone, no husband, no children, no parents or siblings still alive. The few friends she had had over the years had grown old or disappeared, for one reason or another. She had left many of them behind, of course, in the move to Stockholm. It was hard to get old, hard to be alone. No one to talk to, no one to do things with, no one to come to her rescue in a situation like this.

* * *

Katarina was in the kitchen inspecting the contents of Ingrid Olsson's freezer. It mostly contained bread, but also apples and plums parboiled in sugar, and sweetened berries. There were also some bags of homemade meatballs and casseroles. In the refrigerator there were large quantities of potatoes, and in the pantry she found rice and jars of preserves. She would not go hungry; there was food enough to last for weeks.

When she thought about how long this might take, she felt restless. On the one hand, she had an incentive to get the whole thing over with as quickly, and as painfully, as possible, but on the other hand, she knew that the longer it went on, the greater the torment would be for Miss Ingrid. The most important element here was prolonging it, magnifying the old woman's certainty that it would end in death and the uncertainty of how long it would take. That had become the purpose of it all, that it would drag on and on, and that she herself would not take any action.

'Set an example,' she said to herself.

The choice of words was ridiculous because it was hardly worth setting an example for someone who would soon be dead, but even so that was what she would do. She was forced to hold back and not do anything rash that she would regret later.

She peeled some potatoes and put them in a saucepan, which she set on the stove. Then she rummaged around for an old cast-iron frying pan and put in a dollop of margarine. She watched as the margarine slowly melted, and as she shook the pan a little, it started sizzling. The bag of meatballs was rock hard, but by using a bread knife she was able to hack a few pieces loose, which she rolled down into the cooking fat. From the living room she thought she heard smothered sobs, which made her happy, even as the self-pitying and monotonous noise irritated her. There was a popping sound in the pan as the ice melted and a drop of boiling-hot margarine splashed up and hit her in the eye.

Before she knew what she was doing, she was out in the living room and found herself straddling the old woman. She struck her with clenched fists again and again on the face, after which she took hold of her grey hair with both hands and forcefully banged her head against the armrest. There was a crack somewhere inside the thin body below her and Ingrid screamed in pain.

'Be quiet now, you old hag!' Katarina screamed.

Ingrid winced and was silent.

'This is taking too long, much too long! I don't know if I can put up with your ugly mug much longer. So die already! Die, so we're finished!'

It seemed like the old woman was on the verge of fainting. It was probably the broken hip that was so painful.

'Say something!' Katarina roared, continuing to shake her. 'Don't ignore me when I talk to you!'

'You told me to be quiet,' Ingrid whimpered, but her words were barely audible.

'But now I'm telling you to answer. Have you broken your leg again, you bitch?'

Ingrid nodded, and Katarina saw that she was trying to articulate the words 'hip bone', but it disappeared somewhere in the darkness into which she was sinking.

Katarina continued to shake her, but gave up at last when she noticed that the old teacher was now beyond reach.

She got down off the sofa, picked up the remote control on the table and turned on the TV. She flipped between channels for a while and found to her delight that the old lady had MTV. She used to watch MTV when she needed company, and now she sat for a while in front of Christina Aguilera and her well-built dancers, all moving in the same pattern in time with the music. The fury drained out of her as suddenly as it had come. She turned off the TV and went back into the kitchen, where she continued her food preparations.

* * *

When Ingrid opened her eyes again, Katarina was sitting in the armchair, eating.

'Do you feel better now, after you've had some sleep?' she asked in a calm, cool voice.

It was hard to believe this was the same person who a few minutes earlier had jumped on her in uncontrolled rage and hit and screamed at her. For the first time Ingrid felt the terror really take hold of her. Her imprisonment had happened at a leisurely pace and in a controlled way, and she had been more surprised than afraid. But now it turned out that behind the cold, calculating façade there was also a wild, hysterical person, beyond all reason. A person who presumably didn't know herself what was waiting around the next corner.

'You said you weren't going to hurt me,' said Ingrid quietly, trying not to rouse the dormant insanity back to life.

'But I lied,' Katarina answered with an ice-cold smile. 'Can't a person indulge in that occasionally? Life is full of surprises, and I guess that's a good thing. Imagine how predictable existence would be otherwise, and how meaningless, if you already knew how everything would end. You promised that everyone would get to drive the green car, but that didn't happen. I never did. I pushed and pushed for a whole year, hoping to get to drive it at least once, but I never did. You lie when it suits you, so maybe we don't need to turn my statements inside out.'

'What time is it?' asked Ingrid.

Her tongue was sticking to her palate with every syllable. She really needed something to drink.

'Oh, I don't know. I don't have a watch. I don't care about time. This will take however long it takes, and that's how it is with everything else too.'

'Don't you have a job?' Ingrid asked. They might as well kill time by talking. When they talked she could concentrate on the conversation, and then she didn't feel the pain as strongly.

'No,' Katarina answered. 'This is my job – doing crazy things. Before, when I was in the hospital, I was in work therapy, but then they closed that down, so now I more or less do what I want.'

'Where do you live?'

'I live here with you, Miss Ingrid.'

'But before? You must have lived somewhere?'

'I live at home with my mum. If it suits me. In Hallonbergen. Sometimes it does, sometimes it doesn't. Sometimes I live in a shelter on Lidingö. I do what I want.'

Ingrid looked at her for a long time, but Katarina took no notice of that. She seemed to be lost in her own thoughts now, looking dreamily out of the living room window into the November darkness. She was a good-looking girl. She was rather tall, straight-backed with a proud posture, and she had long, blonde hair. She was articulate, and her use of language made a reasonably educated impression. Did it really have to turn out this way, thought Ingrid, with a sudden flash of empathy. Then reality came back to her. She could hardly feel the pain in her hip any more, as long as she lay completely still, but her face ached, her stomach was crying out for something to eat, her mouth and throat for something to drink, and then her hands – the pain refused to go away. She needed to pee again. It had not yet dried completely from the last time before she had to go again. And on top of everything else, she felt humiliated, deprived of all pride and human dignity, reduced to a miserable little creature, lying there helpless, wetting herself.

* * *

Katarina ate her meatballs and potatoes in silence, and without noticing how they tasted. She was thinking about her mother, whom she had not seen since all this started. Her mother was old – even older than Miss Ingrid – and always had been. In photographs from before Katarina was born, she saw that her mother had always looked like an old lady. She wore peculiar hats and her stiff grey hair tied up in a bun at her neck. Even in pictures that must have been taken during the summer, she was unusually well wrapped up, with a warm coat, scarf and heavy winter shoes.

How Katarina had come about was still a deeply buried secret, and no father had ever been mentioned. Her mother raised her on her own, and was very particular about her daughter being clean and neat. That she should carry herself like a little lady and be polite and obedient. She had been too, but still her mother never seemed quite satisfied with her. When Katarina came home from preschool and school beaten up and with her clothes in tatters, she had been met only with curses. Her mother was loving in her own way. Her concern for Katarina took up most of her time, but signs of affection were lacking.

Instead, the time was devoted to her so-called upbringing and schoolwork. Katarina's mother had been as different as you could get from the mothers in the storybooks at the library where her mother worked, and the mothers she saw in the courtyard where they lived. She was more like a kind of governess who sat alongside and studied everything Katarina did for the purpose of judging and evaluating. There had been hugs, at bedtime, but they were too hard and always given along with some admonition about doing better the next day. Katarina always fell asleep with a sense of failure, that she had done something wrong or incorrect that had to be atoned for. Still, she loved her mother. She loved her more than she had ever loved any other person.

These days her relationship with her mother was different. The transformation had happened almost imperceptibly, and Katarina had no idea what caused this disturbance in the balance of power. Perhaps it was simply old age that softened her mother's temperament. Whatever it was, she always seemed happy to see her and made an effort to make Katarina feel welcome, even spoiled – something her mother had previously been terrified of – when she came home. Katarina lived with her mother, periodically, in the apartment in Hallonbergen they had moved to after leaving Katrineholm, before Katarina became a law student at the University of Stockholm. Her studies were interrupted almost before they began, when Katarina was stricken with anxiety, which was followed by one bout of depression after another. Finally, she was hospitalized and spent several years in a mental institution, to which she returned at more or less regular intervals.

She wondered what her mother would think if she found out what she had done. Katarina had always been careful to keep her mother in the dark about what happened at preschool and school, partly out of concern for her, partly because she suspected telling her about it would only have backfired. If the children were mean to Katarina, her mother would have assumed that it was self-inflicted, because Katarina had not followed one or other of her mother's instructions. The consequences would have been worse than they already were, scolding and reprimands about what Katarina saw as the lesser problem: torn clothes, scratched knees and bruises. Katarina shuddered at the thought of how her mother would react if she found out that her nice little girl was a murderer. She would never survive such a thing. She already had a bad heart and such news would surely send her straight to her grave.

Yet she was doing it anyway. Even though she knew how the only person who ever cared about her would react, she did it. Her egotism and self-centeredness had got the upper hand, as her mother had always feared, and now she was busy doing the most forbidden things, simply to give her own life a little dignity and a measure of excitement – and maybe some enjoyment, too.

She shook off the thought with a little laugh and glanced over at the woman on the couch. Was she peeing again? Maybe she should have let her go to the bathroom, anyway; the stench in here would be unbearable if this dragged on. But the humiliation of a grown person peeing and shitting herself decided it. If the old lady was going to suffer, then she should do so properly, even if it created some inconvenience for her too.

She decided to investigate whether there was any alcohol in the house – she had not found any in the kitchen. She opened the door to the basement, turned on the light and went down a steep, narrow stairway that ended in a little hall. There were three doors. The first led to a storage area, containing an old bicycle and a clothes rack with old men's and women's clothes on hangers. The second door led to a small laundry room, with a washing machine, a dryer and an ironing board. The third door concealed a food cellar that was mainly used for jars of jam and preserves – it looked like Miss Ingrid made good use of the fruit the garden offered in autumn – but, more importantly, here she found a bottle of port wine and decided to open it.

Katarina went back upstairs and took a long-stemmed glass out of a kitchen cupboard. As she entered the living room she noticed the stench of urine coming from the couch. She turned on her heels with a contemptuous snort and cautiously cracked open the outside door before she pulled on winter boots and coat and went out. She closed the door quietly behind her and carefully walked down the steps and around the end of the house. Here she found a small white iron bench, shaded from the exterior lighting by the wall of the house. She sat down, enclosed in the dense November darkness, and an ice-cold breeze rushed past her face. It was completely quiet around her, and all she could hear was the distant roar of cars on Nynäsvägen.

She tore loose the foil from the bottle, unscrewed the lid and poured a generous dash. Then she brought the glass to her lips and took a deep gulp of the sweet wine. The strong liquid warmed her chest and clouds of steam came out of her mouth when she exhaled.

'Cheers to us, Miss Ingrid,' said Katarina. 'And cheers to all of you, Hans, Ann-Kristin, Lise-Lott and Carina.'

She turned her eyes to the starless evening sky and raised her glass.

Monday Evening

When the lawyer finally arrived, Sjöberg led him determinedly through the corridors to where the man was being held, brought back from jail to the interview room. Two black eyes had begun to appear and his nose was swollen. Sjöberg knew what had happened, but did not comment on it.

After Sjöberg summarized the situation for the newly hired lawyer, the interview resumed, and this time Sandén and Sjöberg were even more aggressive in their attitude towards the suspect.

'We know you did it,' Sjöberg opened, his eyes dark with conviction and in a threatening voice that was more likely down to his own worry regarding the results of the fingerprint analysis than to any aversion to the accused.

'We have your footprints in the garden, and in a trial that will probably be enough for a conviction,' Sandén lied, but the lawyer was alert.

'And the fingerprints?' he asked. 'Is the analysis of the fingerprints done?'

'The fingerprints appear to belong to someone else,' Sjöberg admitted. 'But we have a witness that confirms that the accused was seen outside Ingrid Olsson's house together with another man at the time of the murder of Hans Vannerberg. We assume you had an accomplice,' Sjöberg continued, now speaking directly to Thomas. 'I know you despised Hans Vannerberg. You hated him with all your heart and you wanted nothing more than for him to die. Do you deny that?'

Thomas exchanged a hasty glance with the lawyer, who nodded to indicate he should answer the policeman's questions. He looked Sjöberg right in the eyes and Sjöberg thought, to his surprise, that he seemed completely sincere when he answered.

'I don't know if I'm capable of such strong feelings. Hans Vannerberg did bad things to me, but I don't want anyone to die. I want people to see me, but at the same time I do everything not to be seen. No one has seen me since I was a kid, and then they saw me because I was so ugly, so different. I don't want to be seen that way, so I make myself invisible. I saw Hans Vannerberg, but I didn't want him to see me. I followed him to see what things are like for a really happy person. I didn't want to kill Hans Vannerberg. I wanted to be Hans Vannerberg.'

Sjöberg was astounded by the sudden profusion of words, but Sandén did not let himself be taken by surprise.

'And yet you killed him just the same!' he exclaimed.

'I did not kill him, I just followed him. But there may be others he treated the same way as me, who have maybe turned out different from me.'

'How, for example?' Sandén continued, in the same aggressive tone.

Thomas sat quietly for a few moments and then answered thoughtfully. 'I think if you have a more aggressive disposition and are subjected to the same treatment as I was while you're growing up, maybe the humiliation is expressed differently when you are an adult from how it is for me.'

'What kind of treatment and humiliation are we talking about here?' asked Sandén.

'Hans Vannerberg was a bully,' Thomas answered calmly. 'He was a mean kid and truly sadistic. What he subjected me to during that year in preschool was pure torture. In his case, it was mostly a matter of physical abuse. He hit me almost every day and encouraged the other kids to do the same. He was tough, strong and good-looking. It was no problem for him to get the other kids to go along with him in just about anything. They tied me up to a lamp-post and threw rocks at me, spat on me and banged my head against the post. They tore my clothes, smeared dog poo on my face, hid my shoes so I had to go home barefoot in the winter, locked me in the caretaker's room, made fun of me, laughed at me, stole other kids' things and put them in my pockets, shoved me, tripped me, hit me. And the teacher did nothing. She pretended she didn't see. If you're strong, you swallow it and go on through life with your self-confidence intact. If you're weak, you become lonely and afraid. I think there may also be a third way. You can go beyond what's normal, beyond what's healthy, and create a separate image of the world for yourself. An image you don't share with anyone else.'

Sjöberg could not help being moved by the strange man's story. He could picture one of his own children, six-year-old Sara, sitting tied up to a lamp-post with a mob around her. He presumed that he would have taken matters into his own hands and fought back, but what would Sara have done if no one saw and no one knew? Sandén sat silent, and Sjöberg assumed that similar thoughts were going through his mind too.

'And which route did you take, Thomas?' Sjöberg asked finally.

'Unfortunately, I'm the weak type,' Thomas answered.

'You don't give a particularly weak impression when you're telling us this.'

'I've never told anyone this before. Maybe I should have a long time ago, but I've never had anyone to talk to. This is my story, and I've carried it with me my whole life. It feels good to tell it to someone.'

Thomas looked at the two policemen and at the lawyer, and suddenly felt embarrassed when he realized that he had exposed himself to strangers. Certainly they looked at him with the same expression as everyone else: contempt. He sensed the colour rise in his face again, and he bowed his head in shame so they wouldn't see him.

But Sjöberg saw him. He saw a small, scared and

lonely person who, for a few minutes, had cracked open his soul, and he did not intend to let it shut again. He felt both warm and completely ice-cold inside at the same time, and he suddenly recalled that they were supposed to be pursuing a serial killer. What if the blushing man with the injured face sitting before him, his shoulders hunched as a shield against the hard eyes and harsh words surrounding him, was really telling the truth? What if there was another person who had experienced the same terrors as him, suffered the same torments as him, but who had reacted differently? Could it be that something, despite the time that had passed, had brought the same memories to life in two different people with similar experiences from a preschool long ago? The same memories, but different emotions. Could it really be that way?

Sjöberg felt instinctively that the man was telling the truth. At the same time, experience and the footprints in Ingrid Olsson's garden spoke volumes. Could this be just a strange coincidence? The fingerprints were undeniably not Thomas Karlsson's, and it struck him that, in reality, *this* was what spoke volumes.

Suddenly something Thomas Karlsson had said several hours earlier popped up in his memory: 'I was afraid that something would happen to her.' And what was it Lennart Josefsson, Ingrid Olsson's neighbour, had said? Something about a strange woman going in the old lady's gate.

Sjöberg leaped up from his chair, which fell backwards and landed with a crash on the floor. The three other men stared at him in surprise, but there was no time for explanations now.

'Make sure he's taken back to the jail, then come up to my office, and do it fast!'

Sjöberg shouted the order to Sandén as he rushed out of the interview room. Sandén had no time to reflect on the situation – instead he phoned reception and asked Lotten to send a constable to the interview room immediately. The constable was there in less than a minute, and Sandén ordered her to take Thomas Karlsson back to the jail, after which he, too, ran up the stairs to the corridor where his and his immediate associates' offices were located. There was Sjöberg, handing out instructions to Eriksson and Hamad, and ordering them to take their service pistols along.

Less than five minutes later the four police officers were in a car on their way across the Skanstull Bridge with the sirens on. Sjöberg had also requested reinforcements, so other cars were en route in the same direction. Hamad was driving the unmarked car, with Sjöberg next to him, and Eriksson and Sandén in the back seat.

'What actually happened during the questioning?' asked Hamad.

'He said, right from the start, that he was worried about Ingrid Olsson,' Sjöberg answered doggedly. 'But we didn't believe him. Then he consistently denied all the accusations, and even though Lennart Josefsson called to say that he had seen a strange woman go into Ingrid Olsson's house, we took no action. This may cost us dearly.'

'But it must be him,' said Hamad. 'Of course it's him!'

'It may be, but my gut instinct tells me that Thomas Karlsson is telling the truth. We can't afford to take any chances anyway, and we should have thought of this before. Now it may be too late.'

'But why is he after Ingrid Olsson?' Hamad continued, still not really clear about what was going on.

'She,' said Sjöberg. 'I think it's a she. And that Ingrid Olsson has committed a deadly sin.'

* * *

Hadar Rosén's office was within walking distance of the police station, although it was on the other side of the Hammarby canal. Petra Westman drove there, however, intending to head home when the meeting was over.

Basically, she thought very highly of Rosén. He was an intelligent man who, despite being ultimately responsible for many of the investigations they worked on, never got on his high horse. At their meetings he mostly listened and let Sjöberg pull the strings. In an exceptional case he might have a diverging opinion, but they always came to an agreement in the end. However, he was a man with great authority, which in most other cases did not scare her. But Hadar Rosén, with his tall, always serious appearance, made her feel like a little schoolgirl. Not many people had that effect on Petra Westman, and she did not like it. Especially not now, when her future was in his hands. It was with a strong feeling of unease that she knocked on the prosecutor's door.

'Yes!' he grunted from within, and Petra did not know whether that meant she should identify herself or just go in.

After some hesitation, she chose the latter. He was pecking at his computer without looking up, and Petra convinced herself that the natural thing for her to do in this situation was to sit down in one of the visitor's chairs and patiently wait until the prosecutor finished what he was doing.

When at last he caught her eye, his expression revealed nothing. He stood up, came around to her side of the desk and looked down at her for a few moments without saying anything. She had never felt so small in her entire life. Finally, he spoke.

'Yesterday afternoon Peder Fryhk was arrested, on suspicion of the rape of a twenty-three-year-old woman in Malmö in 1997 and a thirty-eight-year-old woman in Gothenburg in 2002.'

Petra's heart skipped a beat.

'The detention hearing will take place on Wednesday and we'll be able to raise the degree of suspicion to probable grounds. DNA samples from Fryhk have been compared with those found in connection with the two rapes and shown to match.'

Petra let out a sigh of relief. The prosecutor continued in the same factual tone of voice.

'Searching Fryhk's house, the police found a large number of video recordings of other rapes. It has been determined that these rapes took place in his own home.'

Petra gasped for breath.

'Out of concern for you, I insisted on being allowed to go through the evidence personally before the police. You do not figure in any of these videos. The implications of that you can decide for yourself.'

Before she could say anything, the mobile in her trouser pocket rang.

'Excuse me,' she said as she stood up from the chair.

She took out the mobile and looked at the display: 'Blocked Number.'

'I have to take this, in case it's Sjöberg.'

The prosecutor nodded and studied her attentively while the conversation was going on. It was not Sjöberg calling. It was forensic technician Håkan Carlberg.

'I got the idea that, to be on the safe side, I should also do a DNA analysis of the contents of the other condom,' he said in a tone that was not what she had expected. 'I'm sorry, Petra, but it was not Peder Fryhk's. And this time we have no match with DNA from any previous crime.'

Petra ended the call and met Rosén's gaze. Whether

he had heard what was being said on the other end Petra did not know, but she thought she detected a worried frown. Thoughts were rushing through her mind and she felt completely dizzy.

Neither of them could say anything before the phone rang again. This time it was Sjöberg, and he ordered Petra Westman to immediately make her way to Åkerbärsvägen 31 in Enskede.

* * *

Suddenly she started. Were those sirens she heard somewhere far off? Very, very faint, but still . . . ? Her reaction was both unnecessary and stupid, she knew, but you could never be too careful. No one knew she was here, no one knew that Ingrid Olsson was being held prisoner in her own home. The phone had not rung all day, and Miss Ingrid seemed to have no relatives or friends, as she had noted during the days she had sneaked around outside the house, studying the old woman and her doings. That discovery had given her the courage to ring the doorbell, the courage to ask Miss Ingrid if she wanted to be her friend. But then it was too late. The old teacher was suddenly gone and everything was turned upside down.

The house stood empty for weeks before she dared lure Hans there. She had planned to take them in the order she thought they deserved it. Now it turned out that Miss Ingrid was the worst of all. It could be no other way. She had been a grown-up, responsible for all of them, and yet she had stood on the sidelines and watched as the children crushed her, took her childhood from her, her life, everything. Besides, she was now also ignoring Katarina's cries for help. So Miss Ingrid had been added to the list. She was last, and that was perfect considering the new insight Katarina had. Now she could really draw the whole thing out and make use of all the skills she had acquired in the course of her journey.

Were the sirens coming closer? Now they definitely fell silent. Maybe she had only imagined them. To be certain, she put the cork back in the bottle and set the glass down on the bench. Then she slipped over to the tall hedge that marked the boundary with the neighbour further down the street. The hedge was dense, but there was a space between the branches close to the ground where she could get through if necessary.

She hid by the hedge for a good while before she relaxed. She was just about to return to the bench and the bottle of port wine when she thought she heard something. She held her breath for several seconds, on full alert, trying to locate the source of the sound. It was not a car engine and not human voices either – or maybe that's exactly what it was? Was someone whispering? The sound came closer, and at last she was sure that she was hearing whispering voices and stealthy steps on the asphalt in the street. They were heading in her direction and thoughts buzzed in her mind. What were they doing out there? Did the police know what was going on in the house, and in that case, how in the world had they found out?

Whatever. They would find out from Ingrid Olsson who she was, but they would never catch her. She would have to leave Miss Ingrid to her fate, but she'd given the old preschool teacher some real food for thought anyway, and that was good enough. Seeing that she had a sizeable head start, Katarina squeezed through the obstinate hedge and out on to the lawn of the neighbouring garden, and was swallowed up by the darkness.

Hamad's car, which was first in the group of squad cars headed to Ingrid Olsson's house in Enskede, turned up on to the pavement after the exit from Nynäsvägen, and stopped with the engine and blue lights on. Within a few minutes the rest had caught up and were rolling into the residential area in convoy. They stopped at the main road through the area, just south of Åkerbärs-vägen, and parked in a long row along the curb. The police were getting out of their cars just as Westman arrived in hers. They all gathered in a wide circle around Sjoberg, who quickly relayed his orders. Then, as a unit, they rushed towards number 31.

As they approached the neighbouring house, they slowed down to take the final stretch over to the gate as soundlessly as possible. Ingrid Olsson's garden was silent and deserted. There were lights on in some of the windows, but there was no activity in the house visible from the street. One by one the police officers jumped nimbly over the tall gate and down on to the grass by the side of the gravel path. Sjöberg gave low-voiced commands as the police formed into groups that slipped around to each end of the house to try to see what was going on inside.

The foundation of the house reached a good bit above the ground, which made it difficult to see in through the windows, but Hamad hoisted Westman up to look in across the living room. She couldn't see any movement in the room, but suddenly she caught sight of a pair of feet at the far end of the brown three-seater couch. It was impossible to make out to whom they belonged, but she hissed at one of the police officers on his way back from behind the house to report her observation to Sjöberg. At the same moment Hamad caught sight of the half-empty glass and the bottle of port wine on the little bench.

Nothing else of interest had been seen in the house, except the feet on the couch. Sjöberg stepped up on to the porch and carefully knocked on the door. At the same moment Westman noted from her position out-side the living room window that the feet jerked at the unexpected sound, and for a fraction of a second she thought she saw that they were bound together. Then they vanished into the couch again, and now almost nothing could be seen of the still figure. Hamad let go of his colleague. Westman landed with a light thud on the damp grass and ran around the house back to the porch.

'I think she's tied up,' she whispered excitedly to Sjöberg. 'Her feet jerked when you knocked, but then she was still again.'

'Let's go in now,' Sjöberg hissed to the police force now gathered at the bottom of the steps. 'You two go to the left, you to the right, you up, and you down into the basement. You stay put outside. Weapons drawn, understood?'

The officers nodded in response and took their guns from their holsters. Sjöberg stepped up to the front door, while the others took a few steps to the side. He placed himself to the side of the front door, took a deep breath and pushed down the handle. The door flew open and the police rushed into the house. Sjöberg ran into the living room and indeed – there was Ingrid Olsson, bound hand and foot, staring at them, her eyes wide with terror.

'What's going on here?' asked Sjöberg as he got down on his knee beside the couch, where the shaken old woman was lying.

'She went out,' said Ingrid Olsson in a weak voice. 'It can't be more than fifteen minutes ago.'

'What does she look like?'

'Long, blonde hair and a navy-blue coat.'

'Take care of Mrs Olsson,' Sjöberg ordered one of the young constables.

Then he hurried back into the hall and called out to the officers.

'She's out there somewhere,' he said. 'Unfortunately, she happened to be outside when we arrived, but we'll get her. She has long, blonde hair and a navy-blue coat. We'll send the dog after her.'

'Wait a minute,' said Hamad. 'There's a little bench around the corner. I saw a bottle of sherry or port wine and a glass. Let the dog sniff that first.'

'Good idea, Jamal. Show the dog handler,' said Sjöberg, then he gave the sign to the police officers to go out again.

The large German shepherd sniffed the glass curiously for a few seconds, then she started tugging eagerly on her leash. She rushed over to the hole in the hedge and quickly ran through. The dog handler had a tough time following her without letting go of the leash, and it was not much easier for the other officers. At last all the police were through, but at this point the dog and her handler were far ahead.

After that it got easier. The hunt went through a dozen gardens, until they finally found themselves back at the main road. Then it continued across the road, over a fence and into a small patch of forest, where she seemed to have wandered around before deciding which way to go.

Back in another residential area they thought they caught sight of her, but it proved to be another blonde woman out for a walk pushing a pushchair, and she looked in amazement at the line of panting police officers running past. The detached houses came to an end, and a group of poorly maintained apartment buildings took over. They hurried on between them and across a playground, and Sjöberg felt his age starting to take its toll. He considered giving up and letting the younger officers continue without him, but when he caught sight of the stocky Sandén some fifty metres ahead of him, in a thick overcoat and loafers, he changed his mind.

They soon came to a small street parallel to Nynäs-vägen, which at first glance seemed to be an entry ramp to the main road. When he had run a hundred metres along the small street, and the dog handler and several other officers had already disappeared from view ahead of him, he suddenly realized that it was not an ordinary entry ramp he was on, but instead a street that led up to a bridge over Nynäsvägen. Far off on the bridge, almost at the opposite side, in the glow of the orange lamps hanging on large, ghostly steel frames over the road, he saw a figure trying to climb up on to the railing. Despite the dim light, there was no mistaking it: a woman was hanging on to the railing, and she had long, blonde hair and a dark coat.

The dog handler, who was quickly approaching the solitary figure, now let the dog loose, and she reached her in a few leaps. Barking, she jumped up towards the woman several times and finally caught hold of a corner of her coat.

'Stop, Katarina! Don't do it!' Hamad shouted. He was the officer closest after the dog handler.

With the dog lunging at her, Katarina almost lost her balance and fell back down on to the bridge, but at the last moment she managed to wriggle one arm out of her coat. She heaved herself once again up over the railing, clinging on firmly with her free hand, and let the coat slide off the other arm too.

When he caught sight of Katarina on the bridge, Sjöberg stopped where he was, where he could view the whole drama from below. He watched the coat glide down to the ground and settle in a small heap, right next to the railing. Katarina heaved herself up with strong arms and brought herself nimbly into a standing position on the narrow railing.

There she stood now, her eyes sweeping over the cars below, and he could have sworn their eyes met. Then her gaze ran along the line of still running police officers until at last it settled on Hamad. The whole time she had a triumphant – and, as he would recall it, very beautiful – smile on her lips. She raised her hand as if in greeting.

'No!' shouted Hamad. 'No! No! No!'

It was as if time stopped, and everything became quiet around them while the traffic moved in slow motion down on Nynäsvägen. She raised her arms like wings and then left the railing, the police and life behind her and flew out into the cold night air.

An awful thud broke the spell. The sound of brakes, broken glass and crushed metal cut through the air after Katarina Hallenius's final act.

Stockholm, December 2006

Once again Thomas was sitting at his kitchen table, and once again he was looking dreamily out of the window. But nothing was the same any more. Something terrible had happened – four people he once knew had been murdered. Four people who had lived different kinds of lives, some happy and some, perhaps, unhappy. It was hard to say.

But he was sure of one thing: none of them wanted to die, and none of them deserved to either, at such a young age and so inconceivably brutally. They had done terrible things, but they had only been children, very small children. They probably had no idea what damage they were doing. They were children who, without adult supervision, had been free to do what they needed to secure their own little territory and social position.

And Katarina had struck back. She had done it for her own sake, but Thomas felt that somehow it was for his sake too. For that reason, he received the news of the resolution of the whole tragic story with mixed emotions. Katarina had no doubt been a very sick person, but she had been a person. Their lives had run in parallel, without either of them knowing it. If only they had met! If they could have sat together and talked about childhood and life, been company for each other for a while. Perhaps they could have become friends, united by a broken childhood and a life of solitude. Maybe everything would have been different then, for both of them.

Nevertheless, Thomas felt that Katarina had given him redress. Her outrageous, unforgivable actions had freed something inside him. He despised what she had done, but he could not despise her. He understood her, but not completely. She was the stronger of the two, the one who came straight-backed out of a humiliating situation. She had always looked happy and proud, apparently easily able to put up with the harassment, while he sank deeper and deeper into depression. But somewhere along the way she had taken a step in the wrong direction, and her choice had been devastating for everyone involved.

He himself was not guiltless. His testimony in connection with the first two murders would have been of great value to the police. By telling what he knew he could have prevented further bloodshed, but it had not occurred to him until he read about the murder of Lise-Lott Nilsson, and then he had been paralysed by his own marginal involvement in the whole thing.

Yet it was as if a stone had been lifted from his shoulders. Katarina had liberated him from his burden, though she perished herself. Now it was time to start over, to try again. Take responsibility for his own life. For Katarina's sake.

He felt a sudden longing to go out. It was a quarter past five and the streets were filled with people, people on their way home from work and people getting a head start on Christmas shopping. Sunday was the beginning of Advent and it was snowing again. Snow was falling in large flakes, whirling beautifully in the light under the streetlamps. He wanted to be out there, he wanted to be part of the throng of people down there on the street, and he didn't intend to be scared of them any longer.

He put on his shoes and jacket and jogged down the steps, out on to the pavement and across the street. Then he turned and looked up at the façade of his own building. His eyes wandered from window to window and stopped at last on his own. A warm, welcoming light radiated from inside the kitchen, softened by the lined curtains – blue checks against a warm yellow background, just right for a kitchen. And, in the middle of the window, between two thriving poinsettias, an Advent candle spread its friendly rays. He turned his face up towards the sky, closed his eyes and let the snowflakes melt against his warm skin.

THE NEXT CASE FOR CONNY SJÖBERG

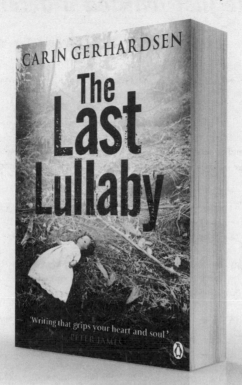

CARIN GERHARDSEN

The Last Lullaby

'Writing that grips your heart and soul'
PETER JAMES

IT'S THE CALL EVERY OFFICER DREADS

Stockholm Criminal Investigator Conny Sjöberg finds a mother and her two young children lying peacefully in bed, their throats coldly and efficiently cut and no signs of a struggle.

As Conny and his team get to work they draw a blank on both motive and suspect for these cruel, senseless murders. The only lead they have is a mysterious benefactor of the family – who eludes their every search.

Distracted and hampered by the mysterious disappearance of one of their offices, Conny's squad struggles on – until an astonishing discovery turns the case upside down and threatens to tear his team apart . . .

He just wanted a decent book to read ...

Not too much to ask, is it? It was in 1935 when Allen Lane, Managing Director of Bodley Head Publishers, stood on a platform at Exeter railway station looking for something good to read on his journey back to London. His choice was limited to popular magazines and poor-quality paperbacks – the same choice faced every day by the vast majority of readers, few of whom could afford hardbacks. Lane's disappointment and subsequent anger at the range of books generally available led him to found a company – and change the world.

'We believed in the existence in this country of a vast reading public for intelligent books at a low price, and staked everything on it'
Sir Allen Lane, 1902–1970, founder of Penguin Books

The quality paperback had arrived – and not just in bookshops. Lane was adamant that his Penguins should appear in chain stores and tobacconists, and should cost no more than a packet of cigarettes.

Reading habits (and cigarette prices) have changed since 1935, but Penguin still believes in publishing the best books for everybody to enjoy. We still believe that good design costs no more than bad design, and we still believe that quality books published passionately and responsibly make the world a better place.

So wherever you see the little bird – whether it's on a piece of prize-winning literary fiction or a celebrity autobiography, political tour de force or historical masterpiece, a serial-killer thriller, reference book, world classic or a piece of pure escapism – you can bet that it represents the very best that the genre has to offer.

Whatever you like to read – trust Penguin.